Tilly Johnson's
Pillow Book

THE *Erotic* Print Society
EPS, 17 Harwood Road
LONDON SW6 4QP

Tel (UK only): 08000262524 (order line)
Fax: +44 (0)20 7736 6330
Email: *eros@eroticprints.org*
Web: *www.eroticprints.org*

© 2006 MacHo Ltd, London UK

ISBN 978-1-904989-30-1

Tilly Johnson's
Pillow Book

EPS

Tilly Johnson's
Pillow Book

Foreword

The Erotic Print Society's Pillow Books are labours of love. They take time, effort, and are hell to organise, but the rewards – your appreciation and enjoyment – are really satisfying. Emily Ford, Dee McDonald, Charlie Webb (who stood in for us during the temporary absence of a Secretary) – and now it's me.

The only obvious break with tradition is my decision to bare all. Somewhere between pages 333 and 353, you will find the Society's first Stripping Secretary. Said distraction, you might think, relieving me of any burden to prove myself to be sexy or cerebral in my choice of this PB's content. But you would be wrong. Hell, I'm not going to let you off *that* lightly.

For a start our authors pull off something that the *Literary Review's* Bad Sex Award thinks impossible: texts that both arouse and entertain. But is it good writing? I hear the greying and inhibited literati ask. Yes, it certainly is, but you can be the judge of that and frankly, my dear reader, I don't give a damn as long as it fulfils those two essential criteria. One of our authors, Christopher Hart, whose story *Latin Lover*, achieves them effortlessly, has even *won* the Bad Sex Award, so what do they know?

New talent Katie Kelly goes to places that chicklit, even in its rudest moments, never thought of going. She now regularly supplies the new EPS magazine, *SEx*, with raunchy shorts, and I'm not talking hotpants. So do John Gibb, Lucy Golden, Kate Copstick and Christopher Peachment (editor of this shiny new organ) whose stories also appear in the pages of this book. Even I've got a column in *SEx*. Which is why I'm taking off my clothes. The first piece I handed in for the mag was judged flat. I was told to try harder.

"Oh," I asked, "have you any ideas?"

"A nude picture by-line might do the trick. Readership of your column would rocket!"

I shrugged off the implication that I was no better than a glorified news bunny, then I shrugged off my clothes and found that I enjoyed doing it in front of a camera. I haven't looked back. I'm no Jordan, but I hope I do a nice 'girl next door'.

And talking of bunnies, there is a warren of them by Fridolin Hase in my Pillow Book. A sort of *Bunny Sutra*. Another of my favourite illustrators, Michael Faraday revisits the *Ten Commandments*, giving it what Charlton Heston never could. The Secret Museum which won the Best Artist category in last year's prestigious Erotic Awards, transports us to Transylvania for a bit of scary lycanthropic sauce. Another gallery is dedicated to Vanya Zouravliov's delicate work, which shows that his talents extend much further than his explicit Past Venus Press work.

Past Venus Press is the EPS imprint that shamelessly publishes the Californian-style pulp porn literary classics of the 1960s and later. Which brings me to the novella, *The Blackmailed Housewife*. A typical bit of Past Venus rudeness, but surprisingly set in Metroland, rather than Pasadena. It has a late-1950s feel to it: *Brief Encounter* goes BDSM. It's short enough to be included in its entirety and it's winningly illustrated by Sylvie Jones.

I hope you like my Pillow Book as much as I did putting it all together. My thanks to Marina Asenjo Gonzalez, the Latin temptress from our Production department who has given me such invaluable help and support. And no, she's not the inspiration for Christopher Hart's *Latin Lover*.

But she could be.

Tilly Johnson

John DuPret *was born in England. A post-war baby boomer, he entered an education system he describes as overloaded and lacking inspiration. He won a place at the local College of Art but his family couldn't support the cost involved. He now believes that frustration drives you harder than easy success.*

In the 1970s, with wife Linda and two young children he moved to New Zealand, then Australia and France. He views his years overseas as strongly formative.

DuPret sees himself as a visual artist, not simply a photographer. Paintings and erotic illustrations have been exhibited in the UK, France, Australia and New Zealand, including regular showings at the NZ Academy of Fine Arts. He works in Surrealist, Orientalist and Anamorphic themes, exploring the energy of the Golden Section. Fetish Photographers of the early 1900s are also an influence.

He works in isolation and lives with his wife and dog in a Victorian apartment overlooking the sea near Brighton, England.

The following photographs are taken from his latest book, SIRENS recently published by EPS and available at £19.95.

John Dupret
Sirens

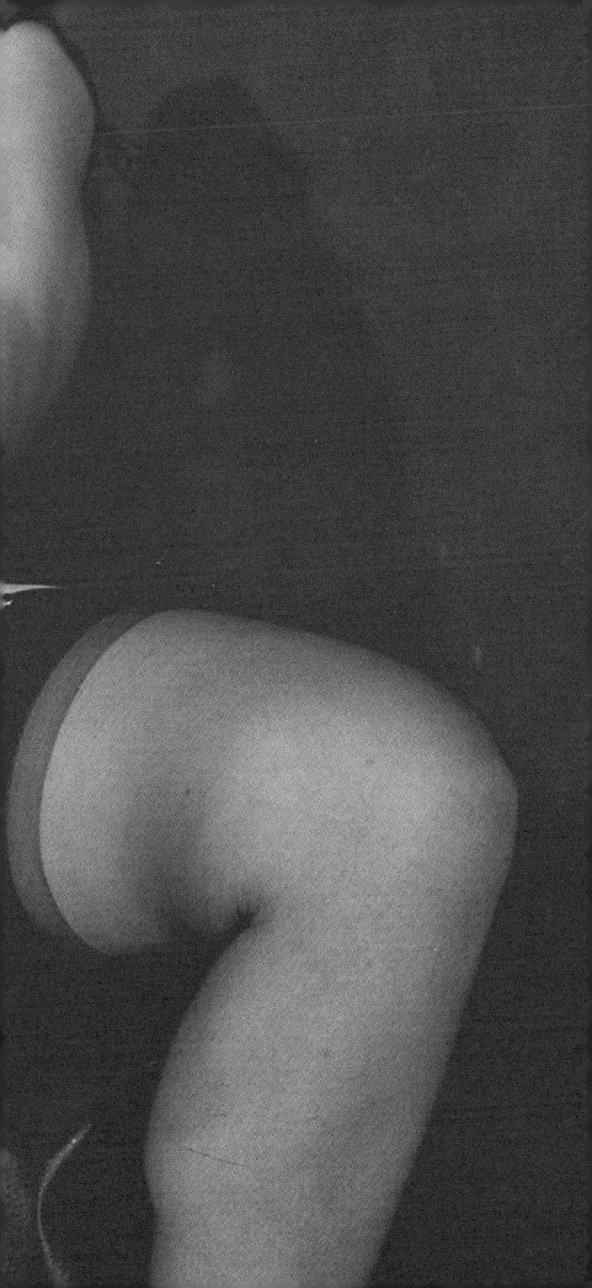

Christopher Peachment *has been many things, including an RAF pilot, a theatre stage manager, main film critic for* Time Out *magazine, Arts and Books Editor for* The Times, *and opera critic for BBC Radio. He has also written two novels,* Caravaggio, *which is about what you would think it would be about, and* The Green and the Gold (Picador), *which is about the relationship between the poets Andrew Marvell and the Earl of Rochester. EPS has published a collection of his journalism,* The Diary of a Sex Fiend, *and he is currently editor of the new EPS SEx magazine. His grossly reactionary views can also be found on the Social Affairs Unit website.*

Christopher Peachment

The Venetian Way of Love

The Venetian Way of Love

Christopher Peachment

The story so far: Guy has arrived in Venice and fallen in love with Federica. He discovers that she is a woman who has been alive many centuries, and, like most Venetians, is still walking the alleys and canal paths. But he cannot determine what sort of ghost she is. Many Venetians have died and still haunt the place. Federica, like a benign vampire, has never died, nor grown old. Like Euridyce, she is trapped in the underworld. She takes him back to the past, and they come upon an incident in which an Englishman shoots a rogue elephant which had escaped from a circus show and killed a soldier. He turns out to be Lord Byron, then staying in Venice.

"Poor beast," said Byron. "It was only in want of its mate. It was in season, and needed release. Jesus Christ, when you look at the damage wreaked in my country by young men who haven't got their end away in a while, this was nothing, *nothing*. I've seen more men killed over a football game. Men have gone to war and killed thousands just because they were horny. The elephant was no worse than any human. If I do not get my piece regular, I do just the same as that poor thing, and rampage about the place." He paused for breath, rather than to let his guests speak.

"Forgive me, sir," he continued, "I drivel on."

After the incident with the elephant, Guy and Federica had followed him at a short distance. It was Federica who had gone up to him, for she already knew him. He had insisted they both accompany him home.

"Under normal circumstances, I would shoo you off, for I hate the English tourist who comes to gape at everything and get the clap and then calls it a cultural education. Forgive me, sir, I see you glower a little, I do not mean you at all. I was about to say that if you are a... what... *friend* here of Signora Zanco, then you are of course different. Very different. So come, come along, we'll go home and have a little something to drink and you can give me the news from London."

He clapped his arm about Guy's shoulders as if they were old friends, and steered them both away from San Marco and towards the Rialto. Soon, they were at his door on the land-ward side of the Grand Canal.

It was a villa on a grand scale, with a luxuriant garden courtyard, and had been owned, so he said, by many generations of the Mocenigo family, a family who numbered several Doges among their ancestors.

"They charge me two hundred a year for this pile. Daylight robbery, but I do like its history. I need a little history around me. Not like those Lakeland poets, all modern and so on. Give me a classicist every time."

He ushered them into the main room on the *piano nobile.* The light from a thin Venetian sun shone through the green and blue panes of bottle-thick glass, making a dappled patchwork of colour on the polished stone flags of the floor and the heavy damask drapes There was a huge table, long enough to seat at least thirty people, with dirty brass eating utensils scattered about on it, as well as a neat row of laundered shirts. A large hookah stood at one end of the table.

"Don't care for tobacco myself, but I like a man who does," said Byron, gesturing that they should sit around the end of the table and indicating a mouthpiece for Guy. "Got the habit in Albania, where I was last. But my lungs won't take it. Specially here in Venice, all the damp, I have to be careful. I got all malarial only a month ago, and there is this damned plague about too"

He paused again, but only to fix a frankly admiring gaze on Federica. "So Federica my dear, do tell," he said. "Where did you find him? And is he one of your kind? He certainly don't look like it."

Guy saw her signal to him discreetly from under her cloak, as if to warn Byron that the subject was as yet not fully explained. Byron nodded imperceptibly, and turned to fiddle with the hookah.

When he had got it lit, he passed a mouthpiece to Guy, who duly sucked tentatively on it, while being careful not to inhale. The charcoal on the central column glowed fitfully with each puff. After a pause in which he looked on Guy's puffing with some envy, Byron rapped on the table and a woman with the startled beauty of an antelope appeared instantly, as if she had been waiting outside. She was however not a maid, as they could see from her informal attitude. She had a slight figure, with glossy black hair and dark eyelids, which looked at first as though she had painted them, but upon inspection proved natural.

"Green tea, I think, Marianna my dear, unless, you would like something stronger," he said turning to Guy. Guy said that tea would be fine.

"Never too early for wine here you know," he said. "The locals are quite unlike other Italians, who don't have much of a taste for drink. Here, they are at it all day long. They have a little *ombra* for breakfast, lunch and supper, and many in between to keep the chills out. I wouldn't be surprised if your average Venetian has never been sober from one year to the next. It's why they never die."

Federica looked sharply at him, and he cleared his throat.

The woman returned, sat down, and passed around the little cups without handles. Guy warmed his hands about the rim and drank the bitter tea slowly.

"Will you join us this evening?" Byron said to Guy. "I have a box at the Fenice, which I keep permanently, though it is a damnable expense, and there is a good opera on tonight. I'm not very musical, but I like a pretty tune. And one does need to be seen about the place. Afterwards we can go to the casino. There's always some high-born woman who will sell you her body to get some money so she can return to the tables. I like to humiliate them."

Marianna scowled and started up from the table to leave. Clearly she was not included in Byron's nocturnal plans. Perhaps she was a servant of some sort, after all, relaxed and informal in manner with her master, but confined indoors. Guy saw him smile warmly at Federica and knew that Byron planned to take her whether Guy went along or not. And he also then knew that they had been lovers at some time in the past, though, he thought, no longer. Guy was not at all sure what he felt about that, and needed time to think about it.

"She is his mistress, the dark-eyed one," Federica whispered to Guy, although from where Byron was sitting he could hear her perfectly well.

He affected to stare out of the window, then said, "She's also me landlady. Which could be damned difficult, now I think of it. No doubt it will all blow up in me face sometime in the future, but until then, the arrangement is practical. Besides, I am enchanted by her. It can only be Venice working her spell for me."

"She owns this place?" Guy said in disbelief.

"No, no. Her husband owns the house in which I first stayed. He helped me find this place a little later. She still comes in though."

"Does her husband not mind?"

"Good God no, he is delighted. Keeps her out of his hair. It is the custom here, sir. Most marriages are contracted for reasons of convenience. As indeed all marriages are everywhere, now I think about it. What is love but a convenience?

But anyway, given the circumstances, it is perfectly reasonable for both parties to indulge in a little loving with whoever takes their fancy. The only difference between this place and the rest of the world is that they display no hypocrisy about it all. And I tell you, that unnerves me slightly.

I approve of it mind you, but not having to keep up hypocritical appearances like you do back home, well, it is unnerving. *There* is this man, a merchant of some sort, chatting to me in a perfectly ordinary fashion about the price of feed, and then he asks if his wife is servicing me properly. And then he brags to all his friends about his lady having an English milord for a *cavalier servente*. It is all quite new to me, and I don't know what to make of it all, except that she is a ravishing beauty.

That flush you see on her cheek, it's because she is always up for it you know. Never says no. God, if ever I had encountered a single English woman like that, I never would have left home."

"I know exactly what you mean," Guy said.

"So you can't stand them, either, eh? Dreary puritanical lot, English women, God knows what their mothers teach them. Nothing to do with the bedchamber, that is a racing certainty.

And now here you are telling me just exactly the same, as I always thought, so nothing has changed. Dear God, it's a wonder the English don't just die out as a race."

"So this woman still comes in to make tea and so on?"

"Not really, she comes in to check up on what I am doing. In spite of the rules and regulations of this place, she does still get jealous something rotten. I had her sister-in-law call on me one evening, just for a little chat, or so the sister-in-law said, though I think there was something else on her mind. Perfectly charming girl, sister to Marianna's husband. And just as we got talking, in burst Marianna, and without so much as a hissing fit starts the most God almighty cat-fight.

I swear to you, this woman has a right hook would floor Jack Johnson. And she used it, too, at least sixteen times on her poor sibling-in-law. Jesus, it was something to behold. She grabbed a handful of hair with her left hand, and just kept her right swinging back and forth across her sister's chops, till she had a bloody nose and was squawking worse than my parrot. And then they started wrestling. Up till then I had been content to watch, but this was beginning to get me going I can tell you.

I was about to dive in and enjoy the attention of two wildcats on heat, when alas her husband arrives home and exchanges a few sharp words about maintaining one's dignity, and jealousy being unbecoming to a woman in her position, and she straightens up and goes all sultry and runs from the room. We tidy her sister-in-law up as best we can, and send them all on their way, but Marianna's blood is up and she comes slinking back to me later in the night and just about kills me with her love-making.

By God she was all over me like a cheap perfume. She's got lovely thick thighs, did you see 'em? She locked those around me tighter than an anaconda, and damn near squeezed the blood out of me. And that was just the start. She all but threw me over her shoulder, and dragged me up to my room, and then she tore...

I am sorry, sir, I see you are a little shy. *Autre temps autre moeurs* eh? Standards do change a bit over time, I know. Still, perhaps you can loosen him up a bit, eh Federica? You're certainly in the right city for a little roving."

"He is a little slow," said Federica, "which I like. We have a long time."

"Course you do, course you do, your kind do have a lot of time," said Byron, then turned to Guy. "I do believe I would like to be like her some day soon. And I would return here too, come back as one like her. It is the best, the greenest place of my imagination, and I could live out several lifetimes here.

Summer is coming though, and it does get insufferably hot here near the main canal. Smelly too, especially when the tides get in the wrong direction and the sewage all backs up. Oh, dear God, it is positively medieval, like living over a midden. Marianna, my love, shall we all go out to the Brenta, sit in that little villa we were wondering whether to take?"

Marianna responded by launching herself at him and wrapping her arms around his neck and squeezing in a way that could have been affectionate but was making Byron's face turn purple. She grabbed his hair too.

"*We* will go there," she hissed in his ear. "And no one else. I don't want that slut near you," she said, nodding at Federica.

"Really my dear, remember what your husband said."

"Don't you talk to me about my husband," she shrieked, and gripped him by the ear, twisted it savagely and kissed him hard on the lips. He flapped his arms about like a wounded bird, unable to break free from her grasp and finally subsided under her fierce embrace.

"All right, all right, I surrender," he said. "Now say you're sorry to Federica, she is with the other Englishman here, and poses you no threat."

"Her kind are always a threat," she hissed. "They hang around forever in this place, centuries, like vampyres. They are worse, far worse, than us ghosts. At least we are normal. We have the decency to die and then we stay down here a while. But her, she's been here forever and her kind don't have any morals."

"Morals, my dear, morals? You yourself are a married woman, and here you are with me."

"That is different, *completely different*; I only take the one lover at a time and so it does not count. When you add up how many she must have had over the years, it is disgusting."

This was definitely something Guy did not want to know about. Byron saw this. Although Guy was very grateful at last for the information about ghosts and vampyres. He was at last beginning to understand   the different gradations. And whatever it was that Federica was. Although exactly how she operated, how she behaved as someone who had never died, was still yet to be found out. What she did for sex, for example, and how, was a question of some urgency in his mind. Or whether she had sex at all. Her skin, after all, was very cool. But Marianna could only be right. After all those years, the number of Federica's lovers must surely be very high.

"It's all right," Byron whispered to Guy. "Don't think of her lovers. It's you she loves, you know that don't you?"

"I wasn't sure."

"Believe me, I know her. It's you."

Guy looked across at Federica, who lowered her eyes.

"So will you join us sir. As I said, I have a box at the opera, and though I am so weary, I still fell obliged to pursue pleasure."

"Don't you find it cloys after a while?"

"Yes, that is exactly what it does after a while, exactly, cloy, what a good word. I will use it in my next poem, you may be sure. And soon, very soon, I must swear off pleasure for a while, and take to one of my sessions of sermons and soda water. It's a bastard of a thing to endure, going without a drink or a piece for a while, but then when I get back to it, ah dear me. There is no pleasure on earth that is not doubled by having forgone it for a while.

So, perhaps after tonight, sir, I will take me off to a monastery. What do you think? Eh?"

"One last fling then?"

"Yes. Last fling, I like that. A very good idea. But what shall be my penance, eh? Where can I go to flagellate myself? Not literally you understand, never did take to that kind of thing. They flogged my bum enough at school for me to never want it ever again. Nothing but pain, there, I tell you, not an ounce of pleasure. Never could understand that side of things."

"What about the monastery?"

"Ah, no distractions there. But I would need something to do."

"It would a perfect opportunity to write your next piece."

"Ah, you might think that. But I am not one of those who needs solitude and quiet to write. Its strange I know, but I write better on the hoof.

I do it best when my mind is exercised over something else. Something not too demanding, like dressing to go out for the evening. I have my man bring my clothes and we choose something appropriate and he combs my hair, and gives me a glass of hock, and all the while I am scribbling lines down at my table. It is often Babel when I come to it in the morning, but it is amazing what a nasty hangover will do for your style. I correct things with an absolute eye. I tell you a hangover is a very good master of bad poetry. Nothing gets past me when I am crapulous.

And then I tie it up in pink ribbon, send it all to Murray in London, though I make damn sure to keep a copy here; you can't trust the couriers these days. And Murray publishes it and sends me some money. I don't know what percentage he keeps though, and I don't know him all that well. Do you think he is trustworthy?"

"Yes he is," Guy replied, recalling what he had read about Byron's publisher in the past.

"Good, I thought he was, but you never can tell with the merchant class, they usually try to cheat me. Anyway, it's an odd method of writing. I am like the tiger in the jungle stalking its prey. I leap and pounce on the words. And when I hit it right, well, it's a smash. But if I miss, then I just creep back into the jungle and lick myself. Hit or miss you might say, but my hits are huge hits, better hits than those Lakeland poets."

"You don't like them?"

"Bah, don't get me started. Pope now, Pope, there was a writer. Worth all of us put together. Because he knew his classics, sir, and that is a fine foundation. The Lake poets, Wordsworth is it? Wittering on about trees and ferns and daffodils, what the blue fucking hell has that got to do with anything, eh? The proper study of mankind is man, and frolicking up and down amid the daffodils trilling about 'clouds of glory' is not going to advance our understanding of man one blasted inch. Gah, I am getting heated, can't have that, or I will fall on Marianna before the evening gets going."

Marianna promptly gave out a whoop of joy, and reached for the hem of her skirt as if to lift it.

"No, no, not yet girl. Dear God, she is insatiable. Federica, can't you amuse her while I get ready for this evening?"

"I think that you are the only amusement she needs," said Federica. "And she doesn't like me, remember? 'No morals.'"

Marianna stamped her heels again and stalked out of the room, breathing loudly through her nostrils.

"Then you stay and talk to me while I faff around, please," he said to Guy. "I like your talk. Good talker, good thinker."

"Guy has in fact spoken exactly eight sentences since you met, and nearly all of them questions. You have spoken non-stop for over an hour," said Federica, her voice suddenly made chilling by being lowered to a near-whisper. "Dear God, George, I don't mind you being so damned full of yourself, but don't pretend you like conversation."

For the first time, Guy saw Byron at a loss. He licked his lips and gave every appearance of having been knocked sideways. He looked about to say something by way of a reply, but then thought better of it.

"Now," he said, staring bemusedly at the table, "which shirt?"

As far as Guy could see they were all the same, laid out in a neat row on the table. All white, all with puffed sleeves and edged with lace here and there. Byron picked one up and held it to him in front of the glass. Then discarded it and held another, repeated this three or four times and finally settled on the one that pleased him. Guy could see no difference between any of them, but no doubt Byron, the dandy, could.

"Something to do with the cut of it," he said, "or perhaps just that I felt right in it. Worse than a woman when dressing, I tell you."

"You cut a fine enough figure, whatever you wear," said Guy.

"Ah, but I don't think I do, and that's the difference."

Like so many egotists, Guy thought, he has little self-confidence. Byron finished by pulling on his boots, grunting and groaning over one of them. Guy was about to offer help, but then remembered the club foot.

"I feel a poem or a play coming on. I will start at it soon."

Oh God, thought Guy, not a play, please God, not a play. He had once had to sit through a production of *The Two Foscari*.

"How soon?" he said.

"After I have fucked myself to extinction. Carnival is coming on soon you know. And then there will be Lent and time enough for writing. Though now I think about it, I write better when I am getting my piece regularly. Tum tee tum:

"There's a whore on my right

For I rhyme best at night

When a cunt is tied close to my inkstand."

"Is that from *Childe Harold*?" said Guy

"No, just a doggerel I wrote in my last letter to my publisher."

"I've heard of carnival."

"Who hasn't? All Europe has heard of carnival, and all Europe wants to join in. You would not believe what happens during it. Everyone takes the chance to change their lover."

"What about Marianna?"

"I expect she will"

"No, I mean her jealous fits."

"They will continue no doubt, nothing to be done about them. Matter of fact, I quite enjoy them. They get her all of a rage, and then she is hot for me. Have you ever made love to an angry woman, sir?"

"No."

"You must try it some... Have you ever made love to a woman at all?"

"Of course."

"Forgive me, I just wondered."

"I... I'm reticent."

"And I am not, forgive me," said Byron.

"He is, in fact," said Federica. "It's just that he likes to tease, and he also likes to push against his own nature. I sometimes think he is just a naughty boy that needs a whipping."

"I've already covered that subject, and no I don't," said Byron, though not very seriously. Guy could see that Federica was one of the few women who could cow him a little. He wondered why that was, and what hold she might have over him.

"None," said Federica, reading Guy's mind again, in a way that unnerved him more than the thought of her having lived for centuries. "I have no hold over him. It's just that I don't care what he thinks about me."

It occurred to Guy that, unusually for a woman, she did not care what anyone thought about her. But then again that was not surprising, given what she was. It seems that the other world does not always relieve you of your troubles. So much for the peace of the grave thought Guy. The revenants get hurt by life just as much as the rest of us. But then she wasn't a revenant at all, not like Marianna. Guy was becoming confused by it all. Perhaps living for a long time made you less anxious about what people thought of you.

"But soon, there is carnival," said Byron. "Already I feel my sword stir in its sheath."

Federica raised her eyebrows at Guy, which Byron saw, and looked shame-faced for the first time.

"I am sorry, I overdo it sometimes. I get so used to annoying the English, that I forget that there are decent folk like yourself. It's a problem. Not that I will change I'm afraid. I keep promising to myself that I will, but it is a hypocritical sort of promise, and one I know well I can never achieve. Still, perhaps even just the thought of the promise, just the realisation I have been bad, is enough. What do you think? Do you think the good Lord will forgive me even though I haven't managed to reform, just because I know that I am as bad as ever? Eh?"

"I believe all that you have to do is repent," she said.

"Yes, but is that really all? I mean, if that is all you need to do to get into heaven, then the Lord does have very low standards. Can you imagine all the riff-raff you would find there? You'd have to sit next to Johnny Keats for a million years, pissing in his bed. Dear God, what a prospect, I'll take the other place, I think."

"Some of us think we are already there."

"Yes, I have some sympathy with that notion. I know I am going to heaven because I have done my time in hell, that sort of thing."

He brooded on that awhile, sitting still beside the table staring at the wall, as the water outside made waving shadows across the plaster, like phosphorescent snakes, and then he looked up and shouted, "Marianna!"

The door opened immediately, and she came back in with a strong light in her black eyes, and a flush to her cheeks.

"We have a few minutes before we go," said Byron to no one in particular as he rose from his chair. His voice as came from the back of his throat and seemed thicker than usual. With a squawk, Marianna turned on her heel and ran gleefully from the room, frisking her skirts, and Byron followed at a brisk step. I looked at Federica. There was no doubt as to what the pair were about to do. A sharp whoop from the floor below, or it might have been halfway down the stairs, confirmed it. There followed gruff noises, as of a distant zoo, though punctuated by human notes too. The sounds were unmistakable, and had the usual effect. While delightful to a participant, there is always embarrassment to a witness.

Guy opened his mouth to make some sort of conversation. But Federica gave a shrug and a smile, which suggested that she was quite happy about it all, and so he shut up.

"It's rather sweet, isn't it?" she said.

"I'm not sure," Guy said, feeling as though ants were crawling out of his collar.

"She is lovely," she said. "Have you ever seen such a look?"

"No," Guy said, and then thought that she was like Federica, or not far off. It was those dark eyes which looked like an antelope. He wondered if Marianna too had been alive for hundreds of years. Then he remembered that it was not good policy to describe one woman as beautiful to another. No good ever came of it.

"She is very sensible about him, too," she said. "She gives him a lot of leeway."

"But what about the sister-in-law? That was hardly cutting him any slack."

"For some reason she only gets jealous of family. Although her husband doesn't. He had other fish to fry. But with other types of women, she never expresses any animosity. She allows him to go with whoever he wants."

"You mean whores?"

She inclined her head to suggest yes, perhaps.

"Christ, why does he need to?" said Guy.

"Wouldn't most men be like that, if they could?"

"I don't think so. I'm always suspicious of men who boast of promiscuity.

What causes it in his case?"

"Vanity, conceit, worry. He wants to lose himself. I've known a few men like him, and they don't like women much. I suspect they were cloaking homosexual tendencies. But him, I don't know.

"You must know him well," said Guy, sadly.

"Yes."

"Were you ever...?"

"He already answered you on that score."

The air in the room seemed to have become thicker, and Guy began having trouble with his breathing, as if the automatic functioning of the lungs had faltered. This was love, no doubt about it, and he was in love with Federica, fathoms deep. Jut what he could do about it, and what it meant to her, he could not even begin to understand. He did not know where to start. Her skin was so deadly cool, and yet she was in all other respects so very much alive. He wondered, again, whether her kind enjoyed sex, and what form it would take.

"Go out and have a look," said Federica, with a smile.

"Certainly not, I wouldn't dream..." said Guy.

"Go on, just a look," said Federica. "You will be amazed. It will answer your worries about me and what I might be like."

Guy saw she was smiling indulgently without a hint of prurience, so he went to the door and opened it.

There on the landing, he saw for the first time something which answered his questions.

Marianna was horizontal, with both her hands resting on the newel post of the carved stone balustrade. Behind her stood Byron, his breeches below his knees, engaged in filling the few minutes "before we go". His face was turned towards the high frescoed ceiling, and his eyes were upturned in their sockets and showing a lot of white. He was gasping for breath. Marianna for her part had her eyes closed and an expression of dreaminess across her happy features. Then Guy noticed something strange. Byron's hands, far from supporting Marianna in her horizontal position by lifting her hips, were in fact resting firmly on the small of her back. As if holding her down, thought Guy.

"Gah," half-shouted Byron, "it's coming..."

And even as he spoke, Marianna let go her hold on the balustrade, floated forward of Byron as if swimming, executed a neat somersault in mid-air, turned neatly over and, still floating, fastened her mouth into the invisible area below Byron's waistband. Her head, Guy realised with some gratitude, was now invisible to him below the parapet. Byron let out a wail, as he approached the critical moment, and there was what sounded like a snort from down below. Guy beat a hasty retreat back into the main room. Federica raised an eyebrow.

"Jesus Christ," he said, fighting to breathe normally. "Can you do that...?"

"I imagine," she said.

"I mean, weightless... she looked like an astronaut."

"Indeed."

"How do you move around normally? You must need diver's boots."

"How literal you are. I keep telling you, things don't work like that down here. We can walk, we can run, when you scratch us we bleed. It's just that we can do other things too, like float in mid-air. But, you have to realise, the man has got to make us want to float." She paused and extended a hand toward Guy, which he took. As usual her deadly pale skin was as cool as alabaster. "Go on, make me feel weightless," she whispered. "Make me walk on air."

I am gone, thought Guy, far gone. Head over heels, lost and gone. What the hell, he thought, there's no going back now. Let love have its way. The madness will pass soon enough, though at that moment he wished it never would.

"As usual," said Guy, "we have to do all the bloody work."

"Might be worthwhile though," she said, and this time there was more than mirth in her smile. Guy began to tremble.

The door burst open again, and Byron came back into the room, ostentatiously buttoning himself up, and whistling between his teeth. He gave no notice of being aware of anything in the atmosphere, which Guy felt was now so thick as to be like a smoke-filled room or swimming underwater. "That got my heart going," said Byron; "nothing like a piece before an evening out to raise the appetite."

In the next instalment: Love at the opera. Love in the Casino.

Die Erbsünde, Walter Klemm

Coming from Behind

Il Tappeto Rosso, Marcello Dudovich

Histoire d'un C, Achille Deveria

Vie de Faublas, Achille Deveria

Some Lithographs, Jean Ignace Isidore Grandville (Jean Ignace Isidore Gérard)

L'Aretin d'Augustin Carrache, author Pietro Aretino, artist Jacques Joseph Coiny

Confidences De Celestine, Anonymous French

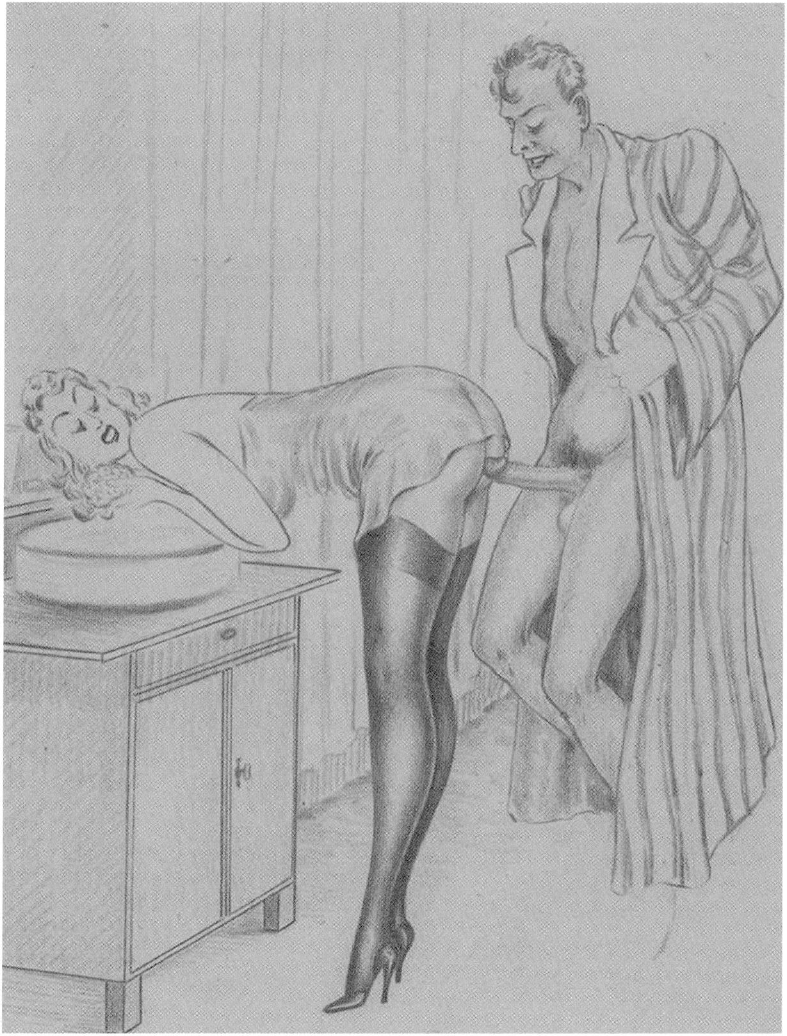

Fetish Album, Anonymous German

La Volupté, Rudolf Merényi

Lucy Golden, *for all her openness in her writing, is a very private person and shuns publicity, considering that what she has revealed is more than enough. And if you were to press us as to what she was really like, we would simply quote her:*

"My books and stories are deeply personal. They are drawn from the very deepest parts of my mind and if you don't know me after reading them, you never can."

Lucy Golden

Finny's Tale

The Creature in the Garden

Finny's Tale, The Creature in the Garden

Lucy Golden

I'd never seen a stripper before Rosie's party. That's not to say that I'm a complete innocent, but it's not a normal part of a girl's everyday life, is it?

I've known Rosie since heaven knows when. In fact it was from her that I heard about this contract devising the new Census Data Collection Forms in the first place. Through her, I joined the contract team, and we shared a flat from the outset. Malcolm joined the team about eighteen months later, and although they hit it off straight away, it was one of those on-again, off-again kind of relationships that you know will never get anywhere.

I was on my own at that time and feeling sorry for myself: Rosie was not the only one to fancy Malcolm. I had managed a few gropes and snogs, but beyond that it never really got going and when his work on the contract came to an end and he announced he was going back home to South Africa, I knew I was going to miss him. Then it emerged that Rosie was going with him and that they were going to get married at some stage, and I knew I was going to miss her. In fact, I was jealous. I mean I was pleased for them, and I am fond of Rosie, but it brought home to me that it could have been me looking so happy and about to get married and it wasn't. And I had been working on this one contract for three years and I was no nearer knowing what I wanted from life, let alone finding what I wanted, than when I started.

I was beginning to feel old.

So I approached their party, a combined going-away, stag party and hen night, determined to have a good time. I knew that most of the contract staff would be there so I was expecting to get lucky even if it didn't last for ever. Sunday morning is the loneliest time of the week if you wake up to an empty bed, particularly when you can hear voices - or more - coming from your flat-mate's room.

It was early July, gloriously hot, and the party was being held in the old Victorian house that Malcolm and the other lads rented out along The Avenue. We held most of our parties there because, although the house was nothing special, it had an enormous walled garden and a wide lawn lined by thick trees and bushes. Alan, Malcolm's best man, had organised 'His and Hers' strippers: a Portuguese girl called Marenia for Malcolm and a gorilla man for Rosie. I drank quite a bit, probably more than I should, and made a last doomed bid for Malcolm which got nowhere; I'm not sure he even fully realised what was on offer. Anyway Alan dragged him back to the living room where, despite Malcolm's pretence of objection, he was made to sit in a straight-backed chair in the centre of the floor. Marenia came down from where she had been hiding somewhere upstairs, the music started, and she began to do her stuff.

Now I am not a lesbian, and I have no wish whatsoever to become one, but she was pretty, well no, more than pretty and not exactly pretty. She was stunning; glamorous, tall and elegant, but strutted with determination and pride in herself. The music was just right. She did two tracks, first a dance number and then a really old slow one called '*Je t'aime*', and she danced really well to both of them. As I said, I had never seen a girl do a strip before, and I didn't realise that she would take everything off and I didn't realise that once she had done that she would drop down into a low squat on the floor and that her legs would be spread wide apart and we would all be able to see her, all of her. Nor that on some girls there could be so much to see.

And I didn't realise that she could do all that in someone's house in front of forty or fifty people she had never seen before, and do it openly, unashamed, uninhibited with total confidence in herself, with grace in her movements and pride in the silent attention from all of us, male and female, her audience.

And I didn't realise how erotic all that could be, how deep an effect it could have when someone, who could be male or female, comes out and does something so exclusively and deliberately sexual in front of a crowd of people, and mostly how much of an effect that could have on me. She had a torrent of black hair which, all through her dance, swooped from side to side so that even after she had taken her top off, when we knew she was only wearing her little knickers, even then this thick wild mane kept tumbling forwards over her front. Her hands would disappear under the curtain of hair and then she would spin and the hair would spread out and suddenly we could see her breasts and her nipples and they would be hard and erect and I knew that mine were as well.

And maybe it was because she was Portuguese, or maybe just confident, or maybe that was just how she preferred it, but she hadn't shaved under her arms so there was thick luxuriant hair there and a sort of soft dark down running over her arms. It was all quite animal and untamed and I felt myself wanting to touch her, stroke her, and not just the hair but the skin too.

So when - finally, after an age of teasing and waiting - she slid her tiny black knickers down her long dark legs, I expected another thick bush of that glorious hair, but she shocked me again. There was none: she was immaculately shaved, revealing thick ripe lips almost pouting at me with another pair of lips pushing out from between them and even her clit poked out too. Everything was being offered to us, visible and available.

She looked so ready, so complete a woman like some kind of erotic fertility goddess. Everything that she had done, every gesture she had made, (and all the little gaps which our minds had filled out) had built to this. Her whole body was primed, totally ripe and ready for sex. And I think I was jealous again. When she was naked she carried on writhing sensuously over Malcolm, resting one foot on his knee then sliding it up his thigh, completely opening herself up for him to see every fold, every glistening crease, every shining pore, everything. Her foot rested in his lap and the toes wriggled around, massaging him gently. At one point she slipped her hand inside the waist band of his shorts and for a few moments, as we all giggled with embarrassment, we only saw the fluttering of fingers beneath the thin cotton. And I was jealous of that too, of the attention that he was paying to her, of the sneaky gropes under her thighs and across her bottom, and of the way she was able to grope him. I wanted it to be me who was doing something so manifestly sexual, me who Malcolm was watching so intently and my body that he was casually caressing. And I wanted to be the one who kept running back to his lap, who could feel his erection, who could hold his head to my breasts and feel his lips nuzzle at me, pretending he was just pretending when we all knew he wasn't.

And at last, as the song sobbed to its wailing end, it should have been me who came up to wrap her arms round him, and me who pressed his face hard against my belly. It should have been my body, my scent, my arousal, he inhaled in those deep slow breaths. Me, he finally kissed.

But it wasn't me and my arousal was wasted and it all seemed so unfair, specially when he already had Rosie, who would be good and loyal, and now he had this girl too, offered in front of all of us, simply as a pleasant diversion. I knew I could have filled either role and I wanted to fill both and I was denied either.

I stayed in the doorway, outside the cheering and the laughter, watching from a safe distance behind the door as she took her bow and collected her clothes. As she left, passing close in front of me, her clothes bundled under one arm, she flashed an excited, jubilant grin and then was gone, a smooth naked bottom scampering up the stairs to get dressed. I wanted to follow her, but for what? To complain that Malcolm didn't want me? To tell her I was jealous? That I wanted her life? That I wanted people to stand round watching me, admiring me, the way they admired her? That I wanted to be her? It would have been stupid and I skulked back into the living room as people were preparing Rosie for her turn.

She too had to take her place on the chair in the centre while a man in a gorilla suit, looking frankly rather silly, came out and started prancing around her. At least, it started silly, but that changed. Again, there was some music and he pulled her up so that he was sort of dancing with her, but his huge hands, all moulded plastic and nylon fur, kept groping all over her, over her bottom and up the front of her tee shirt, and his wrinkled plastic nose sniffed and snorted, pushing under her arms and between her legs and making obscene animal grunts of joy at the smells he was pretending to find. It was well done, and was very funny. Rosie laughed as much as everybody else, but following the girl before and with the thoughts that she had put in my mind, well I am sure in all our minds, the gorilla's game was not entirely innocent. His blank disregard for her attempts to restrain his hands, the complete lack of any expression on his artificial face, his refusal to give any indication that he understood speech, all these together gave it a sinister edge. Like a ventriloquists's discarded dummy, it was both human and inhuman; familiar and dangerous; playful and frightening. Overall, it made him even more uncontrollable and intimidating and yet, somehow, alluring.

He was a big man - and Rosie is five foot nothing in the tallest of her spike heels - so when he picked her up bodily he could turn her upside down ignoring her struggles to keep her skirt from tumbling down and showing her knickers. He simply cuffed her hands away and eventually she gave up, letting the skirt fall down over her head while his unfeeling plastic fingers scratched at the taut material between her thighs, jabbed at the damp crease and plucked at the elastic, threatening always to pull her knickers right off. Then he pulled her up higher, gathering in the skirt but now tugging at her t-shirt where it was tucked in at the waist and finally releasing it. Amid her squeals and giggles, she tried to keep him at bay, but again he ignored her protests and finally pulled it out so the shirt tumbled down to her armpits and her bare breasts were revealed to us all, excited, erect and full. Turned back again, he tucked her under one arm and she made only token resistance when he began to pull her top right off. Once that had been tossed away, she tried to cover herself with her hands but he shoved them aside and scratched around her breasts, flicking at her nipples and pulling, pinching at the real flesh with synthetic, unyielding claws.

With his curiosity apparently satisfied, he laid her down on the floor, but still kept snuffling around at her and preventing her getting up, grunting and then rubbing himself and sort of humping at her. Finally he hauled her up again, threw her over his shoulder and in a half crouch ambled off out of the circle, pausing briefly next to one girl who squealed in real fear the instant he put his face against her. The cheers and laughter with a big round of applause drowned all this as he put Rosie down again, took his mask off, kissed her and took his bow.

When a game of Pig in the Middle started - the lads refusing to let Rosie have her tee shirt back - I refilled my glass and slipped out onto the terrace to get a little air, to sit down and allow my thoughts to calm in the stillness of evening. They had put candles around, little tea-lights mixed in with bigger candles stuck on plates and in bottles so the whole area twinkled. The sun had disappeared behind the gigantic Cedar trees which marked the bottom of the garden, but it was still light and the smell of barbecues and the sound of other music from other parties drifted through the night.

"Lovely garden! Lovely night!" The gorilla man was standing behind me, now in shorts and a striped shirt, gripping a beer can in one great fist and a slice of pizza in the other.

I hated to be so transparent. "I suppose so. I hate gardens."

"Oh," he said. "That's rather a pity." His voice came low and deep from inside his chest and sounded wounded so that I was ashamed of my scorn and tried to make amends.

"But no, you're right. It is lovely."

He grinned. "I'm Jeff," he said and drank most of the beer down in one and then grinned again, mischievous and enticing. "Bloody hot in that suit."

I smiled, or something. He did not look any smaller now that he was out of the gorilla suit but he did seem friendly and his slightly dishevelled fair curly hair seemed almost boyish. I was really fairly drunk by this stage and when he moved on to some vacuous comment about the pizza (he was only making polite conversation after all) I said I thought gorillas only ate bananas. What a stupid thing to say!

"Oh well," he said determined to maintain his jovial mood, "I like them too."

"Mmm," I answered, and to this day I have no idea what on earth I can have been thinking about, but I lifted my eyes to him and then down to an obvious stare at his crotch. "Mmm", I said, "So do I."

He looked at me for a few seconds, taking in my open sandals, my thin cotton dress and bare legs, and the empty glass in my hand and he smiled at me.

"Can I fetch you another drink? I'm getting myself one."

"Thanks, Jeff."

When he brought them back, we leaned on the wall side by side and drank in silence. Inside, everybody else was playing a game, I think it was the truth game with matches because Rosie came to shut the patio doors to stop them being blown out. It seemed private out there, in half darkness, his face - and mine too, I suppose - in shadow from the lights of the house behind us and I asked, just casually; "You live with Marenia?"

"Well we share a flat, but we're not, you know, 'together'. I'm not really her type."

"Ah." I tried to make the sound into an invitation to continue.

"Her partner left her rather unexpectedly and she was looking for someone to help her with the gorilla stuff and I was looking for somewhere cheap to stay for a few months."

"I see." There was another pause.

"You're Finny, someone said."

"Yes, short for Fiona."

"So, what did you think of it? The gorilla routine?"

"Different!"

"Ah." He sounded sad. "You didn't like it. I saw you were hiding at the back."

"Well I liked it, but it was kind of unnerving. Is it all planned out in advance, I mean always the same?"

"No, I discuss beforehand with whoever has arranged the booking to see how far they want me to go, and then I play it by ear, depending on the reaction. Alan had said Rosie was good sport, that she would not mind if I pulled her top off."

"No. There haven't been many parties in this house where her boobs have not made an appearance at some stage."

"I see." He was interested and after a minute's thought said, "And yours as well?"

"Occasionally, maybe; from time to time."

"I am sorry I missed them. Still, I suppose the party's not over yet."

I did not respond and then he dropped his voice, confessing suddenly to the quiet truths that can only come out between strangers in the secure silence of a little shadow world. "I am exaggerating. This is only the third time I have ever done this; I only left drama school six months ago and there is bugger all proper work about."

"Well, it seemed good to me. I mean it! But to be honest, I have never seen one of these before so don't really have anything to it judge by. In fact, don't tell anyone, but I had never seen a stripper before tonight."

"And was it exciting?"

"Which?"

"Both."

"Yes."

"Good." He paused and his voice came through very gently. "But would you like it to have been you?"

"Which?"

"Both."

"Yes." But that was too glib and I needed to wipe away the words I had nearly said. "Yes, I would. Come and do one for me when I leave here." I offered it as a throw away and he knew better than to let on that he knew it wasn't.

"Are you leaving?"

"No."

"Then I had better do it soon."

I laughed at his lack of logic without accepting or refusing the offer but when I shivered in the little breeze, he put his arm around me and I snuggled in close. He may have discarded the gorilla suit, but he was still big and comfortable and secure to rest against. I felt him turn, knew he was looking down at me, considering options, but I did not respond. A gorilla ought to be able to make its own decisions over a mate.

His hand came back onto my shoulder and gently pulled me to him and when

I turned this time he kissed me, first a peck, then a nibble and at last a full, entirely breathless kiss. His hands roamed over my back and down to my bottom and then back up, made the usual circle which is supposed to be so innocent but which we all know is checking for a bra strap. Finding none, one hand worked its way round between us and held me, moulded me, sliding across the front and raising the appropriate peaks of interest.

And then we were surrounded. Half the party poured out onto the terrace announcing that Rosie was leading the hen night down into town where there was supposed to be a Chippendale-type male strip show on. Alan, Malcolm and several others had offered to do their own but since this was conditional on the girls reciprocating, their offer had been rejected. In response they were going to watch a porny video. I didn't care for either option, but Jeff was new and when Alan kept pestering him, he relented: he did not understand how to refuse people he did not know. The girls were all childishly excited and enthusiastic and that just annoyed me. I said I wasn't interested although Rosie and even Marenia urged me to come along but the more they pleaded, the less I was tempted until finally, in something of a strop, I told them to piss off and leave me alone.

They did.

I sneaked back into the kitchen, ignoring the few voices (all male) in the living room, refilled my glass and made my way back out to the garden, through the shrubs and railings down to a small ornamental pond surrounded by low stone walls. Here I settled myself down on the paving, my back leaning against the warm stones, and kicked off my sandals. The night was clear, starlit and open and there were still sounds of cars and people and music somewhere up behind me, but in the little hollow round the pond, it was quiet and private. It looked like being another lonely night, and although I really wanted something less familiar than my own hands for comfort, if they were to be the only hands available, I would make do. I wanted to start straight away in the cool of the open sky with the wide world around and above me, so I tucked the cold beer can between my legs, up high against the bare skin of my thighs and the thin cotton of my knickers where the coolness was needed and where the condensation from the can could refresh me where my own moisture was working exactly the opposite.

All around me the contented rustling of a thousand night creatures made the quiet that bit more comforting until a twig snapped behind me; not close, but close enough. Too loud, too big a twig, to have been a bird or a hedgehog, and I froze. The last thing I wanted was sympathy, someone else coming to tell me to cheer up and come and enjoy the fun, and I pulled my knees up to cover the bare skin and make me less conspicuous. After a few minutes with no further sign or sound of anyone, I peered round the corner of the wall, relieved to find no one there. I relaxed back into my place, slipped a hand back under my dress and, in a sudden silence, heard behind me regular low breathing, not quite panting, more like somebody deliberately trying to make no noise. I carefully put down the glass, peered round the other side of the stones and was confronted by a wall of black fur. I screamed before I saw what it was, I screamed again when it reached out and grabbed my hair and my shoulder and then the huge gorilla pulled me over to its chest, its thick long arms enfolding, engulfing me in the tangle of hair. It spun me around so that my back was against its chest and one long arm reached down over my shoulder and clamped me fast.

My first reaction was simple relief at realising what - who - it was and that I was safe, but when I stupidly said, "Hello, Jeff!" the figure stopped in a terrible ominous stillness and then reached out and deliberately cuffed me with the back of its hand, hard across my thigh. I screamed out a protest, suddenly unsure it was Jeff, wriggled and tried to push him away, but the clamp tightened and the free hand started to creep across me. It did not respond to my struggles, and too strong for my resistance, too uncaring of my protests, it continued to drag over me, pulling at my clothes, rubbing over my chest. It virtually disregarded my breasts, simply ran over my front in a series of big circles that reached down to my waist and up my side and across both breasts. I grabbed his wrist but he was much stronger than me and I could not restrain him; the more I pulled, the more he pushed. The arm encircling my shoulders tightened and the other arm stretched, reached down the front of my dress until the hard pointed claws rasped along skin, hooked under the hem and pulled. Up my legs, up my thighs, my knickers suddenly came into view, white in the dusk, and the dress was pulled higher still. I was now fully encased in his crossed arms, pinioned and captive. Even if I had tried to resist, even if I had wanted to resist, I would have been powerless.

But it was then that things changed, for slowly edging round the far side of the stone wall came someone - something - else; also in a suit of black fur, also ambling, grunting and then, when it reached me, nudging with its nerveless nose at the exposed crotch of my knickers before its moulded hands slithered up my legs, right up under my dress to my breasts. Not quite as big as the first one, it was no less menacing, no less alien and equally uncompromising in its unchanging stare. There was little flexibility in the stubby fingers as they clawed at my nipples, scraped across and over them, but the complete lack of delicacy did not in any way reduce the effect: if anything the opposite. I was helpless in their grasp: held tight by one; accessible to the crude and insensitive maulings of the other. I was frightened, but with the exhilarated terror of the fairground. I didn't actually believe I was in real danger, but neither was I in control. The ride had started and I was committed until it ended, but the ending was not at my bidding. They had chosen to scare me for their amusement, and their next choice could be anything else they desired. For now I was theirs, a captive, alone with them in a deserted garden under the stars.

In retrospect, I do not know why I didn't just laugh. It seems so crazy, two figures in ridiculous party costumes pinning me down in the garden of a suburban house. What threat was there? But we don't live our lives in retrospect and the course of the evening had led me to see these creatures only as they appeared, as wild untameable animals, uncaring and dangerous. More than that, it all seemed vital and passionate and an invigorating contrast to the sterile predictability of the life I had been living. I despised the safe artificiality of the show that the girls had gone to see, trooping off to gawp from a secure distance at immaculate coiffured elegance. I was cramped on the ground with two huge black hairy monsters. It was glorious.

From behind, the first creature pushed me forward up against the new arrival where all I could see was a pair of deep black eyes staring back at me through the mask, moist eyes, shining, full and excited at the knowledge of its power, at what it was doing. The scent of this one was, if anything, stronger, slightly more sweaty and animal than the other so I could not be sure if this was really Jeff, or if the other was; and if this was Jeff, who was the other, the first one? Who was it now behind me, arms embracing me, hands reaching down and pulling insistently at my knickers? Pushing down inside to claw at my own inadequate covering of hair? The front one also joined in, digging at the elastic waistband, scrabbling at the top and trying to get inside or get them down or somehow, anyhow, to get rid of their flimsy protection. Finally it grew impatient and with a sudden yank, the material was simply ripped, torn almost in two and pulled away. For a moment he held the pink clammy remnant up at eye level between us, then clasped it to his nostrils and snorted before it was tossed up high into the air where it flapped once before it disappeared.

I turned back, my eyes drawn to the luminance of my pale thighs shining out in the half-light, to my dress which had been pushed right up during the battle for possession of my knickers and to the point just below the hem where was visible the tip of the slightly darker shadow of my neatly trimmed triangle. The one in front of me now held my shoulders while the other fumbled at the back of my neck. Its claws were struggling to grip the tongue of the zip, and hot gasps of increasingly frustrated breath came onto the bare skin of my neck. Finally impatience took over again and with one hand in the neck band it simply pulled the dress apart, enough to start the zip running down, enough for it to continue and work it down to the bottom where the dress was rucked up around my waist. The other one now took over, pulled at the torn neckline to tug the garment down my arms, simply dragging it completely inside out, over my hips and legs and off. It bundled the cloth up and tossed it away into the shrubs.

That was all I had been wearing, so I lay back, naked, a nakedness made even more complete by the contrast with the heavy masses of animal hair. I was gripped and cradled in the arms of the first one while the second stared at me. My arms were clamped down by my sides and my legs pushed out in front of me leaving me so available, utterly ready for them to take charge.

The one in front of me brought himself up into the same low crouch and taking hold of my wrist pulled me out of the other's grasp and forward onto hands and knees. He released me and we stared at each other while I waited; there was little doubt what was the next step in the game.

They wanted me: they had found me.

They had caught me: they had stripped me.

I dripped.

Suddenly I felt a stinging slap across my bare bottom which made me gasp and turn on the attacker behind, but immediately I turned, I was slapped from the other side and, when I tried to protect myself from this, a long black arm reached out and the cold rigid fingers, like pre-formed claws, pinched my nipple, pinched me hard. Caught between them like this, I was entirely vulnerable. I jumped to my feet and tried to make a run for it, but as soon as I was up, I realised that I was visible to anybody still left in the house, or on the terrace or even in any of the adjoining houses.

I darted behind the fruit-cage but immediately one of them appeared at the corner and although I kept my back to the wall, I was slapped on the thigh, then on the bottom again and then right across the breast, and it hurt. I slipped out between them and across the damp grass towards the shrubbery and heard them lumbering after me as I ran. It was the unpredictability which made it so hard to bear, which undermined me. When they had first appeared, I had been frightened, then complacent; now I was scared again. Sitting in the comfort and safety of a living room surrounded by friends, it may have been stirring to watch the charade of an amorous gorilla dancing to music. It was entirely different to be utterly alone, stripped naked by two creatures who did not respond to any command or any word spoken to them, who reacted only as animals, whose intention was solely their own pleasure, a pleasure which clearly included playing with me like a mouse, and causing me pain by slapping me and pinching me whenever I came within range. I managed to reach the shrubbery, but while I picked delicately across the rough earth between the twigs and thorns, they simply shoved their way through behind me and as soon as I stopped, another stinging slap across my bottom sent me further on.

And still I could not be completely certain who they were. I was almost certain that one was Jeff, but I had no idea at all about the other. It could possibly be Alan, but Alan should have been taller. If not Alan, then who? Malcolm? I would have liked it to be and it seemed the right height, but I could not know for sure. For a minute I considered trying to head back to the house, but there was nowhere there to hide and with no chance to recover my clothes, I could hardly go back to the party. At the far side, where the side of the garage ran very close to the wall of the garden, there was rather more shadow and it did look as if it might offer more cover than was available among the shrubs. I scampered across the lawn and found a tiny area where, with my back to the garage, nobody could creep up behind me and, squeezed between the two walls, I was almost invisible.

I crouched down into the corner and drew my knees up to my chest. The sudden pressure of warm skin on my breasts, even though it was my own warm skin, sent a little ripple through me and, without thinking, my thighs opened a fraction and my hands reached down to cover me, to protect and to comfort me, and my fingertips stroked gently at the little damp protrusion. As soon as I pressed it, the dampness increased markedly betraying how readily my body responded to the attention and stimulation it had already received, and in anticipation of the more there would be to come.

It happened quickly. I heard the unmistakable sound of shuffling feet and the light in front of me was blocked by the black mass of one of the animals. It reached in, grabbed my ankle and started to haul me out and, although I tried to pull back, it was so much stronger than me that, unless I was willing to be dragged across the stones on my back, I had no choice but to concede and worm my way out.

As soon as I emerged, they each grabbed one arm and I was dragged backwards across the lawn and up the steps onto the terrace. As we arrived, a roar of muffled laughter came from inside where the others were still watching their stupid film.

At the top of the terrace steps, they laid me down on the warm flag stones, one taking my wrists, the other taking my ankles and I was spread like a sacrifice. The sky was still bright and with the candles all around, I was plainly visible, a pale virgin star, their play-thing.

Now I was shared; brittle plastic and soft fur scuttling over me, artificial hands to squeeze and paw at my breasts, hands whose cold unnatural hardness made their blunt caresses all the more stimulating. Had anyone else groped me so roughly, I would have protested, or left, or both. This was different. They had changed me: I was as animal as either of them. I could smell their sweat and could feel my own running down me, and it was not just sweat I was leaking. My legs were spread wide, my pussy peeled open and that smell too drifted up to me.The game was over and I was impatient. After all that had happened, I could not wait for any long slow foreplay; in reality the foreplay had begun hours ago when the Portuguese stripper first stepped out onto the floor; maybe that afternoon, when I had taken a shower and changed ready for the night. Now I was entirely ready.

One of them half stood up and shuffled over to the low parapet wall where it selected one of the candles, not one of the neat elegant, dinner table types in their finely painted candlesticks, but a cruder one, thicker one: an altar candle, one whose length and width could not help but stir images in my brain, and - obviously - in the creature's brain too. It snapped the candle free of its saucer, shaking loose the molten wax and extinguishing the flame in the process, and turned back to me, settled onto its haunches between my legs, staring at the deep shadow between my thighs, shuffling up further, closer, pressing down on my thigh and with the candle clamped tight in its hand, reaching forward to pull at my pussy lips, opening me, running the candle once, twice along the side and then - with no preparation beyond a low grunt - simply twisting it in, deep, deep in. I moaned. Its free hand was still rasping over me, up my thighs, across my stomach and raking through my pubic hair, but the sharp point of the thumb nail kept returning to ride my clitoris, running spirals up one side, across the far too sensitive top, and back down the sides. At the same time, the candle never stopped: sliding in and out of me in a brutally careless piston, relentlessly lifting and exciting me however much I tried to dismiss it all as sheer mechanics.

What attracted their attention, the men who had stayed behind to watch stupid films? A sound that I made, although I had tried to be quiet?

A sudden movement from one of the beasts? The erratic flickering, part obscured, of the row of candles? I heard a single low call, just the one, and then the patio door was being pushed open and as I looked up from the ground, they poured out, fifteen, twenty maybe, excited grins already flooding over their faces. They formed their own circle around us, a ring beyond the two creatures (who had anyway entirely ignored them), from where they could watch me, watch what was being done to me, and I could watch them watching me.

If I hadn't called a halt before, this should have been the moment to stop the game: I knew many of these men, worked with them, would meet them in the office again in two days time. I would have to face them while we both remembered the sight I now presented. I should have stopped then.

But it was too late. Powerful hands were still scraping and pinching at my breasts: a cruel and relentless assault, exquisitely painful. The smaller one stayed crouched between my legs, intently focussed on its thumb nail rasping at my clit and its fist driving the candle, a constant unbearable rhythm that was irresistible. I no longer cared that I was so publicly exposed and humiliated: I just wanted them to go on. I heard myself moan, looked up to see the mocking reaction of my spectators - yes, Malcolm among them: now he could see how much better he might have done if he had chosen more carefully - and saw the concentration on all those faces as they watched the crude simplicity of the candle pounding in and out of me. I moaned again and this time it was just a single wail as the intensity of it all became too much and the stimulation of watching, of being watched, of being so simply and unambiguously treated, all of that finally pushed me over the edge into an extended sobbing orgasm that washed away any other thoughts or feelings, that obliterated all thoughts of the people around me and I no longer cared for what any of them saw or thought as long as the feelings would just continue for ever.

It wasn't forever; it was all too brief. But it wasn't completely over.

The candle was pulled away and the two animals spun me round, hauling and twisting me to the position they wanted until I was clamped against the second one's chest while it was the first one, who had been behind me, who now shuffled up close to take his place squatting between my legs, gripping one ankle in each huge fist, lifting and spreading me wide again.

And he didn't want the candle: he was fiddling with the crotch of his costume, awkwardly, almost comically but I was too impatient. I needed more and brought my knees up, the better to open myself to him, lifted my hips to offer myself to him and reached down to squeeze my clit to make sure I would be fully ready when the time came. I separated my lips and, dipping a finger deep inside, smeared the abundant wetness across both swollen sides and up the whole length of my crease. He was trying to concentrate on his costume, but distracted by watching me and even the hands across my breasts froze as both of them paused to watch the spectacle; at last I taken back control. I heard the expectant silence from the outer ring of spectators and was tempted to carry on. Now I was the centre of attention: that stripper had not dared to go this far. I did; I dared. Lying naked in front of all of them, I had let myself be fucked by a candle. In a minute I was going to be fucked by a man. Before that, I might, if I chose, if I felt they deserved it, I might let them watch me masturbate.

Even the thought was almost enough to make me come a second time, but I was on a plateau and I had been waiting long enough and needed something more, so I did not protest when my fingers were pushed aside by a long claw which slithered down my front, came to rest in my lap and started to dig its way inside me. It dug at the moisture it found there and brought it out and up to smear it over my nipples.

At last the other creature eased his costume open and a glorious erection appeared, pink and slightly incongruous surrounded by the sea of artificially black hair, but I didn't care. It was there, visibly hard, erect and ready; the ultimate compliment to my offering. He moved up to squat over me and ,as my own hands were pinioned by the other creature, he swung his huge erection across my face, slapping my cheeks with it, teasing and prodding at my mouth, but quickly pulling away every time my tongue reached out for him.

As soon as he crawled back down between my thighs and I felt the tip of his cock nosing around me for entrance, I reached down, took hold of him in my fist and fed it in. I was so wet he almost slipped straight out again so I grabbed tight handfuls of hair on his sides, locked my ankles behind him to make sure he could not escape. His hips lifted back and then dropped as he slid far in and the first beautifully vicious thrust knocked my breath out; I heard and felt a gasp as the shock drove me back further against the figure behind.

The black mask loomed over me, and it was that which I was most aware of, that which I still recognised as my lover. Ridiculous, yes, but still powerful, still strong and intimidating. As well as that, the mask prevented any kisses or tenderness, so that his grunts, coming muffled through it, were not of love but of animal passion, of lust. He was clearly as ready as I was. Before another steady dozen bruising thrusts had driven me back still harder into the arms and the caresses of the figure behind, I was lost, the trembling beginning somewhere way down deep and mushrooming up through me in a flood. I clamped his hairy black shoulder in my mouth and lifted my bottom to meet him, pushing back with my hips as hard as I squeezed in with my thighs to force every atom of pleasure out of him and into me and I heard my own voice screaming obscenities of encouragement out into the night air, encouragement which he didn't need for he was already pressing ever more savage thrusts at me, animal grunts from both of us and somewhere above me, chanting from our watchers. It was short and rough and brutal and wonderful and nothing since has even come close.

When finally it had been enough, and I realised that he had stopped his thrusts, in fact that my slot was now as full of his wetness as of mine, I slowly relaxed my grip and let him ease away, nursing his bleeding shoulder where my teeth had bitten right through the costume. We sat back, panting, both shocked by the force of the encounter, by the way we had been entirely taken up in the parts we were playing. He eased the mask off and for the first time I could see Jeff's face as he leaned back down to kiss me. He reached his arms around me and hugged me up to him and this time it really was Jeff, not some wild creature that was embracing me, kissing me, whose tongue at last met mine, whose breath mixed with mine. But such subtlety was lost on our cheering circle of spectators, whose laughter and clapping embarrassed me so that we broke apart. I remembered the other creature and immediately looked round for him but he was gone, no sign beyond a black shadow pushing through the grinning circle which closed up behind him.

So I still don't know who that other person was. I have a few suspicions and a couple of clues. I never saw them stand up straight so I cannot judge the height and I never heard them speak so I cannot judge the voice, although that may be a clue in itself. I do know two things. Three things.

First, when I looked into the mask, and even allowing for the whole face being entirely unlit, the eyes looking back at me were a very dark brown, almost black. I don't know any of the guys I have considered who have eyes quite that colour.

Second, thinking back over the sequence of things, at the end I was lying in their lap and in spite of everything that had happened and was still happening, in spite of it all I could feel no bulge, no erection under my back. But I was cradled against a very soft chest.

Third, the two of them never spoke, as if words were not needed for a game which they had played together before. And Jeff only knew one other person at that party.

I don't know what to think.

Fridolin Hase *is a German freelance illustrator who has a serious penchant for conies. Her love of this small furry animal is such that she has invested them with some important human attributes. She is working on a* Bunny Sutra. *Viva rabbit lib!*

Comme des lapins

Fridolin Hase

86

Spot the Seven Differences

Katie Kelly *is one of the latest contributors to SEx magazine and is as beautiful as she is wise and as bold as she is brilliant. She makes grown men whimper and Chick-Literati turn pale chartreuse. But read her story and be the judge of this yourselves.*

Katie Kelly

Let 's put this to bed

Let's put this to bed

Katie Kelly

This is not a story of romantic love. This is the tale of my first (last? Better not be hasty!) foray into bad love, a so bad it's good love, resplendent in its many guises. I intend to focus on the physical one you'll be relieved to hear. I'm writing this down for two reasons. The first is self-indulgence. I don't talk about those few months spent embroiled in you anymore, so by writing this I get to relive those amazing moments without having to relive our messy demise. The second is simple. I want to; I need to forget you. Memories of you have, for too long, saturated my thoughts and as frequently my knickers. So I shall write this down, read it one last time and then burn it and kiss you goodbye, beautiful man.

Where to start? Should it be in your bed, where we ended up after two years of restrained, polite conversation? Pants were yanked down, t-shirts discarded and mouths hungrily explored. "We shouldn't have sex," I whispered in your ear. Forty-seven minutes later you were fucking me on all fours on the floor in front of the full-length wardrobe mirror. My knees were glowing for days afterwards. So too, unfortunately, was my nose which took the brunt of your 3 am stubble. What I've glossed over though in my recollection of that night, is how rough we were. I scratched up your back; you repaid the favour by digging your fingers into my ass with impressive fervour. You bruised my mouth with your kisses, pulled me off the bed onto the floor and laid me on my front.

"I want your ass in the air"

I faltered for perhaps, hmmmm, a second and then, pulling myself to my knees, arched my back and gave you an unrestricted view of my soaking wet, pink pussy. Spreading my cheeks apart you sank your face right in and devoured every drenched bit. Then, for want of a more romantic phrase, you fucked me really hard; on my back with my feet on your shoulders, against the wall with my legs wrapped around your waist and bent over the bed, clinging onto sex sodden sheets as your cock hit that spot over and over. In the morning, by which I mean after perhaps an hour of sleep, we did it all over again, adding some shower action to our repertoire. Later, as I meandered in a dazed and confused state towards the station, I felt for the first time an unfamiliar but indescribably sweet ache in my pussy.

Pain maintained a shadowy and persistent presence throughout our time together. I was self-obsessed, caught up in dramas, which you had no choice but to take a second place to. You'd take your revenge later, when you had me naked in your room. Instinctively we knew how to hurt each other and not just verbally. Perversely though, the nastier we were, the better the sex was. It was only a matter of weeks before you were taking your frustrations at our failing relationship out on my ass.

A white-wine-induced tirade (mine) was halted abruptly when you pulled me over your lap, yanked down my knickers and spanked me until my shrieks of rage faded into a muffled apology. An apology, which quickly turned into a stifled sigh of wanting, as your fingers sank between the slick heat of my cheeks and worked my pussy into such a state of excitement, and I was soon feverishly grabbing for the remnants of the bottle of Pinot Grigio stashed by the bed. But you got yours too, didn't you? We were always equal when it came playing the bitch with a whip routine, and I had you over a pillow once, remember? I was playing with your ass, a finely gym-honed vision of suntanned pert firmness. I gently nipped your cheeks with my teeth, grinning as you wriggled. Then edging your thighs apart I ran my tongue deep in between from the base of your cock, to your ass hole which is where I lingered, gently flicking over this most sensitive place. With each measured stroke of my tongue, a shudder ran through your body and you'd squirm, only to be stilled by a stinging slap to your ass. Your ass was tongued and spanked until I reached underneath and felt you ready to explode. Murmuring, "Turn over," I slid happily onto your hard cock and rode you like an over enthusiastic pony-club virgin.

Though it was already blatantly clear now that this was going to be a love of the self-destructive variety, destined to end in therapy not marriage, I couldn't stop. Alarm bells should have triggered the first time you pushed me down onto my knees, by my hair and told me to suck your cock. I stared up at you incredulously. "Suck my cock," you ordered again and then, using your fistful of curls, forced my head towards your groin. As I struggled to pull away, your other hand reached between my thighs. I was soaking and got more so as you spread me wide and spanked my pussy. Gently at first, then a little harder. I moaned and with one fluid movement, you took advantage of my distracted state and slid your cock deep into my mouth. There was no gentle love for us, no lazy early morning spooning whilst you kissed my neck and stroked my hair, not when there was a sofa to be bent over, a table to be fucked on, handcuffs to be used, a ruler to be brandished, an argument to be had, a cutting comment to be made and retribution to be delivered.

The end came as violently as I always did. We'd been bouncing barbed emails back and forth all day. I was wearing a skirt you thought was inappropriate for the office. One that looks deceivingly respectable lying on the bed, but entirely not so when wrapped around a well shaped female behind. A black pencil skirt that touched my knees, but was tight enough to transform my walk from a confident stride, into a languid saunter. You used to love this skirt. Happy you were not, and you got less so when I decided to join my team for a few drinks after work. I knew I was taunting you but I didn't care. I went out to the bar next to the office and ignored your texts and phone calls. Particularly when they became increasingly frequent after ten. Midnight, and as I made my way towards your apartment, my defiance was steadily losing a battle to nerves. I had been an utter bitch and you were not known for your patience under such circumstances. Unfortunately I couldn't slip in unnoticed. The entrance to your building was through an underground car park and I had to call for you to buzz open the main doors. The phone rang and rang. You picked up only to hang up immediately, cutting off my hello. Looking up I saw the lift from the light flick on, signifying someone was on the way down. I leant uneasily against the bonnet of your car, and waited. The entrance doors opened and there you were, still wearing the suit you'd had on that morning, standing a few metres away from me and not smiling. I tried a hesitant grin. It elicited no response. If anything your jaw clenched shut an extra millimetre or so.

"Ok, I'm sorry!" I exclaimed. "I'm sorry for ignoring your calls, I'm sorry for not.."

"Turn around", you interrupted. "Put your hands on the bonnet of the car and please just shut the fuck up."

Now would have been the time to shake my head in offended disbelief and walk away. But having heard the story so far and witnessed my somewhat positive response to imminent chastisement, I'm sure you won't be surprised to hear that I didn't take that course of action. Instead I obeyed, turned around and placed my hands on the car.

"Now pull up your skirt"

Jeeeeeeeesus. I looked over my shoulder, were you joking?

"Pull it up, don't make me come over there." It would appear you weren't.

Flushing slightly and whispering an apology to my feminist sisters, I inched my skirt up. Not an easy task but with a bit of strategic wiggling it crept upwards, navigated my undeniably round ass until it rested, belt-like around my waist. My knickers were displayed to you in all their scanty glory, sheer and black, hugging my cheeks. Nervously I shifted from one foot to the another. I heard the gentle hiss of a belt being pulled through trouser loops. Footsteps brought you closer to me. I could feel your stare, moving heatedly up my legs, resting on my ass. I wasn't expecting to feel though your hand rest on my hip. Your palm felt cool against my skin. Your fingers curled around the waistband of my knickers and slowly, slowly pulled them down to beneath my ass, then down to my knees. Your hand moved back up, cupped my left cheek and gently squeezed it, assessing the fullness. Did you mean for your finger to brush over my pussy as you did that? It sent a jolt through me, my hands slipped over the polished surface of the car and a small moan escaped, cutting through the silence. Moving away from me, I looked back and saw for the first time the belt in your hand, folded over. Having enjoyed many an Indiana Jones fantasy ever since watching Harrison brandish a whip in *Raiders of the Lost Ark*, the jolt of fear I felt as I saw that belt took me by surprise. Feeling the flood of wetness to my pussy however, did not. Would you really do it? Surely not. My deliberation was rudely interrupted by the whistle of a belt in flight followed by a sharp crack as it connected beautifully across my ass. You barely gave me time to gasp before delivering the second stroke, which landed perhaps a centimetre above the first. Tears prickled insistently. It hurt, you were hurting me and I still wasn't moving. Again I turned to look at you, your arm was raised, the belt loose in your hand and as it fell once again, hitting the very top of my thighs, that tender skin beneath the swell of my bottom, I bit my lip and you saw a tear slip out, slide down my face and splash onto the surface of the car. Angry, I twisted my head away so I didn't see you move until you wore against me biting my neck, whispering that I had to learn my lesson, that I was a bad girl. Your hands travelled to my ass, traced the hot marks the belt had left, then in between, enjoying the slippery warmth and the force with which I pushed back onto your fingers. Deftly, you opened your trousers. Your cock sprung out, thick and hard and then you were blissfully deep inside me. You fucked me with all the anger you had, months of it hoarded and now tinged with regret. But it felt so good and though we both knew we were, in our own fucked up way, saying goodbye, we savoured every last second, every last thrust, every last caught breath. Bruised you left me. I watched you walk away.

So that's how it ended. Ended? I'm wincing as I write that. I did love you my beautiful man and I wish I'd been nicer, but I'll take my 'what-ifs' with me and let you go.

Now where are the matches?

Maybe I'll read through this just one last time.

MANUAL OF CLASSICAL EROTOLOGY (De Figuris Veneris), author Frederick Charles Forberg , artist Paul Avril

Anal Sex

Eveline. Léon Courbouleix

Les Exploits d'un Jeune Don Juan, author Guillaume Apollinaire, artist Louis Berthommé de Saint-André

Jeunesse, André Collot

Outdoor Perversions, Anonymous European

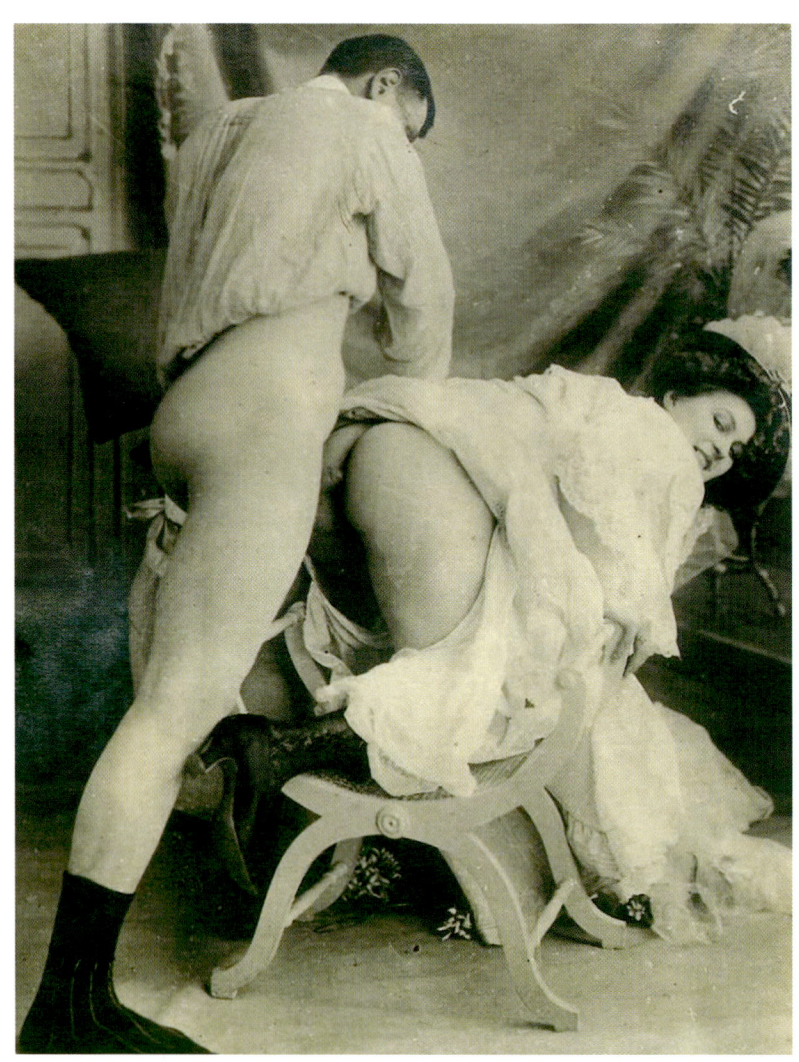

1900s Vintage Photography, Anonymous

Berlin Années 30. Dessins germaniques d'H, Ernst Hildebrandt

Fetish Album, Anonymous German

Pybrac, author Pierre Louÿs, artist Louis Berthommé de Saint-André

John Gibb *started writing rude stories for* The Erotic Review *when it was the only monthly magazine in Europe committed to serious sexual fiction. He now writes monthly for* SEx *magazine. He learnt his trade as a journalist writing about crime for the London* Evening Standard.

John Gibb

Four in Hand

Four in Hand

John Gibb

I won't forget December 23rd 1983 in a hurry. Holiday time in the West End and I was on my way to pick up Fowler and take him for lunch at Bentley's. I arrived at Soho Square early and decided to take advantage of the warmth of the recording studio. A black Daimler parked on the kerb, half on a double yellow line had blocked the way in and I was forced to squeeze between the car and the front door. It was a sharp, clear day, no warmth in the sun and the vapour from the car's exhaust rising in a plume to join the sooty effluvia which in those days, floated like grey gas above the London roof tops. A man in a heavy Crombie lounged against the car studying his watch. Plod, I thought, doesn't look happy. As I climbed the wooden staircase, I could hear raised voices, one of which was Fowler's. An argument seemed to be in progress and by the time I reached the fourth floor, words, louder and more formal than is acceptable in polite conversation, were becoming clear: "You may think yourself qualified to advise others about pronunciation, but these are my words and it is what I say that goes" To which Fowler replied in that infuriating way he had, eyebrows half way up his forehead, and almost certainly with his fucking monocle jammed into the side of his face. He was employing his calm and patient voice, "I have to produce a recording of your book which the public will buy, which is why I have been employed to record you reading it. Perhaps if you spent more time mixing with real people instead of having them served up to you like biscuits, you would be aware that EQUERRY is pronounced 'EQUERRY' and not 'EQUAIRY'." I reached the top floor where there was a single closed door above which a light glowed red and a sign screwed to the wall beneath it reinforced the warning with SILENCE in neon. Insipid daylight seeped in via a grubby sash window and I could see storm clouds gathering black above the City which meant that snow was on the way. Beside the closed door, perched on a typist's chair was a girl in a riding coat. She stared at me, a handkerchief entwined between her fingers. I said, "who are you? What's going on?" She shrugged. "It's the Duke," she replied, "he's not happy at all." For a moment, I failed to understand and said, "What Duke? When is Fowler going to finish?" And it was some moments before I remembered that he had been working for months to publish a book about driving teams of horses with carriages at speed about the countryside. "Christ," I said, "you mean the Duke?" And her nod coincided with an explosive and uninhibited retort to Fowler's remarks: "Who are you to tell me how to read English; anyway, who's President of the fucking English Speaking Union? I'll tell you who is, I fucking am and either we do this fucking book my way or we don't do it at all." An impasse, it seemed to me which would result in Fowler saying something like, "OK, if you want to make a fool of yourself, who am I to get in your way?" Which in the event was exactly what he said. It was probably time to go, I felt.

I looked at the girl, now on her feet. She was tall and fresh faced, cheeks pink, hair in a bunch. "Do you fancy lunch, it looks as if I'm going to be stood up?" And she smiled and nodded and we set off downstairs, and that was how I met Nellie.

I'm Nellie Wallis and I work as a groom at Ronnie Whistler's yard in Larkrise. Sometimes the Duke passes the word that he needs a couple of lads to act as back-steppers for his four in hand and he's chosen me ten times in all. I have to hang on the back of the carriage and move about while he barks away at the front and we canter around the obstacles. He kits us out with black riding pants and boots and he looks after us with a good feed and a bit of jocularity. On this particular day, he's picked me up at the yard and we've gone to Windsor and spent an hour or so on the marathon course and then he's told me to come with him to London because he's going to record his book on Competition Carriage Driving and he might need someone to run a couple of "errands." Well, of course, we all know what that means, but it never amounts to anything much and it's nothing I can't handle. Then he's fallen out with a beard in the recording studio and seems to have forgotten about me and then this man appears and offers to take me out for tea. He's a broomstick, slick hair with curls on his neck, seems to have broken his nose at some time; pin-striped suit and silk shirt and tie. Probably a bit of a rascal. On the way out I tell Sergeant Hoskins that it looks like being a long day and I'm going to find something to eat, while my new friend whistles up a cab.

As we progress slowly down Old Compton Street, he says his name is Porteous. He refers to himself only by his sir-name, shakes hands, shoots his cuffs and smiles. Perfect gent. "Fancy a spot of fish?" He says as we arrive in a lane somewhere at the bottom of Regent Street and a man in a heavy blue coat steps out and opens the cab door and ushers us into Bentley's Oyster Bar. It's a wide, cream painted restaurant with a zinc topped bar and little booths where waiters in white aprons are serving oysters and champagne. The downstairs room is full of smart looking, well dressed gentlemen drinking out of silver tankards and reading the *Sporting Life*. These are big, well fed, pink-faced boys in Holland suits and pale blue ties. Porteous says this is where old Rugby players eat when they're just past their best and bored with training. "Bubbly?" he asks and passes me a heavy goblet of Champagne. He opens his wallet and removes a wad of notes which he passes to the doorman and turns to me: "Handy chap, Coleman; places the occasional investment for me over the road.'"

"I'm Keith Coleman and I have a small property in Esher, next to the cricket ground. I earn a fair wage doing the door at Bentley's and I've been greeting at lunchtime during the week since 1966. My Father did it before me and passed on all the ins and outs. In the evening I do alternate nights at the Café de Paris and sometimes help out at The Savoy. It was December 23rd when Mr Porteous came in for luncheon with a tall girl in a heavy riding coat which he slipped from her shoulders and handed to me to deal with. She's a striking filly underneath, long legs in a pair of black riding breeches and boots and a saucy little bum-freezer jacket. I have a feeling that I may have seen her in the ring at Epsom from time to time. I never forget an arse and I can see that Mr Porteous has decided to make a modest investment in the hope that something positive may come of it. He passes me a wager which I take across the road to Ladbroke and when I return, they're sitting down to a couple of dozen "Extra Fine" and flagons of Black Velvet. Nice."

At Bentley's, Porteous is secure in his metier; he finds himself in the company of men he feels at home with; rugged characters with whom he collides on muddy Saturday afternoons at Richmond and Harlequins and who he plays golf with on Sundays at Royal St. George's. These men are the salt of his earth who on weekday evenings, congregate at the Clermont and Boodles and take their pleasures discretely; men to whom the sacrament of comradeship comes first and foremost. Today he has acquired the accoutrement of a girl who has appeared out of the blue and, he has to admit, taken his breath away. It seems to him that she is perfectly acceptable; she is after all, known to the Duke and is familiar with the social and sporting intricacies of the turf. He glances covertly at her across the table; takes in her eyes, wide apart, her generous mouth, skin firm as an apricot. She knows how to handle an oyster, lifting the slippery meat to her lips and sliding it across her sharp tongue with relish. He has noticed the muscular swell of her thigh as she slides behind the table onto the soft, leather seat. He wants her and has it in his mind to take her back to his pied-à-terre in Albany. "I want to show you my little place round the corner," he says as the waiters clear away "Edward Heath has an apartment there, so does Buccleuch." Nellie looked at him. "Who?" she says. "Well it's a good place for coffee and a brandy. Perhaps a smoke? Get away from here."

The girl considers him. Well watered as she is, she has a strong head and is in control. She has become bored with the ferrety attentions of priapic National Hunt jockeys and likes the look of this runner and is happy to let events take their course. She smiles across the table and the deal is silently done.

It is at this moment that the head waiter, Stokes, sidles up to the table and says, "Mr Porteous, sir, I have a call for you," handing him a bakelite telephone and bending down to plug the cable into a socket by the table. It is Fowler. "Slight difficulty, old boy," he says. "The Duke's on his way down and he's not at all pleased. He says you've kidnapped his groom and he needs her for an errand. He has his personal protection officer with him and they'll be with you in five minutes. I should scarper if I were you." Porteous quickly fishes out another wad of crisp notes, slips them across the desk to Stokes, nods at Colemen who is watching from the door, and has Nellie in the back of a cab heading south as the bonnet of the Ducal Daimler noses into the top of Swallow Street.

Albany will turn anyone's head; cut off from the chaos of the city, it is a refuge for powerful men just to the north of Piccadilly, accessed through a discreet wicket gate where residents and their friends are welcomed and strangers eyed with suspicion. Porteous has inherited his apartment from his father and the faded art deco would have been what Wodehouse had in mind when describing the bachelor Wooster at home. He sits and watches the girl looking down across the gardens, her shape at the window caught in black silhouette against the weak afternoon sun. He stands and slips his arm around her waist and she rests her head on his shoulder. He kisses her as she turns in his arms and clings to him and he feels her hard breasts against his chest. There is always a moment as Porteous starts a relationship with a woman, when his heart becomes saturated with heat, causing a shortness of breath and light-headedness. It is a physiological manifestation of his astonishment that a woman is prepared to react to him in a sexual way.

Nellie, swept along by strange events is herself light-headed, her breath coming in short bursts, her face flushed, a pulse beating in the sinews of her neck. She sinks to the floor where Porteous, spread like a crucifix on the deep carpet, lies waiting for her. He submits to the girl, who is slowly filleting his clothes, de-boning him of his pants until everything has been peeled away and his cock lies fresh as a tropical fruit across his stomach and she can slip from her jacket and kneel between his legs and take his arms and pull his hands into her clothes and he is able to tug the riding tunic over her head. And she sits back and he pulls down the boots and slides his hands into the waistband of her breeches and the Christmas sun squats, scarlet, on the rooftops of Mayfair and floods gold through the window and catches the gold of her hair. And when Nellie takes him in her hands for the first time, Porteous immediately ejaculates sumptuously into the valley of her breasts while he gazes, terrified into her startled face.

Nellie knows instinctively that moments like this can be an end or the beginning and she says, "Hello, you certainly needed that didn't you. Now it's my turn," and she takes his hand and places it deftly between her thighs. She sits, facing him, legs apart, her back arched like a bow, her index and central fingers holding the lips of her vagina apart and, while she sorts out his hand so that he can do what she wants him to do, she says, "some days the fever comes at you without warning." And she takes his fingers and sets them to work in her wet, rustling, fecund sex and as she writhes and moans, she holds his gaze and all the gathering shocks and nervous impulses and waves of breathless fear and passion are passing through her eyes and after a while, she falls forward, her body curled, across him until she lies, breathless along his chest, and his hand deep in her groin and her mouth on his as she shudders and brings up her knees and he feels the wetness flooding from her.

And as the afternoon turns to dusk and the lights come on across London, Porteous discovers an unknown world inhabited by a girl whose sole desire is to bring him to life. On the bed where his father had died, she resuscitates him impatiently and guides him inside her for the first time, operating him like a muscular machine until he feels that his body will explode; she makes him examine every intimate inch of her body, guiding his tongue and his fingers into her perfect, wrinkled little anus and demonstrating to him the budlike button of her clitoris and showing him how she likes it to be touched, particularly when "I am out and about during the day and you can find a quiet moment," and for hours they lie entwined, her pussy spread across his eager face while she takes his cock into her throat and makes him wait until finally she sucks his impatient come from his shuddering body.

Dusk has come and gone and once more they are looking down at the gardens, illuminated now from a scattering of brightly lit sitting rooms around the square. Porteous lies on top of her, his cock resting in the valley of her bottom, when he sees the little wicket gate open with a jolt and the Duke stalking into the glow of light from the porter's lodge followed by Sergeant Hoskins, holding his bowler hat in his hands and looking self conscious. Porteous stands up, "It's him," he says, "'and he's brought his bloody policeman with him."

Nellie rolls over, pulling on her pants and is dressed before Porteous can find his socks. "Give me the keys," she says, "I'll deal with this," and she is away leaving him to stand forlornly in his underpants, watching from the bedroom as she appears standing by the gate, arms on her hips, and having one of those conversations with a man who is somewhere in line to the throne. In five minutes it is done with and the Duke is passing an envelope and touching his rat catcher as he turns to go.

"Got any eggs?" she says when she returns, "We need building up." And Porteous looks at her and says, "What happened?" Oh well I gave him a piece of my mind, told him to stop following me around and to behave himself and he said "he'd only come to give me the wages he owed me for today."

Porteous takes her in his arms and breathes deeply because from that moment he knows he is enslaved. "Early night?" he says, and so they have supper on the carpet and go straight to bed.

Vania Zouravliov, *born near Moscow, attended the Vladimir Art School at the age of ten. His work soon gained recognition in Russia, but he moved to this country in 1993. He has illustrated several books for the Erotic Print Society.*

Christopher Hart *was, for several years, the literary editor of* The Erotic Review. *His published novels include* The Harvest, Rescue Me, The Venetian Carnival; *also published is a collection of short fiction,* Rogering Molly & other Stories. *He is currently a theatre critic for* The Sunday Times.

Christopher Hart

Latin Lover

Latin Lover

Chris Hart

She was quite old for the profession, at least in this part of the world. About mid-twenties. Her hair was very dark and her eyes black which made the bright red lipstick seem dark and dirty. She came over to me, curvetting, reached out and touched me on the thigh.

"Hello honey, you like to buy me a beer?"

I bought her a beer and we sat together and she glugged it back very fast and arched her back and stuck her breasts out and burped and then wiped her mouth. She wore a tight red crop-top and black miniskirt. Whores at these latitudes do not wear stockings, alas. Changes of latitude, changes of attitude, as Jimmy Buffet once sang. But you could put up with the absence of stockings, because attitudes here were very, very good. She touched her tongue to the mouth of the beer bottle one last time, eyeing me from under her false lashes, darted her tongue inside, then set the bottle back on the table. The foam slid down inside the dark green glass. She smiled. She had a room of her own over the street, she said. Did she now?

Less than a couple of weeks before, we had both gone back to that room of hers and lain on her bed for a while and kissed, and I had my hand running up beneath her miniskirt and plucking at the elastic hem of her knickers when we were rudely interrupted by the return of her husband. She froze. That was him, running up the stairs, she could hear him, she knew his tread. I'd cautiously opened the door. And there he was, small and wiry, dull lizard eyes, coming up two steps at a time, mean little mouth set very firm beneath his iron-grey moustache. The type you really do want to avoid. Besides, I'm a lover, not a fighter, as Michael Jackson once sang.

"Quickly," she said, "you get out this way." And, very conveniently, running down from the balcony outside there was a rickety old wooden staircase where I could make my getaway.

Only afterwards did I realise my wallet was gone.

Now here she was again. But she had already forgotten me. I suppose she saw a lot of men each day, over the course of each week. But it was just as well.

Two days earlier I had got drunk on aguardiente with the local police chief, a huge sweaty dimwit called Balboa, and we had soon ended up talking about women, and the horses locally. Horses? Whoreses, he meant. He spoke some bad English but got confused about his plurals. 'She is a whores,' he said, jabbing his thumb over his shoulder at a passing schoolgirl. 'And those two, mother and daughter, they are both whoreses.'

Mine, it turned out, was not a whores but a cheat. A very bad girl. She cheated on her customers, but hey, it was usually rich gringos so what did that matter? Balboa looked at me slyly. I bought him another drink. Although lately, he went on, he didn't think this little one – María de la Adoración Rodríquez García was her simple, peasant name – had been paying him his full whack for not interfering. He wouldn't tell me how much. I bought him a couple more drinks. He told me.

I unfolded my plan, even pushed a note across the table in advance payment. He grinned blearily in my vague direction. I don't know why I do the things I do, as was it Frankie Avalon once sang? I felt only a strange, horny determination.

We were now on our way back over the street to her room again, for the second time in a fortnight. I put my arm around her waist and pulled her close to me. She giggled and pretended to pull away but I held on firmly to her body and she didn't resist any further. When we got to the permanent puddle in the middle of the dusty street I lifted her up altogether so she wouldn't get mud on her little jewelled plastic sandals.

"Oh honey, you are such a gentlemen," she murmured in my ear.

How very untrue that was.

As I released her again her miniskirt rode up against me and in the window of the Jesus Cristo Es Mi Salvador Internet Café I saw our reflection and her bum barely covered by her skimpy black panties. We went on in and up the stairs to her room hand in hand.

She was very amenable about kissing and she brushed her hand over the front of my shorts and murmured outlandish compliments about bulls and stallions. But I knew why she was quite relaxed about it. It was for the same reason she kept glancing at her little pink plastic wristwatch. I tweaked at the back of her croptop and pulled it up but she wriggled away. I looked puzzled. Did she want paying now? She looked hurt.

"No honey," she said. "Come here. I'm just a little shy."

I returned gratefully to her arms and we kissed a little more. Then I tried to pluck at her croptop again, and again she demonstrated that she was a little shy. So I changed tactics and pushed her back onto the bed, lying heavily on top of her. She tried to say something, to express the unaccustomed shyness and modesty that she was feeling, perhaps, but my mouth closed over hers. It was very strange, and a rather unexpected part of my plan, because the moment we returned to kissing she was not at all shy. I might even have said that she was enjoying it, at least this part of it. But only in anticipation of getting her little paws on my wallet, of course.

Then I attempted the removal of her clothes for the third time, and this time her resistance was to no avail. In fact she had just moved her right hand down to massage the front of my shorts again, which seemed to conflict with her overall plan, for by now, by rights, her reptilian little husband should have been scuttling up the stairs and there was no need to entice me further. But this meant that I was able to trap her right hand where it was, and only had to pin her left hand back above her head on the bed as with my own right hand I pulled up her croptop around her throat and bent my mouth to her chestnut nipples. Now she began to fight and thrash in earnest, wriggling that firm body beneath me and, any moment I feared, ready to deliver the coup de grâce with a straight upper cut of the knee between my legs. At which point I deftly rolled to one side and, my right hand still resting gently around her perspiring throat, murmured tenderly, "What is it, *mi querida*? 'It is my husband,' she said. "I have this terrible fear he is coming back." "You have a husband?" She lowered her eyes sorrowfully. "He does not know I work." She raised them again, beseechingly. "It is for my family you know, my mother, she is very old, very sick. I … but now I am so afraid. I am sure my husband is coming back."

I had rolled off the bed and glanced out of the window before she could say any more. And there, some way down the street, was the huge, sweaty figure of my great friend, Benjamin Balboa, much-respected officer of the law around these parts, leading a small, wiry little man away towards the station for serious questioning. The little man gestured wildly and frantically, with many a glance back up the street – in the direction of this very room, in fact – but it was to no avail. Balboa was determined. The little man looked quite hysterical.

I was back on her in a trice. "I do not think your husband is coming, my kitten," I murmured softly. "Do not fear. We have all afternoon ahead of us."

She tried and failed not to look appalled.

I had to be very quick and deft. These things are not so simple as you would imagine. In fact, lying directly on top is not the most effective way, because although it might keep her pinned down, it means that removing her clothes is much more difficult. Not that I am an old hand at these things. I wouldn't want you to think I was some kind of serial violator of young ladies. In fact, this was the first time I had ever tried such an uncompromising approach, and even now I wasn't sure how far it would go, or what my motives were. Perhaps I just wanted to give her enough of a fright to get my wallet back.

Nevertheless, with a deftness that surprised me, I did as I had planned in my head, and managed to restrain her with my left arm while with my right hand I forced her thighs apart and plucked at her panties. When she drew breath to scream I bent and kissed her again. Curiously, instead of turning her face away and screaming anyway, she seemed to want to kiss me back. Her silken, chestnut, thighs were still squeezed together as demurely as a virgin schoolgirl's at her first communion. She was deeply conflicted, poor girl. She needed help. And I was all too ready to assist in a sensitive resolution of those inner conflicts by sticking my hand up her skirt.

I forced my hand up between her thighs until I felt my forefinger against her mound and the black material of her panties and... they were wet. Not just from the perspiration of having to fight off some vile gringo ravisher either. She was still struggling, though her inner conflicts must have been a terrific drain on her energy, so I had to move quickly. Is it possible to rip a young lady's panties off by main force, in one swift and gallant movement, as they do in inferior erotic fiction? Perhaps those little lacy nothings are made of stronger material than they look? I took hold of the elasticky hem and pulled.

They're not. They tore and were flung God knows where, and my hand immediately delved back in between her thighs. I pushed up against her mound and felt kissed by her weeping lips.

Her thighs moved apart. Slowly and full of shame, they parted. I looked down at her and her eyes were half closed and she didn't look as if she was about to scream. Not in that way anyway. I moved my fingers a little faster, wider and then closer again. She breathed faster. Her mouth was open now. I could feel her panting on my face. She looked at me, our eyes met.

Then it all happened very, very fast. She was kissing me again urgently, driving herself harder and harder against my working fingers, and dragging off my shorts all at the same time. Half sitting up, moaning 'Oh baby, baby, my darling, *mi querida*' and other tender endearments, before seizing my very expectant cock and pulling it into her. As I slid inside, there were two simultaneous sighs, those sighs which say, "Ah, at last, that's where it belongs. Home."

And we had all afternoon ahead of us.

After I'd kissed her a very fond farewell, some three hours later, and was heading off to find Balboa and pay him his filthy fee, she pulled at my hand.

'What'll you tell your husband?' I said.

'I tell him I bit you.'

'You bite a lot of men?'

'A lot,' she said. 'Very often.'

I kissed her again, on the top of her head. She looked up at me under the false lashes, still feigning shyness. 'I not working tomorrow,' she murmured. 'My husband is not around, he's over in Trujillo, so I can't work.' Then her shyness dropped away and she smiled mischievously. 'But, fuck my husband. You wanna come round and make love with me for nothing?'

Surely the most sweetly-worded offer I have ever heard.

I Watch Myself

Jessica Roder is a new photographer-writer who will soon be publishing her first book with the Society. This is a preview.

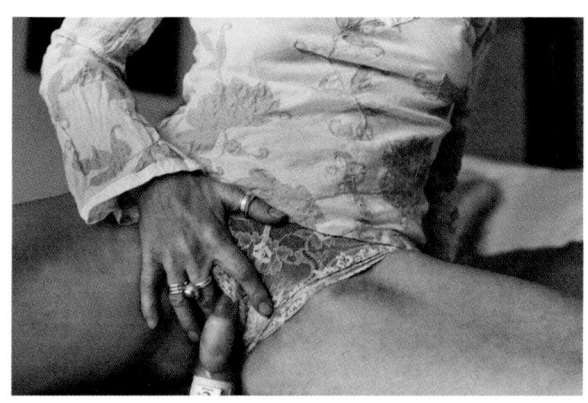

The hand between my legs is stroking the lace around my crotch. I know I am beginning to get really turned on as I feel myself getting wet. Tucking my fingers in behind the fabric I feel that moist place. It's soft, hot, yielding. Withdrawing my hand I take up my vibrator and turn it on so it begins to buzz gently. I tuck the tip of the vibrator in behind the fabric and slowly move its tip around the entrance to my vagina.

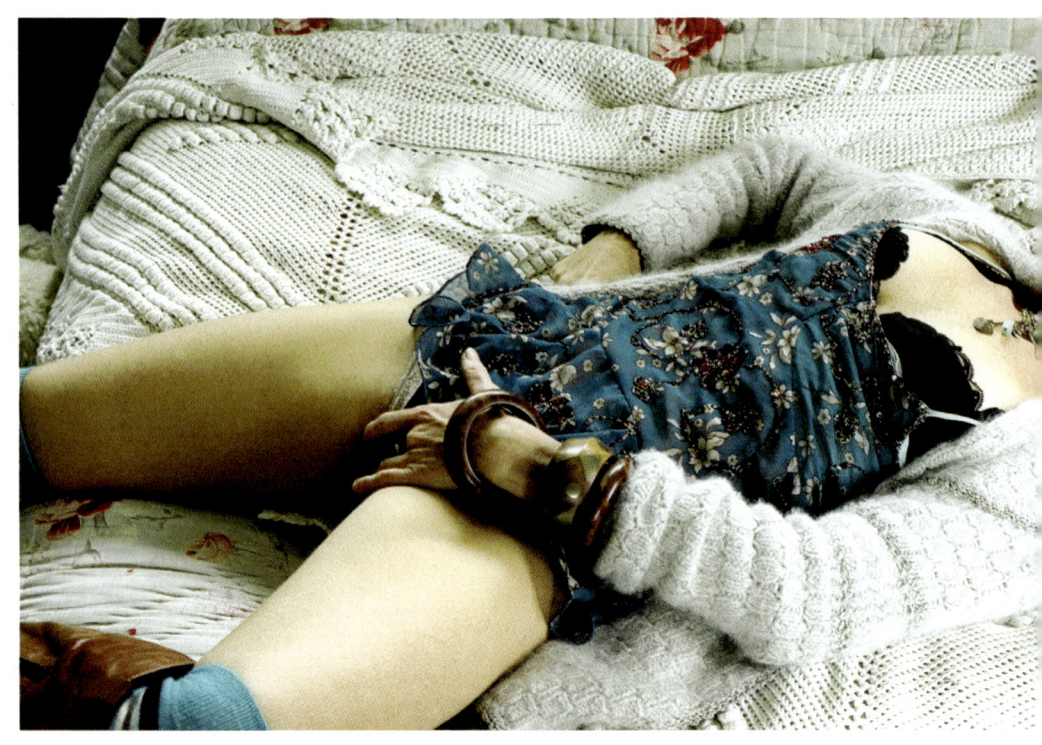

I watch myself in
the mirror as I start
to turn myself on.
I begin by pulling
up my skirt slightly
to reveal a bit of
the lace around the
top of my stocking.
The skin around the
lace looks inviting.
I stroke it softly.
With my other hand
I undo a button on
my shirt to reveal
my bra. Stroking my
breast, my nipple
feels hard through
the fabric. I push my
bra down to expose
the nipple, which
I touch with my
finger. It feels good
and parting my lips
just slightly I let out
a barely perceptible
moan.

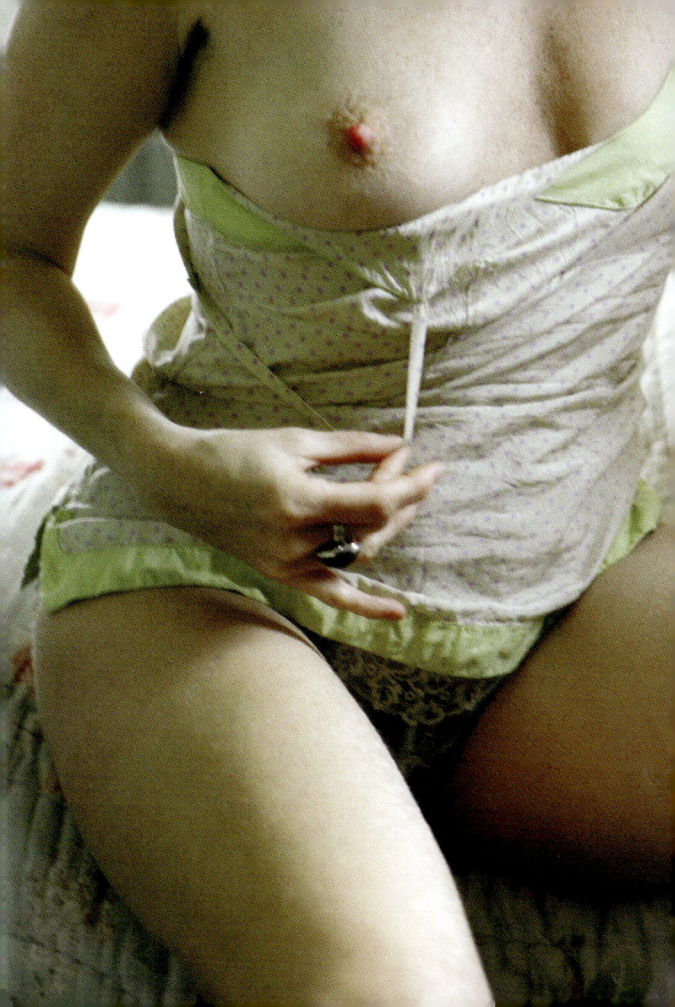

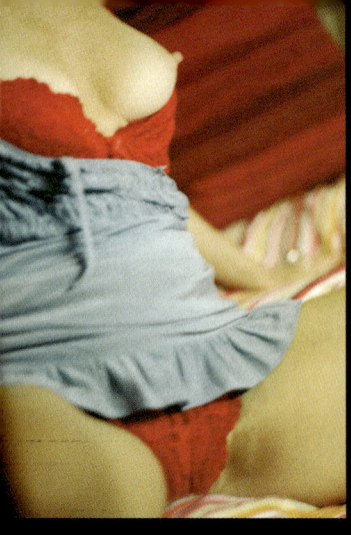

I always like to dress for the occasion. I adore sensual, sexy clothes over pretty, lacy, frilly underwear. I also like to see myself i a mirror, getting u close and watchin only selected area of my body in motion...

I like to look at my sex getting wet and horny, swelling, as I get more excited. I sit or kneel, legs open to get a good view in the mirror. I work my hands down over my belly, often feeling silky soft fabric, which I carefully gather up to expose my panties, parting my big outer lips to feel that soft place inside getting wet. Pulling my panties to one side I may massage that area carefully, sliding

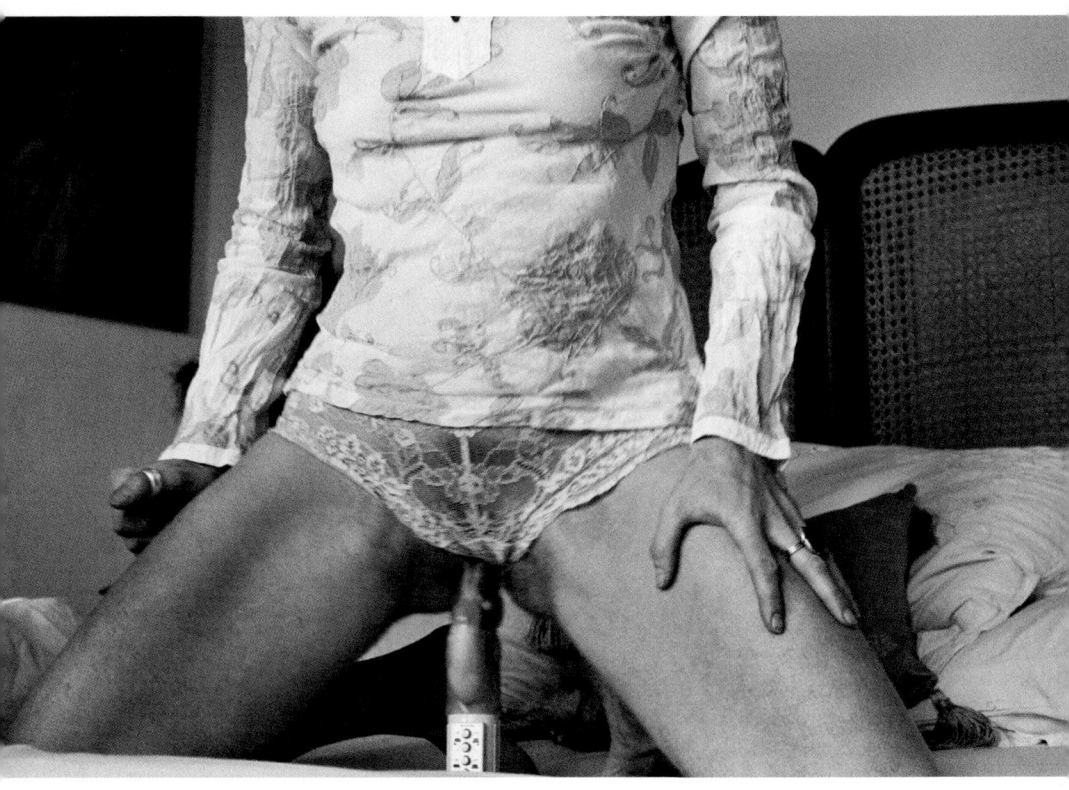

my fingers in and out for a while. But really I like stimulating my clit wiwth the vibrating ears of my bunny rabbit. The sensation it makes down around my sensitive areas is electrifying. I imagine a tongue and fingers exploring those parts. I can spend a lot of time rubbing myself against those vibrating ears.

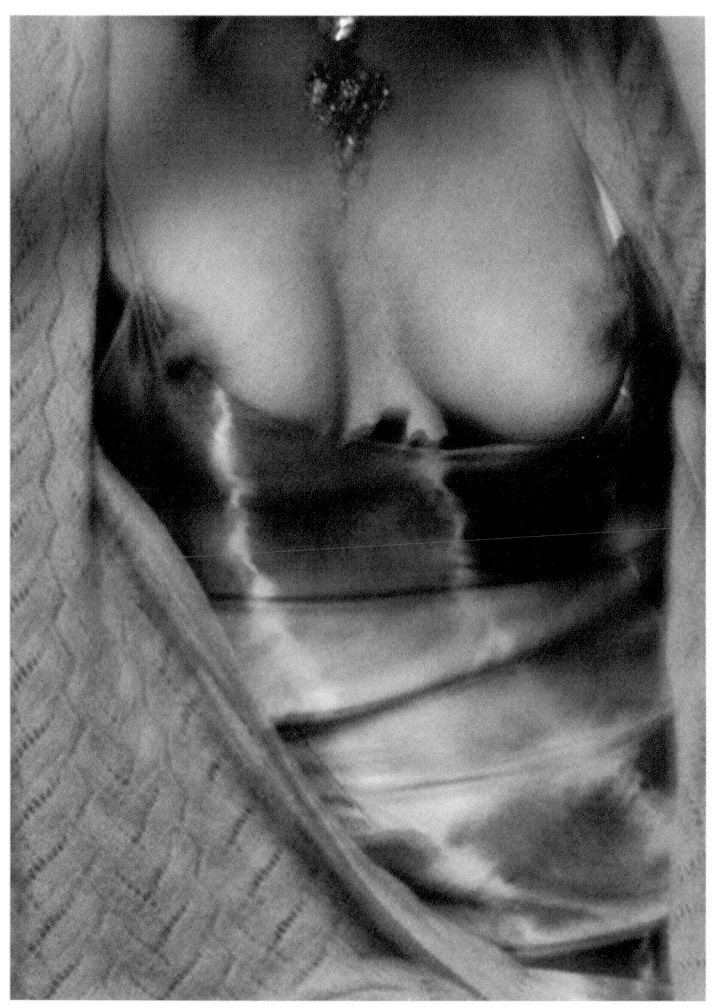

Kate Copstick *is as close as we'll ever get to Renaissance Bi-Woman. Being a happy, self-avowed, bi-sexual, she has written and continues to write, perceptively, wittily and controversially about sex with an authority that boggles the mind of those with a narrower sexual orientation, (i.e. most of us). She is also a television actress, presenter, writer and director. She founded the Children With Aids charity for which she is a tireless worker.*

Kate Copstick

Threesome

Threesome

Kate Copstick

Ask any heterosexual man – and I do – what his favourite fantasy is and he will reply "two women". His eyes will widen and his pupils will dilate at the thought. He will be imagining two mouths on his cock, two tongues flicking and licking at his balls, twenty soft fingers running over his body and a quartet of breasts into which to plunge both face and cock. Get the positioning right, and he could do both at the same time. Two cunts, two arses to be fucked and licked and fingered and filled in a myriad delicious combinations. Marvellous stuff.

Or at least it can be.

But the truly great threesome is a thing of delicate balance, no matter what the three might be. It is not to be entered into lightly. It can happen spontaneously, in a little chemical explosion of mutual desire, which is wonderful, or it can be planned in advance, like a dinner party with each other as the edibles. Either way, if it is not right, it will be very, very wrong.

Too often the threesome is an embarrassing affair instigated by a man with a fixed idea, a malleable partner and no concern about anyone else in the bed having a good time. I meet these people all the time in my capacity as an available, bisexual woman about town with an open mind and no desire for breakfast. But add another female to a couple like this and what you get is not a threesome, but a two-on-one. This is about servicing, not great sex.

It is like being asked out for a romantic dinner by a man with the devil in his eyes and then finding out that he wants you to cook it and your best friend to bring the wine.

Swingers clubs are full of couples looking for a third, although the man tends to look more enthusiastically than she does.

And, girls, beware. If you are not into the idea of a woman in bed beside you, then the arriving will be even more embarrassing than the travelling hopefully.

There is a feel to the skin of a women when she is lying beside another woman and doesn't feel comfortable about it. There is a way that she kisses, a hesitancy about where she lays her hands, a tension to her legs as you part them, while her husband watches and hardens and breathes more heavily.

I am lucky in that I have always been bisexual and more than happy to explore the sexual possibilities of anyone. Although I have an aversion to women in make up and men with hairy backs. And vice versa.

But I have found myself, several times, beside a happy man with a hard-on and a woman having a hard time looking happy, trying to create the sort of sexual dynamic that we can all enjoy. The possibilities here are as follows:

1. She lies back looking ill at ease and gazing intently at the ceiling as I kiss her and play with her breasts, licking my way down the curve of her waist and round her thighs before parting them and letting my tongue play on her clit as a kind of warm up cabaret for Hubby. While he engages Madame Palm and her Five Lovely Daughters to keep Mr Happy pointing in the right direction.

Result: her lower back goes into spasm because she is so tense. And I work my way to an aching jaw, a crick in my neck and a bit of a tetch.

2. He suggests she reciprocate. She looks dubious. He smiles and insists. I kiss her. She pulls back. He takes her hand and places it between my legs.
Result: she runs from the room crying.

3. We both go down on him. I sit on his face while she desperately sucks his cock. She sits on his face while I deep throat such as there is of Mr Happy.
Result: she is paranoid about my giving better head than her, territorial about him and nervous about being this close to me, because she doesn't do women.

4. He fucks me while she watches.
Result: tears, fraught atmosphere. I don't know whether to make "this is the best fuck I have had since Jordan had her own breasts" noises and upset her by seeming to enjoy him too much. Or make "look I have an appointment with my Sky Planner at 11pm, what did you say the time was ?" noises and upset her by not enjoying him enough.

5. He fucks her while I watch.
Result : boredom for me. I work out the menus for a variety of dinner parties in my head. There is usually slight embarrassment for her.

None of this is conducive to anyone's greater happiness. And it is a tragic waste of time and sexual energy. It can even break up relationships.

So, in the interests of the greatest happiness of the greatest number I would like to share what I feel to be the secret of the truly great threesome.

Real bisexuals. We might be amoral, greedy, shiftless, irresponsible, selfish creatures hell bent on immediate satisfaction, incapable of honour or commitment and a threat to the fabric of decent society, but you'll never manage a decent threesome without us.

Whether two men or two women are involved in your sexual triptych, they need to be bisexual. They need to be able to give and receive pleasure to each other and not just to the opposite sex. Then and only then will your threesome develop a life of its own. The right combination creates something akin to a sexual centrifugal force and it is a thrilling, exhilarating experience.

It took me some little time to get the whole multiple partner sex thing out of my fantasies and into my bed. But now, I am delighted to say that many of the little doors that line my memory's lane have behind them a Gordian Knot of limbs and the scent of serious satisfaction.

For Christmas one year there was the sound technician who used to fuck me on the floor of my dressing room just after the fifteen minute call. He introduced me to his sweet, blonde girlfriend, a girl who, he told me, had been lesbian till meeting him. The first time we fucked was on a pile of coats at a cast party. My tongue was in her pussy as his cock was in my ass. If I ever get to heaven, that's the kind of thing I'll be doing a lot. He used to fuck us side by side as we kissed. Now that was a threesome.

Then there was the summer nights I spent with a fabulously alpha male of my acquaintance, and his beautiful doll-like mistress. I was having lunch with some friends when he called me up after the wild salmon and before the lavender pannacotta and said, "She desperately wants to have sex with a woman, but she wants me to be there too. It's her birthday tomorrow, and I wonder if you'd like to be her present from me." I was duly giftwrapped and delivered. We kissed and sucked and fingered and fucked all night. She came as I played between her legs, and when, in less time than it takes to say "Happy Birthday to You", he came too - all over her face - I licked it off. The phrase "many happy returns" suddenly developed new and heartfelt meaning for all of us.

I remember with great fondness a delicious episode involving my then girlfriend and the gorgeous, ostensibly straight and happily married lady with whom she had enjoyed a teensy horizontal adventure. The turbo-charged flirting between the three of us was thrilling. And where it led was even better. There is something about the way a woman who is turned on by women, but hasn't had much experience of them, has sex. There is a delight, a hunger, and a thrill tempered with wonder that is tangible in her. And she had the prettiest cunt I have ever seen. Sweet and neat and pert. Like a little half open rose. We three had a sexy time until the sunshine and the birdsong.

And then there are those other threesomes. The threesomes where I am the only one without a cock. But the same rules apply. And this experience is one, to quote Julie Andrews, "of my favourite things".

I cannot tell you how pore-openingly, cunt-moisteningly exciting it is to watch one sexy man fuck another. It does it for me every time. I could just watch and come. But that would be, under the circumstances, a waste. Because it would be missing out on the joy that is going down on a man in tandem with another man. Or having a beautiful boy go down on you while both of you are rocked by the thrusting of the man with his cock in your pussy-licker's ass.

There is always the option of having all the attention on you and you are so thrillingly full of cock that you reach new levels of satisfaction. Having two cocks inside you is an incredible feeling, whether it be one in your cunt and one in your ass or one in your mouth.

But again, the dynamic has to be right. Everyone has to enjoy everyone else equally. Being spit roasted by two guys who are paranoid about their cocks touching is a much less exciting experience. Although I wouldn't say no.

Foursomes can be fun. Personally I prefer a proper foursome, as opposed to two couples. Once again, the greatest joy to be had from a foursome is when all four participants are bisexual. Call me biased, but when we, bisexuals, become involved, the possibilities are sufficient to make it worth setting a day aside.

After that the centre cannot hold and the experience becomes either orgy or gangbang. Each with its own special charm but like the difference between having three tasty courses beautifully served to order, and plunging into the maelstrom of the all-you-can-eat buffet.

Another Christmas provided such a buffet for me and others when a game of Truth or Dare degenerated into a sensual and then a sexual free-for-all. We were a catholic assortment in the Presbyterian West of Scotland and the slithering mass that came together, like egg yolks emulsifying in oil, became a carnal mayonnaise of gay and straight, eighteen year old and forty-something, couples and singles. God it was glorious. There were mouths and holes everywhere, fingers and phalluses, sweat and saliva and cum. This was whole body-everybody sex. I really don't know to this day to whom or with whom I did what. All I know is a very happy memory.

So, more than two in a bed might not be your thing. But don't knock it till you have tried it. And don't try it unless you are going to do it properly. For properly minded triers, I can always be contacted through The Erotic Print Society.

Some Aquatints, Paul Marc Joseph Chenavard

Voyeurs

Some Etchings, Henri Monnier

Confidences De Celestine, Anonymous French

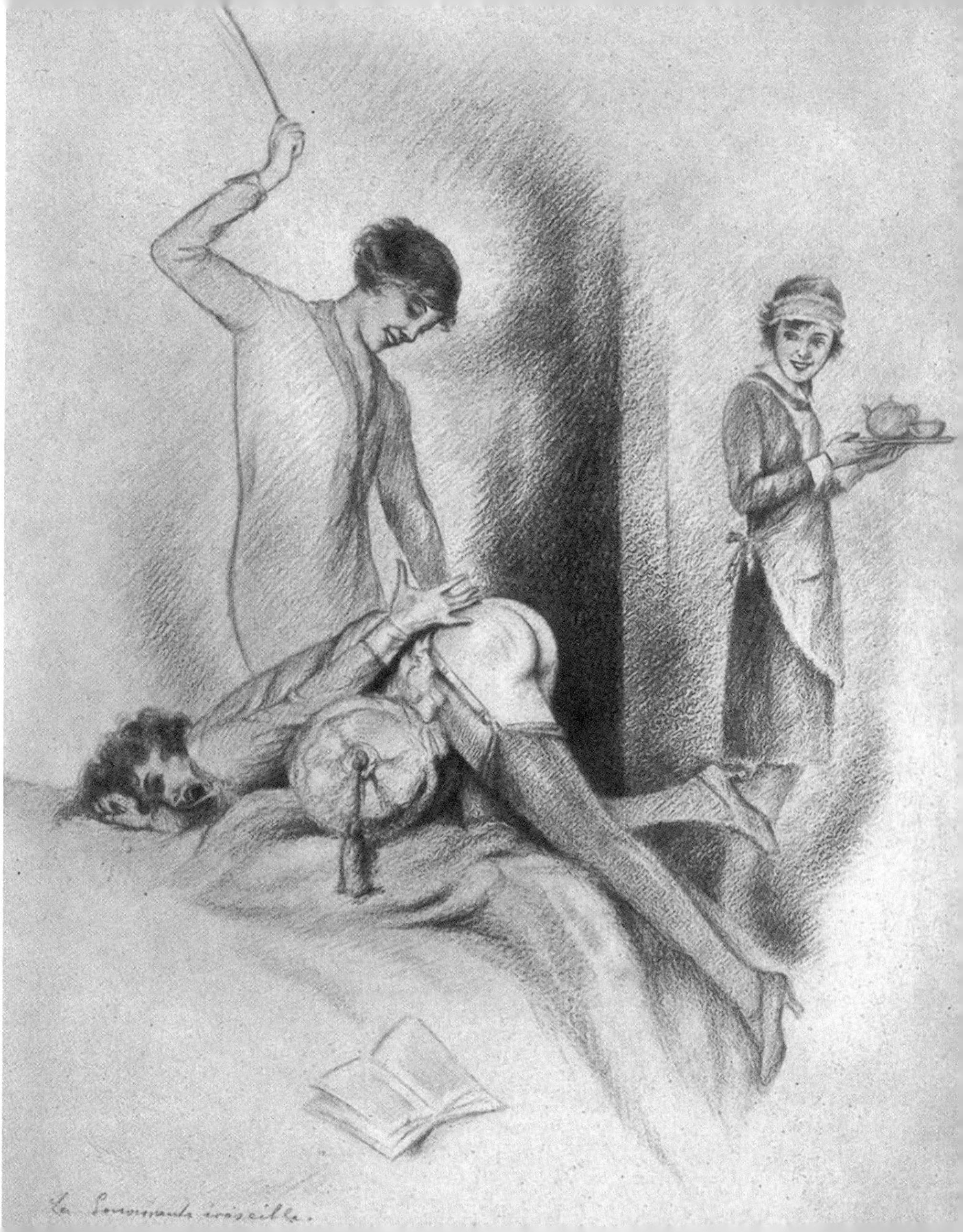

Autour de l'Amour, Eugène Reunier (Carl Breuer-Courth)

La Grande Danse Macabre des vifs, Martin van Maele

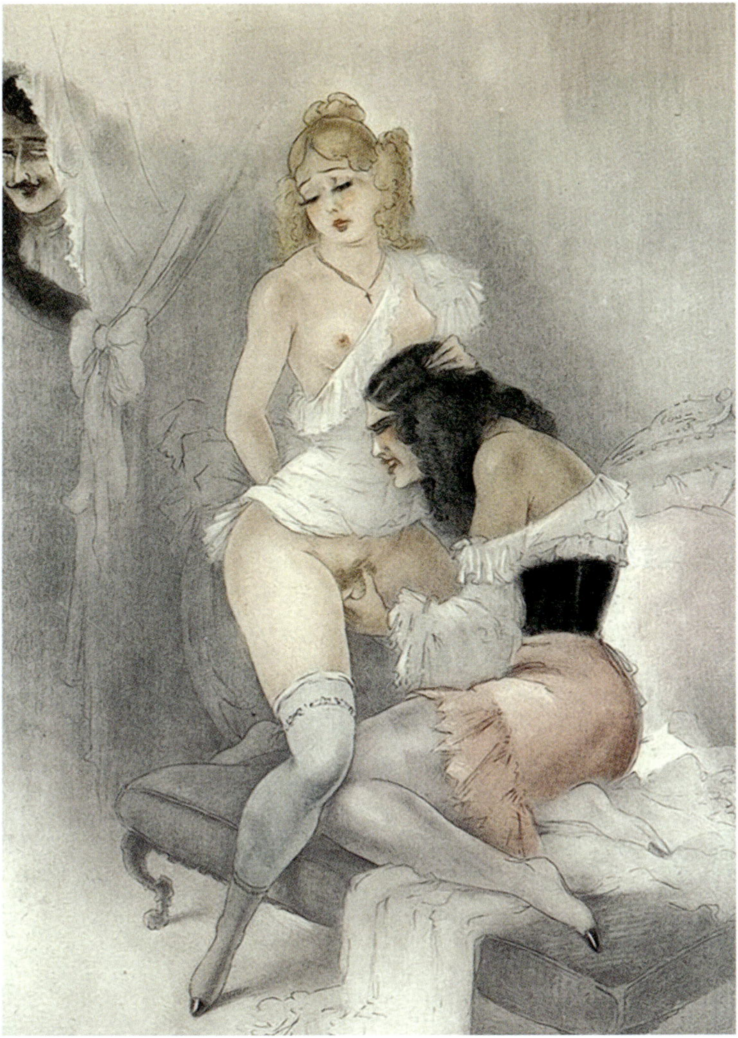

Scenes from the Jazz Age, Jean Morisot

Scenes from the Jazz Age, Jean Morisot

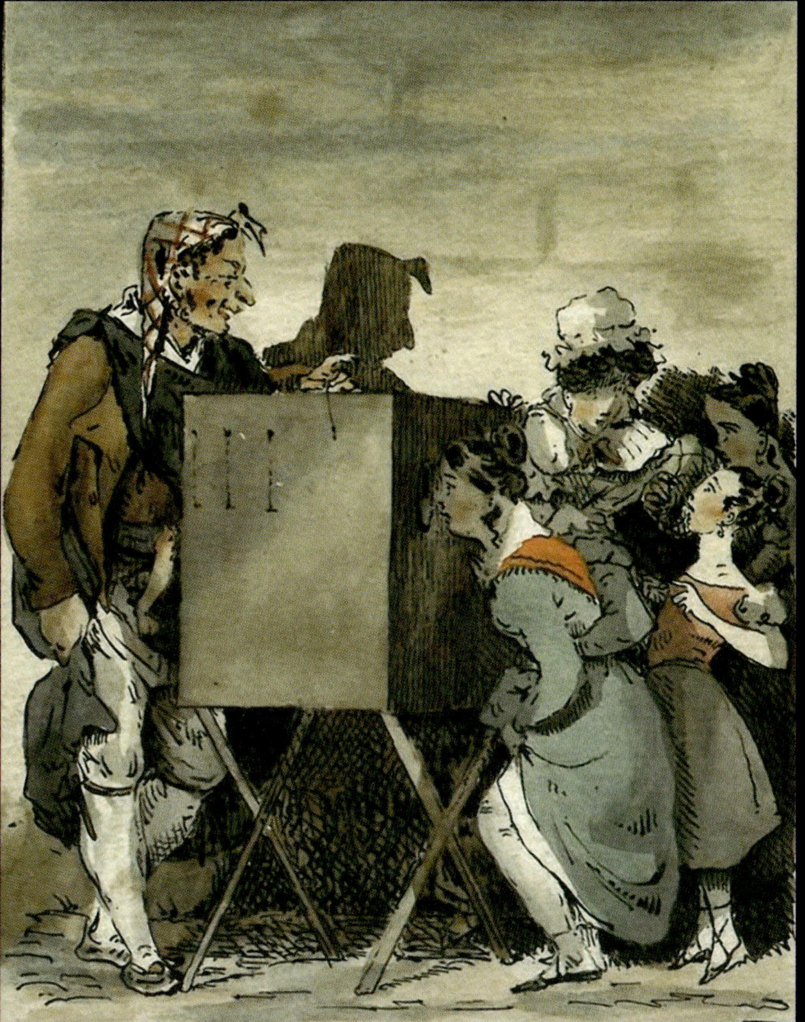

Some Etchings, Henri Monnier

Voyages de la Cristaline, Achille Deveria

Gravures, Paul Gavarni

Yellow 44 is a piece of work from The Secret Museum - a repository that proves that the categories of Art and Pornography are not mutually exclusive. The Museum contains many exhibits, each of which is finely crafted not only aesthetically, but technically and intellectually. These works must be examined closely to reveal their multitude of facets. In many cases narratives are built up through layers of detail and seemingly disparate fragments.

The Secret Museum is itself an enigma. It hovers somewhere in time and space in a version of London that is somehow timeless. Though references can be found that tell visitors on how to reach the building, nothing seems to exist in the real world and it is the website to which baffled travellers must return.

The Secret Museum can be found at: www.thesecretmuseum.net

YELLOW 44

By:
The Secret Museum

2006

We shall prevail

The 2 Heral

Thursday the 4th of April

[handwritten notes in margin:] This is getting up early makes a man quite idiotic

[handwritten stamp:] Received... LS...

Brave female pilot shot down

Yesterday one of the Royal Flying Core's female pilots was shot down in a dogfight over the Eastern Front. It is thought she parachuted to safety but her current whereabouts is unknown.

Squadron Leader Dorothy Evans, 24, engaged two T.A.F.S. "Bosporus" class fighters at about 4pm yesterday. Though she was outgunned by the two superior machines, her skill in piloting her Sainfoin Kitfox landed her a kill before she was shot down by the second. The MoD says a witness reported seeing what he presumed to be the young pilot's chute descend to the tundra. For security reasons her last known position cannot be divulged.

Air Vice Marshal Winterton, Evans' superior, said to the press, "The War has claimed yet another bright young woman and this should give us all more reason to increase our efforts to overcome the threat posed by the Trans Asian Free State."

Painting Stolen

John Singer Sargent's famous portrait of Madame X was stolen yesterday from the Sir John Soane's Museum in London. The painting was on loan to the museum from its home in The Metropolitan Museum of Art in New York and was left unattended in a cupboard due to building renovations. Staff reported a man with long grey hair and sunglasses leaving a 2pm – shortly before the theft detected. The portrait had featur news recently after Mr Kars CEO of Sainfoin Inc. Corpor made an unsuccessful bid painting for his person

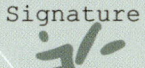
Office stamp: **Model used:**

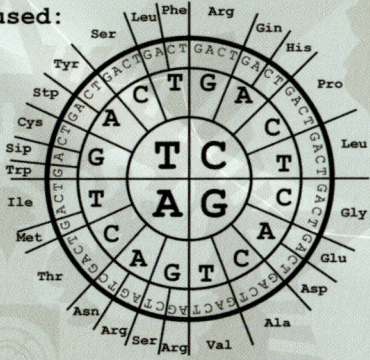

Paste results below:

```
     Query: 1      cagOtaHcaHgaOtWtItcLagaOacVaE
                   | | | | | | | | | | | | | | | | | | | | | | | | | | | | |
 Subject: 4096     cHattEtaaggcRataaPcgOtaWgcatD
```

```
     Query: 2      caEtactaRgatYgacgSataacKcaIgg
                   | | | | | | | | | | | | | | | | | | | | | | | | | | | | |
 Subject: 4096     cgNttaAaNcgDgataTtcHatEcgcWta
```

```
     Query: 3      cgAtacYcgIataTcgcBccRatUIaStt
                   | | | | | | | | | | | | | | | | | | | | | | | | | | | | |
 Subject: 4096     cgEttaSaacgSgataOtcgatacgcata
```

What a demanding Job I've chosen!

Mr. Samsa,

What's the matter? You are barricading yourself in your room, answer with only a yes and a no and are making serious and unnecessary troubles for your parents.

Suitable

Carrier

Suitable

Infect

Acquire

Suitable

Madame Blatevsky

Mme Blatevsky has foreseen:

I saw the girl again. She was not afraid this time for she was with the only one of them who had been kind to her. She loved him.

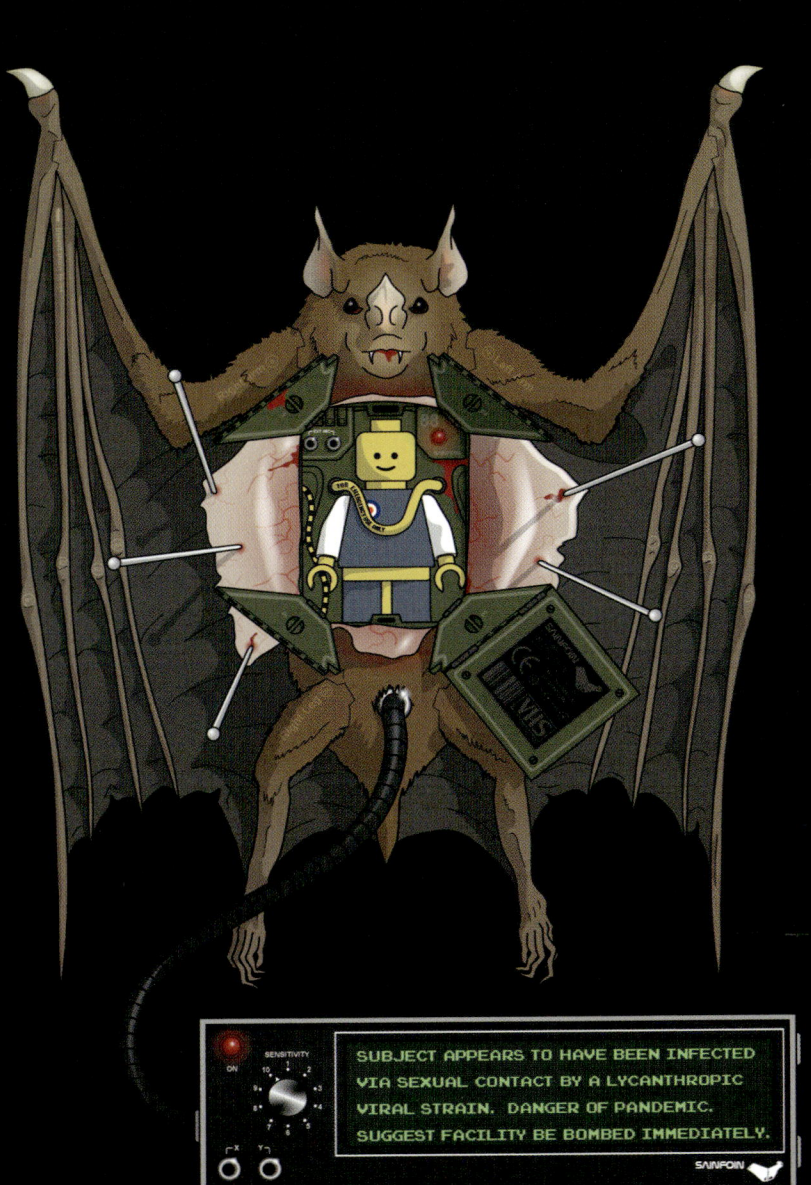

SUBJECT APPEARS TO HAVE BEEN INFECTED
VIA SEXUAL CONTACT BY A LYCANTHROPIC
VIRAL STRAIN. DANGER OF PANDEMIC.
SUGGEST FACILITY BE BOMBED IMMEDIATELY.

Past Venus
The Blackmailed Housewife

The Blackmailed Housewife

by Anonymous

Chapter 1

"How do you feel, Susie?"

"A little woozy! I'll be all right, though – I'm just not used to having so much to drink; but don't worry Bill – I'm not drunk!"

"I'll take you home – a nice fast drive with the hood down will set you up. Let's say goodnight to Mrs Jordan."

"Susan – you look quite starry-eyed!" exclaimed their hostess. "Better watch *her*, Bill!"

"Oh, it's just the booze," smiled Susan. "Good job my husband isn't home – he'd think I'd been out on the razzle! Thank you for such a lovely party."

"When shall we be seeing that handsome husband of yours – He always seems to be away," asked the older woman.

"He's due home next week, actually."

"He simply must come to our next. Tom was asking about the Major – he's such fun. I rather suspect he's so popular around here for his pungent brand of army jokes!"

"Yes – I'm afraid he has some stinkers! And, incidentally, it's Lieutenant Colonel now."

"Does that improve the brand of joke?"

"Maybe a little more flowery," murmured Bill.

"You never had any inclination towards army life?" asked Mrs Jordan.

"One member of the family is enough. I prefer to make money."

"Army pay is very good, though, nowadays, isn't it? Especially for a lieutenant colonel."

"Not as good as the stock market. Besides, I haven't got my brother's disciplined mind."

They said their goodnights to several other guests and took their leave of host and hostess.

"Whew! That's better." Susan sat back in the front seat of the car and let the wind play on her face.

"It was very stuffy – I think that helped as much as the drink."

"So would you like to go back to the party, now?" Near her home, he slowed down.

"No fear!" She waited as he turned the car into the driveway and stopped. "I think I should like another drink, though. Care to join me?"

"Why not? The night's young!"

"Hm. Not young enough for that niece of mine, though. I see she's still up; I'll pack her off to bed."

They went into the library and the blare of a particularly loud pop number playing on a tape recorder assailed their ears; a pale, rather angry-looking teenager with short black hair and dressed in a pair of tight jeans and a leathery-looking black shirt looked round almost irritably, then got up from her chair, sucking in her cheeks and giving them what came close to a dirty look.

"You're back early, Aunt Susan."

"Early for grown-ups, perhaps, but not for you. Off to bed with you, now, like a good girl."

"I'm not a girl," she answered sullenly. "I'm sixteen now."

"And midnight is long past a sixteen-year-old's bedtime. Off you go!"

She took her time picking up her tapes and packing up the

tape recorder.

"And don't keep that thing going half the night, please, Liz," she begged as she carted them out. "Goodnight, dear."

"Goodnight," muttered the girl sullenly, nodding shortly to Bill.

"Pity there's no National Service for girls, if you ask me; I'm afraid my sister and her husband have just let her walk all over them. And I have to put up with another ten days of her."

"I hate to say it, but she looks a bolshy little specimen to me; there's an unhealthy look about her – she's so pale!"

"She gives me the creeps at times, the weird way she looks at me," Susan shivered. "Let's have a drink… Scotch?"

"Fine." He sat in an easy chair and she brought the drinks over, resting a shapely bottom on the arm. "How does she look at you?"

"Oh, you know, undresses me with her eyes. One expects that sort of thing from a boy her age, but not from a girl. And she's not fussy whether I notice it or not. There's something in the look – a sort of – of *knowing* stare – as though she – well – knows exactly the sort of things she'd like to do to me if she had a chance."

"Gosh, you mean you think…"

"No. I don't think. I just *know* that young Liz's going to be a lezzie when she grows up."

"Oh surely not! It's probably just a phase she's going through and she's simply got a crush on you. Anyway – you're a beautiful woman, Susie. I'll bet she's not the only one who looks at you like that."

"Yes, but a sixteen-year-old *girl* – and her own *aunt*! No, Bill – I can't help it – I've always felt that there's something not right about her – unhealthy, as you put it."

She finished off the rest of her Scotch. "Let's have another one"

"Here we are." She re-seated herself on the arm of his chair. "And thanks."

"Thanks?"

"For telling me I'm beautiful. I haven't had anyone tell me that for a long time."

"Doesn't Peter take care of things like that?"

"Sometimes. When he's home!" She got up and switched on the radio, found some dance music.

"Dance with me, Bill."

She drifted into his arms as he came over.

"That's a slinky dress you're wearing."

"Hm? Slinky girl inside it, too," she grinned and pressed herself a little closer; it was good to be this close to a man again, to feel his arms around her, body moving against hers. She closed her eyes and rested her head on his shoulder, her lovely chestnut hair falling against his cheek and the slow, easy movement made her generous breasts roll pleasantly against his chest. Her bra was one of the new, no-bra types: a transparent nylon that held the breasts in check so that they needed no uplift. It was as though they were bare beneath the dress, nipples rubbing against the material. She pressed closer.

He felt the movement and looked down at the rich, chestnut hair; impulsively his arms tightened about her. She abandoned herself for a moment to the erotic excitement that welled up within her. Her nipples began to tingle. This was madness! Her husband's brother! Abruptly, she pulled away.

"I think we ought to have another drink."

"Steady on, old girl, that was why we left the party, remember?"

"I'm in the mood, now. Got the taste!"

He remained standing where she had left him, watching her as she poured two over-generous measures. She was, indeed, a beautiful woman. Tall, full-breasted, wide-hipped and with a bottom that was positively mouth-watering. How old would she be now? he asked himself. His brother was five years older than her. That would make her thirty. Nice age for loving. Matured and experienced in sex, young enough to enjoy it to the full. And definitely *not* a good age to be left alone by her husband for several months in the year.

He looked into her eyes as she walked back towards him. Starry-eyed, Mrs Jordan had said. Well, if she could see her now…

"Want to dance some more?"

"Um – I think not Let's sit over here and talk for a while." She took his hand and led him over to a window seat.

"What about this niece of yours, then?"

"Liz? My sister will be collecting her in about ten days' time. I can't say I blame her for not wanting to take her on holiday with them. She'll be leaving the day Peter gets home. Peter can't stand her."

"Can you?"

"Oh, I have to. She's my own sister's child. All the same, I'll be glad to see the back of her. She… she disturbs me. Elsie, our maid, doesn't like her either. Liz looks at her in the same way. And there's another thing. You know the balcony that runs along the back of the house? My bedroom window opens on to it and I'm certain she stands outside sometimes in the hope of seeing something – I almost caught her once."

Without asking him this time, she fetched the bottle and refilled both their glasses. Then she took a good pull at her own.

"For someone who thought they'd had too much only an hour ago, you're hitting that bottle pretty heavily."

"I'm in that kind of mood now. Sort of reckless."

"Dangerous! It may catch up on you and hit suddenly. Then I'd be having to put you to bed!"

"Put me to bed?" she repeated archly, giving him a cheeky grin. "Sounds interesting!"

"*Susan!*"

"Hm. Sorry. Shouldn't have said that, should I? It sounds all so nice and cosy, though." Her voice was smoky, sexy, smouldering. She swallowed some more Scotch, topped up the glass and slopped some more into his before he could pull it away. She let her head rest on his shoulder again. And once more, he felt the soft hair, her warmth, smelt her lovely perfume.

Now he was beginning to feel reckless himself, and by no means entirely through the Scotch. Susan was warm, beautiful. She was all woman! He downed the Scotch in one.

"Now who's hitting the bottle?"

Susan looked up at him; her eyes flashed, she drew a deep breath and downed her own in one, too. Putting her glass on the sill, she got up.

"I think I'd like to dance again now," she said, her voice very slightly slurred.

This time neither of them attempted any dance steps. They just stood very close, arms locked about each other, their only gesture towards dancing, a gentle swaying, roughly in time to the music. She lifted her face. Her mouth looked soft. The lips trembled a little.

"Kiss me, Bill," she whispered.

He felt her body shiver as their mouths touched. He felt the pressure of her breasts as her lips quivered and came alive against his own. The movement of her breasts quickened, her mouth opened to his, he felt the soft pressure of her lips against his own, and then her tongue, wet and gently inquisitive, met his. She drew away, breathlessly.

"I-I think we… you'd better put me to bed," she said quietly, not looking at him, but keeping very close.

"Susie, I…"

"No, Bill, please. Please don't say anything. I know it's all wrong. Terribly, terribly wrong. But… but let me worry about all that in the morning – please? You want to… you know… don't you?"

"I'd be a case for the loony doctor if I didn't, but…"

"Well, come on, darling. I shall probably hate myself in the morning, but just now, it's a must."

She took his hand once more, and led him from the room.

Looking back at him over her shoulder she put a finger to her lips.

"Quitetly, now."

They crept up the stairs. She paused outside her niece's room, listening.

"Not a sound! She must be asleep by now." She led him to her bedroom, and once they were inside, she turned the key in the lock and quickly faced him. "Ohhh… dizzy!"

He held her shoulders as she swayed.

"Susie, do you want to call it off? You've had an awful lot to drink, you know."

"No, I don't. And I'm not drunk, either. I've had enough to lose a few inhibitions, that's all. There may be some remorse in the morning, but I think we should both spend the rest of our lives wondering what we might have missed if we didn't go through with it after getting this far. So, no more talk now, dear."

She went over to the bed and picked up her nightdress, looking back at him.

"You won't mind if I undress alone?" She looked down. "I-I don't think I could just strip in front of you and do it in cold blood."

She stopped and stood on tip-toe to kiss him on her way to the dressing room.

"And don't look so *worried*, darling," she whispered. "You're not exactly forcing me into anything, you know. I actually do want this."

He watched her as she went into the little dressing room that led off the bedroom. Her buttocks rolled softly under the tight, shimmering skirt, showing the faint ridge of her panties in an acute 'V'. She was right. This was something that had to be done now, he reasoned. He had to know her, completely. He had to learn every intimate part of her body, its feel, its smell, and its taste!

Shaking his head as if to clear it of the whisky fumes, he took off his clothes and climbed into an unfamiliar bed. His own brother's bed. Yet far from brooding over the sibling treachery that he was about to commit, he simply kept his eyes glued on the closed door of the dressing room.

When she emerged, she paused in the doorway and looked over towards him. She blinked once or twice as if she were surprised to find him still there. She wore black silk pyjamas, with a bolero top, giving tantalising glimpses of her large, shapely white breasts as she walked slowly towards the bed. She stood looking down at him for a moment. He looked back towards her, up over her flat stomach, her navel peeping above the waist of the pyjama trousers, the up-curving undersides of her breasts, their deep valley leading to an alabaster neck, and finally his eyes met hers, full of amusement and anticipation. She gave him a lop-sided smile.

"Oh, darling," she breathed. Then she had pulled back the covers and climbed in beside him.

She leaned over him, giving him her mouth, arms circling his neck as he held her, stroking the bareness of her back under the bolero jacket. Kisses became more searching, tongue met tongue in a brief encounter. She threw one leg across his and he felt her start as her thigh encountered his erection. He stroked the smooth softness of her flanks, upwards, to her armpits, down again, to caress the sides of her breasts, then inwards, to palm the erect nipples. Gently, he squeezed the warm resilience. She took her mouth from his and put her hands on either side of him, lifting herself.

"Just slide the jacket down if you want to see them."

She knelt upright then, a knee between his thighs, her arms at her sides.

Slowly he slid the bolero down her arms, uncovering his brother's property. But now she was no longer his sister-in-law, she was a warm, vibrant woman, exposing the loveliness of her intimate person to her lover. He removed the bolero entirely and looked up at the rounded fullness swaying above him. He reached out and lifted her magnificent breasts, holding their weight, his mouth half-open in wonderment.

"Nice titties?" she whispered.

"Beautiful!" he breathed.

"Kiss?"

"Mmm!"

She lowered herself, offering the left one, holding it in her hands, touching the hard nipple to his lips, pressing forward to push it in when he opened his mouth, as she might feed a baby. She let him suck on the hot, fleshy little nub for a while, then gently withdrew it and presented the other one.

She lay on top of him, her naked breasts flattening slightly against his chest. He stroked down her back, slid his hands under the pyjama trousers, clasped the firmly up-thrust buttocks. Her mouth was warm and wet against his. Once more her arms were around his neck. The hardness of his penis matched the firmness of the pelvic bone it throbbed against.

He kneaded the velvety dough of her bottom and she squirmed against him. His fingertips encountered wetness in the cleft of her buttocks.

"I-I'm ready now, darling," she breathed huskily, rolling over to lie beside him. "The trousers slide off too."

He started to slip the pyjama bottoms down over her hips.

"Please – put the light out, darling."

In the darkness there came a whispering rustle as bed-covers were thrown off, silk pyjama trousers were discarded, a male rose to

cover a female, long, shapely legs were thrown wide, exposing the sacred portal between them as she was mounted. A soft little cry on penetration, and then a long sigh.

"Oh, darling, you're inside me!" A whispered declaration.

There was a vague sound of movement, getting louder, more purposeful. A definite rhythm established itself, becoming faster, more urgent, accented by the soft slap of flesh against flesh. Heavy breathing was replaced by gasps, then gasps by moans of pleasure.

A last, frantic thumping.

"Now, darling, *now!*"

"I-I'd better pull…"

"No, it… it's all right – let it go in me! Ohhh, darling, I-I…"

A soft cry, followed by a long, drawn out, shuddering sigh, and then, for a while, silence. Presently, a woman's suppressed sobs.

"Oh Susie, I'm sorry… I…" A male voice brimming with concern.

"No, Bill, it was beautiful…" A female voice, tearful, but full of gratitude.

Chapter 2

As the early morning light began to filter between the half-drawn curtains into the room, Bill roused and sat up. He looked down almost unbelievingly at the still slumbering Susan, so perfect in her sleep. He had to get out of the house before either the maid or the niece were up and about.

Deciding to try and slip out without waking Susan, he got out of bed, collected his clothes, and crept into the dressing room. He dressed quickly, the memory of the previous night coming back strongly at the sight of her frock and underthings draped over the back of a chair.

As he went back through the bedroom, she awoke. He stopped and went over to the bed. She blinked up at him for a moment, her chestnut hair a dark pool under her head on the pillow.

"Bill!" She sat up with a jerk.

She was still naked and her bare breasts bounced gently with the sudden movement. She looked down and her hands lifted involuntarily to cover them. He picked up the bolero from the end of the bed and handed it to her. She quickly pulled it on.

"OK, Susie. Call me whatever you like. I don't quite know what to say. But I definitely took advantage of you last night."

"I wasn't going to say anything like that at all, dear," she said quietly. "We'd both had a little too much to drink, or we should never have done what we did. As far as I can remember, though, it was me who initiated the whole thing."

He grinned a little sourly.

"What I should have done was smacked your bottom and put you to bed, clothes and all, then gone home."

"No, it was something I had to have at the time. Something I have probably wanted for a long time. I think if I analysed my feelings yesterday evening, I'd find that I had purposely consumed all that alcohol to give me the courage to do what I wanted to do."

She looked up at him steadily for a moment. "But it must never happen again, Bill. Never. If I ever get that way with you again, you must…"

"Smack your behind and put you to bed! From your point of view, Susie, I'm sorry it happened, but I can't help feeling that Peter could do more than he has been doing in that respect. You're a full-blooded woman. You shouldn't be left on your own for so long. There must be many times when he could take you with him."

"Yes, I know. There are too many nights when I could just cry with sheer frustration. Now let's try and forget that it happened. Does that sound terribly selfish of me, dear?"

"No. I understand. Well, I'd better get out before the rest of the house wakes up."

"Yes. My sweet little niece would be bound to add two and two and make five out of it. I'd love to ask you to stay for breakfast, but under the circumstances…"

"That's all right, I'll get something in town. Try not to worry about it, eh? God bless." He turned towards the door.

"Bill!"

"Yes?"

"Kiss me. Just once. Please?"

He went back to the bed and bent to kiss her. Her arms circled his neck as their mouths touched. She clung to him tightly for a brief moment.

"Goodbye, darling." Her eyes were misty.

"That sounds so final. We'll be seeing each other again."

"Not in this way, though. We shall be two different people again."

He went out, unaware of the choked sob that followed the close of the door.

Susan got up a few minutes later, feeling a little better after a cry, but unable to go back to sleep again. She went down to the kitchen and made herself a pot of coffee. By the time the maid arrived she had drunk it all and had started another percolating.

It was a heavy day, added to which her niece seemed more than usually insolent. It certainly didn't help Susan's state of mind. When she went back up to her bedroom, she realised with a shock that she hadn't drawn the curtains the previous night. She didn't worry too much about that, however, remembering that she had stopped to listen outside her niece's room when coming up with Bill.

As the day wore on she kept recalling more and more little details of the previous night. Accompanying the deep feeling of guilt was the natural fear of being found out, but weaving through it all were the sharply remembered thrills of forbidden sex.

Bed didn't seem the same that night; she had lain with her husband's brother, given herself to him without reservation. She dozed… she was lying naked in Bill's strong arms again. There was a noise out on the balcony. Lying beneath Bill, she was looking towards the balcony window. Her niece was walking towards them. She stopped at the bottom of the bed, looking down at them. Her face changed to that of her husband. From her incongruous position she was explaining to him how it had happened…

"It was the alcohol," she was muttering as she woke up. But in the secret darkness, her heart admitted that she had wanted it so much for so long, that she would have found some other way if booze had not been available.

She rose the next morning after a night of fitful, guilt-ridden dozing, finding no joy in the brilliant sunshine that poured into the room when she drew open the curtains.

She followed the routine of the previous day, starting with a pot of coffee in the kitchen. The maid gave her an anxious look when she came in.

"Aren't you feeling well, Mrs Barrow? You've been looking so pale these last couple of days, and you don't usually get up this early."

"I'm all right Elsie, still recovering from that party I went to the other day. Bit of a prolonged hangover!" She forced a smile.

"Is that niece of yours getting you down?" asked Elsie darkly. "I can see she's been getting *you* down. What's she been up to this time?"

"Nothing you can put your finger on, as usual. It's the way she looks at me."

"Never mind, she'll be going back in about a week. I'm afraid I can't do much about her looking at you. I get the same sort of treatment."

By late afternoon Susan realised and faced up to the fact that the ache in her heart and fluttering in her stomach had little or nothing to do with a guilt complex. It was a longing to have the strong arms of her brother-in-law about her. She wanted to feel his nakedness against her own, pressing, rubbing… entering.

She held out against the desire to telephone him for the rest of that day, then the following morning she received a letter from Peter. His return had been postponed for another three weeks, until the end of the month.

Early that evening she phoned Bill at his flat.

"Bill? It's me, Susan." Her voice was quiet, but tense. "I'm sorry dear… I-I'm afraid I'm going to make a nuisance of myself. I want to see you again."

"You'll never be a nuisance, Susie, but do you think it wise? At least until Peter comes home next week. By that time, the other night will have faded. If we meet shortly before he turns up, there's no knowing what might happen and he'd be bound to notice the atmosphere."

"I had a letter from him this morning. He won't be back for another three weeks. Please, Bill. I know I said we must never let this happen again, but you must see that that isn't possible. We can never regard each other in the same way as we did before this happened."

"I knew this. I had intended keeping away for a while, and, in any case, only seeing you while Peter was home." He drew a deep breath. "Very well, dear. Want me to come out to you?"

"Better leave it until late though. We don't want Liz or the maid around."

"Righto. Say midnight?"

"Make it one, just in case."

"All right. I'll park the car at the end of the drive and walk up."

"I'll watch out for you. 'Bye dear. And thanks!"

"See you at one."

Her niece seemed to hang around later than usual that night, playing her tape recorder in her favourite haunt, the library. Several times she went into her, finally ordering her to bed just before midnight. This time she didn't even bother to look round and Susan, with a glint in her eye, grabbed her arm and spun her niece around to face her.

"I told you to get up to bed, young lady!"

She staggered a little, her open hand started to come up, and for a moment, Susan thought that Liz was going to hit her. Then she seemed to have second thoughts and her hand dropped.

"Want to get rid of me?" she sneered

"I want you to go to bed!" Susan snapped back, nevertheless feeling a tightness in her stomach at her obvious insinuation.

"You don't like me very much, do you?"

"I don't think you do very much to endear yourself to anybody. I think a word with your mother wouldn't do any harm. Do you behave like this at home?"

"Like what?" There was an open challenge in her narrowed, defiant eyes.

"This... this rudeness, insolence, disobedience. And those horrid jeans. I think you've worn them since you arrived here nearly a month ago. I think you could find a hairstyle that would make you look more… feminine. Short hair's all very well, but you're just too young to… I don't know. I just hope for your father and mother's sakes you behave a little better when you're home."

Her niece had been gathering the recorder and the tapes and now she went to the door. She looked back at Susan, a slow, burning gaze of pure insolence that could almost be felt.

"Well. I hope for your husband's sake you behave a little better when *he's* home!"

"And just *what* do you mean by that?" Susan hissed, after a stunned silence, but the click of the closing door provided the full stop to her little speech.

She started after her niece, but changed her mind. What could she say that wouldn't make her look even guiltier? Of course, it could be no more than a shot in the dark. Or could it? The hour before Bill arrived seemed interminable.

She let him in quietly, the hall lights out, and took him straight up to her bedroom.

"In her own mind, she probably thinks she's being hard done by. I should think that's what she meant," suggested Bill when she told him about the incident in the library. "After all she's only sixteen, you know."

"The way she looks at me, she could be an adult lesbian, and an experienced one at that! Oh Bill, do you really think that was all she meant?"

"I'm sure of it. She couldn't have been referring to me. I'm a fairly regular visitor, but it's always been open and above board and she knows I'm Peter's brother."

"Bill, I forgot to draw the curtains the other night," she told him quietly.

"Oh? But the light wasn't on for very long after we came up here. Anyway, you listened at her door before we came in. Her light was off and she would have been asleep by then. Don't worry about it, Susie."

"But what about that remark?"

"As I said, she's sixteen and she's just being defensive and defiant."

"I feel a lot better now you're here." She stood close to him, her hands clasped behind her back, looking up into his face. "I'd feel better still if you kissed me."

She threw a glance over her shoulder in the direction of the window. "I've remembered to draw the curtains this time."

She clung to him fiercely, her mouth open under his. He gently disengaged her arms from about his neck.

"Susie, I…"

Gently she placed an index finger against his lips to silence him. "No, darling. No talk, please!" Her voice had changed with emotion, smoky and deep. Her body was taut and vibrant against his, her face lifted pleadingly for more kisses.

"But Susie, where is it all going to end?"

"Does it have to?"

"Just what are you saying?"

"I've thought it all out, dear. Nobody gets hurt. Peter is away more than he's home. You're close and I have nobody. I could still be a good wife to Peter when he's home. I could be a good one to you when he isn't." She moved away from him, shaking her head. "No, no. Everything about it is wrong, isn't it?"

She was leaning on the end of the bed, her back to him, head bent, her rich chestnut hair fallen forward about her face. He went over to her, his arms slipped around her waist, he heard her little gasp as he kissed the nape of her neck, then she had taken his hands and lifted them to her breasts.

"Let's go to bed, darling," she whispered.

"Like this?"

"The clothes are detachable. Help me?"

"No dressing room this time?"

"No dressing room. If you look down, you'll find a zip just under your chin. Pull it!"

He found the zip and pulled the tag halfway down her back; she pulled another at the side and drew the dress over her head.

She had no slip on underneath and his head swam as he beheld her in wispy black and red nylon panties and bra. Slim black suspender straps held her stockings taut to her tapering thighs. She saw him gazing at her and smiled, swivelling this way and that for him, like a catwalk model. It then occurred to him that the only intimate parts of her he had actually *seen* were her breasts. Navels could hardly be termed intimate any more, he supposed, being available for view at any beach or swimming pool.

"Don't just stand there looking at me, darling! Unclip my bra and get your own things off."

She turned her back to him, waited while he unclipped it, then, still keeping her back to him, drew the straps from her shoulders and tossed the bra on to the bed.

He started to take off his jacket and stopped halfway with an audible gasp. She had bent forward to unfasten her suspenders, thrusting out her perfect bottom and threatening to rip the flimsy panties apart. The cleft of her buttocks could be seen beneath the sheer material, darkly spreading as they were stretched. He heard her giggle, although she didn't look round.

"I warned you not to stand looking at me!"

"Now I know why you used the dressing room the other night. It was for my own good!"

He shed the rest of his clothes, but without taking his eyes from his nearly naked sister-in-law. She kept her back to him the whole time, putting each foot on the side of the bed as she rolled her stockings down her legs.

Finally she straightened momentarily to hook fingers into the waist of the impossible panties, then the slimness of her waist and the width of her hips were accentuated as her bottom moved leisurely from side to side. He saw the pants slowly easing down, uncovering the round globes of her buttocks. She completed his devastation by bending right down to take the panties to her ankles. She paused there for a brief second, giving him a rear view of the forbidden fruit: peeping from between the backs of her well-shaped thighs he could see a downy ovoid, dissected by the slim line of her closed vulva. Above nestled the little tan pucker of her anal aperture, tempting and full of mystery.

She straightened up and turned to face him at last, her beautiful breasts swaying excitingly. She had a lovely body. Although it gave the appearance of height and slimness, in fact her breasts were deliciously large, firmly upcurving, her hips wide and her buttocks full-fleshed. His gaze dropped to the dense, dark triangle of pubic hair at the junction of her thighs and stomach.

"I think you're nice, too!"

"What? Oh!"

He realised that he had been staring intently at her for a long time. They both laughed and she came into his arms.

"And did you like what you saw?" she whispered. "Oh! Something hard sticking into my tummy tells me you did!"

The warm, pliant masses of her breasts pushed against his chest and her soft stomach rolled gently against his hard penis as they kissed. She could feel a little moisture leaking from its tip.

"Bed now, darling?"

There was only one answer to that question.

For a very short while they rolled, kissing, on the bed. Hands began to wander, and then seeking, slim fingers closed gently around a hard, fleshy shaft. Soft, creamy thighs parted to admit a questing hand. Stronger, thicker fingers probed and parted swollen, hairy lips to encounter wet, slippery membrane. A fingertip found a small, sensitive protruberance.

"Oh darling!" Susan's thigh closed on his hand, holding it prisoner in the warm, flooded softness. Her thighs opened again and she pulled at him to get him on top of her.

"Lights out, Susie?"

"No, not this time. I want to look at you as we do it."

Her smooth knees bent, thighs falling open, making flat planes of her rising loins as she lifted from the bed to meet him. The bared, purplish head of his thick cock lowered, aiming at the vulnerable entrance, no longer defensible. Her plump labia were blotted from view as he mounted her. Susan made a sharp intake of breath as the hard, rubbery glans made contact with her softness. These became almost moans as his shaft sank further in and was engulfed by the clinging wetness of her tight vaginal tunnel. In and in he went until her cunt was fully penetrated. She clasped him tightly to her.

"Hold it there for a little while, darling. Mmm… wonderful! I can feel it throbbing inside me… so hard and big! I think the tip is just touching my womb!"

She wriggled beneath him. "Ohhh… I felt it jump then."

She started a gentle rise and fall of her lower body.

"Kiss me," she gasped.

He covered her mouth with his, covered her body with his, filled her sex with his. Squirming and jerking beneath him, she kept her legs wide as he sawed in and out of her.

Suddenly her thighs lifted, legs locking over his. She wrenched her mouth from his kissing lips.

"Ohhhhh… I think I'm going to… it's coming…" she panted, urgently thrusting her pelvis violently upwards so that her sex was filled again and again by his long shaft and her clitoris ground into his pubis. "Yes… now… *now!* Oh, darling, I love you! Ohhhhh!"

Both madly jerking now, there came the stifled female cry of fulfilment as Susan reached her climax at the moment she felt her lover's semen spurt into her in great gushing jets.

"Darling," she whispered afterwards, lying back and looking up at him with shining eyes. "That was so beautiful, I could cry. No, don't pull out of me; let him stay in there until he wants to slip out himself. Just hold me."

"Don't you do anything about preventing babies, Susie?"

"Sometimes, but this is my safe period. I worked it out a long time ago. Don't worry, darling, you won't give me a fat tummy!"

Before going back to his flat in the early hours of the morning, he took her again. On this occasion his entry was smoother, less urgent and they took their time, only climaxing together after a satisfyingly long bout of lovemaking; he left a contented Susan to sleep, this time without either tears or remorseful apology. The balcony was cloaked in darkness.

Chapter 3

Susan felt better that day than she had done since the beginning of her liaison with her brother-in-law. Not only did she feel sexually satisfied, but the worry of how she had obtained the said satisfaction seemed to have faded into the background of her mind. Had she been a cat, she would have purred. She was even nice to Liz when the teenager joined her at breakfast, although she seemed to be in an even more churlish mood than was her wont.

Her niece went back to her room immediately after breakfast and spent the rest of the morning there, a fact which pleased both aunt and maid alike.

Liz was silent all through lunch, answering the small talk her aunt attempted with grunts or nods. Afterwards Susan started to help Elsie to clear the lunch things away, but Liz got up and stood in front of her.

"Can that wait for a while? I want to talk to you privately. In the library, I think, would be best."

Susan looked at her. There was a strange expression on her face, half triumphant, half nervous. She sensed a tenseness.

"Is it really so important?"

"Very important."

The accented 'very' made her put the dishes she had been holding back on the table and follow her niece into the library. Liz waited until her aunt was through the door, then shut it and turned the key in the lock. Now Susan felt real tension.

"What on earth did you do that for? Unlock the door at once!" She made to brush past and unlock the door herself, but Liz stood with her back against it.

"I don't think you would want the maid coming in in the middle of this conversation." She moved away from the door. "Of course, I was only thinking of you. Call her in to listen, if you like."

"Listen to *what?*" Susan's heart was pounding now. She realised that something dreadful was to follow.

"Over here." The teenager walked away from her to where she had her tape recorder already plugged in and a tape on the deck.

"What is this conversation you wanted with me?"

"Oh, I think this will explain it all. Just listen."

She switched on the machine, ran it fast, then switched to 'play', standing back and folding her arms, eyes on her aunt's face. There were a few clicks and rustles, a sound of breathing, then "*Ohh… dizzy!*" Her voice! "*Susie, do you want to call it off? You've had an awful lot to drink, you know.*" "*No, I don't. And I'm not drunk, either. I've had enough to…*" There was a scraping sound and the tape went blank.

Susan swayed. She felt faint, and leaned heavily on the back of one of the library's armchairs for support.

"Well, what about *that*, Auntie?" The last word was delivered with a definite sneer.

"You… you little *beast!*" she whispered. "You nosy little bitch!" Numbly she picked up the decanter from the drinks trolley and poured herself a liberal measure. She swallowed, gagged, swallowed again. It was brandy and it burned all the way down, but it took the numbness out of her body. Still holding the glass, she stared at the wall.

"How long have you been snooping like that?"

"In your bedroom? Only that night. You both had that lovey-dovey look, so I guessed what might happen and put the mike just inside your window. All I had to do then was wait on the balcony until you both came up, then switch on."

"So now I suppose you're going to tell your…"

"That could be avoided."

"By money?" Then, suddenly, she remembered something and her heart lifted. She still couldn't face her, but Susan's voice was more confident.

"That conversation doesn't mean anything, you know, it could have taken place at any time and he could have been referring to the dance when he asked if I wanted to call it off. Your tape broke down on you, didn't it?"

"Yes, it did. The lead was at full stretch from my room and the plug pulled out of the socket. It didn't take long to fix that."

Susan heard another click. "…anything, you know. I want it." There were a few more clicks and she heard her niece race the tape. Stunned she listened on: "*Oh, darling.*" A breathy whisper, but unmistakably her voice. There was a lot of rustling after that; several gasps, then her own voice again: "*Just slide the jacket down if you want to see them.*" More rustling, then: "*Nice titties?*" Susan's face burned as she faced the wall in silence. "*Beautiful!*" "*Kiss?*" "*Mmm!*"

"Alright. You don't have to go on, you… you despicable little beast!"

"Oh, Auntie… I think this bit is well worth hearing."

She heard the tape deck race for a couple of seconds, then "*I-I'm ready now, darling*" and "*The trousers slide off, too*" Rustling… "*Please – put the light out, darling.*"

"Stop it for God's sake!"

But she didn't. The tape ran on: "*Oh, darling, you're inside me!*" Gasps. Moans. Thumps.

"STOP IT!"

Susan rushed towards the tape recorder, but Liz stepped in front of her and held her off, the wiry sixteen-year-old's arms surprisingly powerful as she gripped her wrists. Susan winced with pain. She realised with a shock that her niece was physically stronger than she was. The tape ran on as they struggled: "*Now, darling, now!*" "*I-I'd better pull…*" "*No, it… it's all right – let it go in me! Ohhh, darling, I-I…*" A soft cry, a long sigh…

Liz must have seen the desperation in Susan's expression.

"It's no use. You can take that tape if you really want to. I've made a copy."

She let her aunt's wrists go and went to switch the tape recorder off. Susan retreated to the drinks trolley and poured herself another brandy. Her hands shook and she had difficulty in controlling her voice.

"All right, how much do I have to pay for the tapes and your promise of silence?"

"That's better."

"How much?"

"Well, I haven't really made up my mind about the financial side. But you can let me have a tenner to be going on with."

"To be going on with?" Susan whispered, sensing the menace. "When do I get the tapes?"

"When I've finally decided what I'll let them go for."

"In the meantime, you can go on getting tenners out of me whenever you want them, is that it? This could go on for years, couldn't it?"

"I suppose it could, but…"

"I'm not a rich woman. I don't have very much money of my own. If you plan to bleed me, it won't go on for very long."

"Oh, I don't know. Your boyfriend must be pretty well-heeled and Uncle Peter is worth quite a bit."

Susan swung round at that.

"How could I possibly ask them for money? You surely don't want me to tell my… er… Bill about this, do you? He'd kill you!"

"I'm sure you could make up a story about needing money for something or other."

"But I'm not going to. Look, you've been beastly enough as it is. Why can't you make a straight deal and tell me how much you want? I'd try and meet it in return for the two tapes and your solemn promise never to mention it again."

"I might even do that. Could you meet, say, five hundred?"

"Five hundred pounds! That's quite a lot of money. I… I think I might be able to. I'd need time to raise that amount. I should have to sell some securities."

"That's all right. I'll be here another week. I want to work one or two other things out. In the meantime, you can let me have that tenner."

"Very well. I'll have to fetch it."

"No hurry," she drawled as Susan unlocked the door to leave.

Feeling as though she were going through a particularly nasty nightmare, she went up to her room to get the money. She knew and had already faced up to the fact that there was nothing she could do about it. Her niece had her dead to rights and, if she didn't pay up, would have no compunction about giving the tapes to her husband.

She also realised that she dared not tell Bill. She wouldn't put it past him to turn violent, put the girl over his knee and give her the thrashing of her life. And if she knew anything about teenage psychology, that would have the same effect as refusing to pay up. Liz would go straight to her husband. She was the sort of girl who was capable of doing that. No, her only chance was to pay what she asked and pray she would keep her word and hand over the tapes.

Back in the library she found her niece with a glass of brandy in her hand. Automatically she reached to take it from her.

"You know you're not old enough to drink! What would your mother say if…"

"None of your fucking business!" Susan recoiled at the harsh aggression of her niece's reply, and the girl easily avoided her aunt's grab for the glass. "And furthermore, she's never going to know, is she? I think you're forgetting that I'm the one who gives the orders from now on."

For just that one moment she *had* forgotten. Liz had merely been her sister's child, whom she was looking after.

Susan looked at her niece with new eyes. She was certainly no longer a child. The young woman who stood before her was just as tall as she was, if not a little taller, with a slim boyish figure. Her short, jet-black hair was so badly cut that Susan couldn't help speculating if she had done it herself. The salient features of her pallid face were strong, almost masculine eyebrows above piercing black eyes, a sharp inquisitive nose; her broad, thick lips seemed almost shockingly sensual in one so young. Were it not for her habitually saturnine expression, Liz could be extremely attractive to the opposite sex in a *gamine* sort of way, Susan guessed. It was true, that of her bosom there was practically no sign: just two little bumps, and those only visible when she wore a tight crew-neck sweater to go out. Her hips were slender, although she had long, shapely legs and a pert bottom. But there was no doubt that, given some more attention to detail, Liz could be an extremely attractive girl. Susan handed her the money and Liz thrust it into the pocket of her jeans with hardly a glance at it.

"I don't need to count it. I trust you!" she grinned.

"But am I to trust *you*, though?"

"Well, I don't think you have any option."

"Are you going to stick to your bargain and let me have those tapes?"

For a moment or two, Liz looked maddeningly undecided.

"I haven't exactly *made* a bargain, yet. I only asked if you could meet five hundred pounds."

"Well, when *will* you make up your mind, then? How long are you going to keep me in suspense?"

"I think I'll be able to come to some arrangement before I go home. Let's see, that's in exactly eleven days. As I said, I still have one or two things to work out."

"What sort of things?"

"Oh, you'll find out, Auntie." She raised her glass at the older woman in a mock toast. The audience with her niece, Susan realised, was at an end. In any case, she could no longer bear to be in the same room with her. She wanted to get away to be on her own and think things through. But as she went to the door, Liz started tinkering with the tape recorder once more.

"Susan!"

Her face went hot as she stopped and looked back at her.

"Just so you don't forget, how about this?"

She started the tape again. "...*feel it throbbing inside me… so hard and big! I think the tip is just touching my womb!*" She switched it off and Susan went out, her face flaming.

She went through the rest of the day on automatic. Several times she nearly phoned Bill, but always changed her mind. She couldn't do anything that might cause Liz to inform her husband of what had happened between her and Bill. She squirmed with shame every time she thought about those tapes. To think that she had been outside the window, listening and worse: she had probably been able to see them that first time, before Bill had switched the light off.

Late that evening she decided to phone Bill, just for the comfort of hearing his voice. Using the phone in the hall, she began to dial the number when her niece came out of the library and saw her. She came straight over and jabbed a finger on the rocker.

"I wouldn't, if I were you! If you do and he tries any rough stuff with me, then there'll be no deal and I'll send the tape straight off to Uncle Peter."

"I wasn't going to tell him. Now go away and mind your own business. I don't have to put up with your intrusion in my private life in addition to being blackmailed by you."

"Don't bet on it!" came the furious reply. Nevertheless, Liz took her hand off the phone and went back to the library. She turned at the door. "And don't make any dates for tonight, either. I want to see you after supper."

She decided against ringing Bill after that in case her voice betrayed her and he came over. If he saw her that night, he would know something was wrong.

Although she hated having to face her, she felt some slight relief. Her niece's wanting to see her after supper obviously meant that she had made her mind up about what sort of deal she was going to make.

Liz kept her hanging around, taking her time over her supper, a meal Susan had no appetite for that evening.

"Well?" she said, when Liz finally stood up from the table. She came over to stand close to her. Susan couldn't bear to look at her and turned to lean on the mantelpiece, looking down into the empty grate. "Have you decided on the best way of blackmailing me?"

"Now, now, no need to be unfriendly about it; it could be a very pleasant little deal."

"Pleasant! For whom? I think we can dispense with the light conversation. Just come to the point and tell me what you want. If you'll settle for the five hundred pounds, I think I shall be able to let you have it before you go home."

"Five hundred will do for the cash side of it." She was standing close behind her.

"For the cash side of it? What do you mean? What other side could there be?"

Suddenly Susan stiffened and stood stock still, unable to believe what was happening. Liz's arms had slid around her waist and she could feel the teenager's breath hot on the back of her neck.

"You're quite a dish, Aunt Susan. And we know you love sex, so I think you'll find this part of the bargain OK!" Then Susan felt her young niece's lips on the nape of her neck. So all her suspicions had been right all along! Liz *was* a homosexual, even though she was only sixteen! She was actually attracted to other women. The touch of her lips on her neck snapped her out of her shocked immobility. Susan's beautiful face twisted in disgust as she turned and wrenched herself from the precocious young lesbian's grasp.

"How *dare* you!" she said, her eyes blazing.

Liz was not so easily deterred. She moved after her aggressively, both hands reaching out and clumsily stroking the silk-covered mounds of her aunt's breasts, fingers coming together in an attempt to locate and pinch the nipples. With a gasp, Susan hauled off and fetched the girl a ringing slap across her face. A red handprint was clearly visible on the teenager's pale cheek. Her eyes narrowed and her expression was one of suppressed rage. Liz raised her hand as if to strike back but she just managed to check herself and gave her aunt a sickly-sweet smile instead; suddenly Susan was not only physically afraid. There was something utterly evil and calculating about this girl. If she had struck back, things might have developed into an unseemly cat fight, but at least that would have been a more normal outcome to what she was witnessing now: a smouldering rage, but one that was very well contained. Such control in one so young was truly terrifying.

"You'll pay for that, Auntie dear," she hissed venomously.

Without answering, Susan left the room, both angry and scared by this weird turn of events. Liz followed her into the hall and shouted up the stairs after her.

"And you needn't think that's the end of it. For the next ten days I'm going to make you wish you'd never been born! I know you never liked me…"

"Quiet!" hissed Susan. "Elsie will hear you!"

"I don't care who hears me. You better listen good if you don't want your husband to know about…"

"Oh, very well! But for heaven's sake keep your voice down. I'll come down."

Susan went back down the stairs, knowing she had no choice, but dreading whatever was coming next. Her niece stood at the bottom looking up, her eyes roving over her body.

"There, that's better," she smiled sweetly, when Susan reached her. "Now, apart from the seven hundrend and fifty pounds…"

"But you said five hundred pounds!"

"That was before you made the serious mistake of slapping my face! I should have spanked your bottom, but we can always get around to that later on…"

"You… you insolent…"

"It would have more effect if you received it on the bare bottom, of course…"

"You beastly little…" words failed Susan as she glared at her niece, her face blazing with embarrassment. She had to clench her hands at her sides in case she made things worse by hitting her again. But she hadn't heard the half of it. Inconceivably worse was to follow. Liz felt herself the complete mistress of the whole situation and played it to the hilt, as a sixteen-year-old girl might who suddenly found a grown-up in her power. Especially when the grown-up in question was an extremely attractive woman and the sixteen-year-old was a lesbian with an extremely twisted mind plus a knowledge of sexual matters well in advance of her years.

"And talking of taking your panties down, well, that's the other part of the bargain. After all, if you let yourself be fucked by your brother-in-law, why shouldn't your own niece have a go, too?"

There was another moment of complete silence, as Susan looked at her in shocked horror. Everything started to reel around her and she thought she was going to faint. Then her vision cleared and Liz's leering face came back into focus.

"Never!" she hissed. "Never, you… you *monster!* Tell my husband and be damned!"

She left the girl standing at the bottom of the stairs and went up to her bedroom.

Chapter 4

After a completely sleepless night, during which time she had almost made up her mind to pack a bag and disappear, she spent most of the next morning alternating between coffee and brandy and smoking incessantly. Her hated niece was not in evidence until nearly lunchtime, and then she looked into the library, where Susan sat holding a glass of brandy and staring sightlessly out the window.

"I thought you might like to know that I'm just going to the Post Office to send one set of the tapes off to Uncle Peter." She held out a small parcel long enough for her aunt to see her husband's name and army address.

"What will you do now, dear Auntie Susan? Leave home?" she grinned. "Well, ta-ta, I won't be long!"

"Wait!"

Liz turned, her grin widening as she sensed victory.

"Changed your mind then?"

"No... I... oh, God!" She covered her eyes with a hand. "Give me time to think. Have you no pity? You're playing with the lives of three people – you could ruin them forever!"

"Pity? None. Not a shred. And just who was playing with whose lives when you asked your brother-in-law to fuck you?" Her voice, which had risen with self-righteous indignation, now fell to a normal level. "I'll give you until after lunch. Then I'll post it."

The young lesbian left her with her chaotic thoughts. Elsie came in to announce lunch, but she waved her away, preferring another brandy and a cigarette.

She had to acknowledge the fact that she had been the chief instigator of the whole chain of events; she had insisted when Bill would have backed out. The two brothers had always been very close and she would be the cause of the inevitable divorce. She'd have the contempt of her husband, and Bill would have nothing to thank her for. A sorry mess for the three of them.

That brought her to the next consideration. She shivered as she thought about her niece again. Those hands on her body. Liz's mouth touching hers... and worse. She took a quick swig of brandy as the mental image of herself lying naked beneath the girl's body flashed across her mind.

What of the price of getting out of it? Five hundred pournds, or had Liz meant it when she had upped it to seven hundred and fifty pounds? She could still find that amount by selling most of her jewellery, but the rest of it – to go to bed with her sister's daughter! Her own niece! And one who filled her with nothing but revulsion. What had she called it? 'Taking her panties down'! Her stomach crawled at the thought of exposing her person to the younger female – and to let herself be touched intimately by a member of the same sex!

However, she forced herself to think about it. It was the only answer to the problem she herself had created. If she could do it, she would have paid her debt and be free of this blackmail. Or would she? How long would it go on? How long would Liz continue to hold those damnable tapes over her head? Supposing she found the pleasures of sex with her aunt and the occasional tenner whenever she asked for them more desirable than the lump sum? It could go on for...

"Well? What's the verdict?"

Liz was back. Her time for thought was up. Now she had to make a decision.

"If I agree to your proposals, then how long would it be likely to continue? When would you give me those tapes?" She stood facing the window, her back to the girl.

"On the day I go home."

"What of your promise not to speak of this to anyone? Could I keep you to that?"

"I won't tell."

"No. You probably realise that without the tapes, no one would believe you anyway."

Susan was silent for a moment. Liz licked her lips nervously. It was in the balance, she knew, but the odds seemed in her favour. She saw her aunt's shoulders straighten as she took a deep breath.

"When would my ordeal begin? Right away, I suppose. Tonight?"

"That's right, and no changing of your mind afterwards, or I'll change mine, too."

"I wouldn't do that; I want those tapes. I… I take it I wouldn't have to do it… *every* night?" she asked quietly.

"Perhaps. Depends on how I feel." Liz knew that she had her, now. "Well, what's it to be?" She scented victory.

"Very well," Susie said in an almost inaudible voice. She already felt dirty, somehow.

Liz feasted her eyes on the shapely back of her aunt as she stood facing away from her, her head bowed in defeat. The young lesbian let her eyes wander over the curves of her hips and settled on the woman's lovely backside. Hers! All hers for the next week! She wanted to strip her on the spot, but restrained herself. Elsie was about, and it and would be all the better for waiting anyway.

She was almost blinded by lust as she visualised what her aunt might look like in the nude. This proud, beautiful woman, whom she had dreamed of having in just this situation. It made it even better that she would hate every moment of it. And Susan had no inkling of the punishment she would receive in addition to the sexual indignities that Liz had planned for her. She'd make her suffer for that slap that her aunt had given her the night before too. She grinned to herself, her glance once more falling to the woman's magnificent bottom. She would take it out on that. That would really be a little surprise for her. The mere thought of beating another woman made her heart pound.

Susan turned and brushed past him with a look of pure loathing. She stopped at the door.

"I expect you'll tell me when… when I'm required." Then she went out of the room without waiting for a reply.

"Oh yes," said Liz quietly to herself. "I'll let you know alright…"

Chapter 5

Susan went out shortly after the interview in the library. She needed some fresh air to clear her mind, to get away from the house, the silent witness to her coming shame and from the person who was to be its instrument.

Finally, after crossing two fields she found a place to sit down and think things through. How had things escalated to a point where she was soon going to sleep with her niece… her sixteen-year-old niece, at that? She was nearly thirty, almost twice the girl's age. If it ever became public knowledge, she might not be found guilty of any crime, but the scandal would be enormous. Yet how could she avoid it?

And how many times would she have to do it? Once? Twice? Every single night?

She had no idea of the girl's sex-drive. She would just have to see.

After dinner, Susan waited in the library. By ten o'clock, she was feeling like a condemned prisoner. Her niece was not in evidence. Half an hour went by and she began to start at the slightest sound. The little sadist was making her suffer in anticipation for as long as possible, knowing how much she would be dreading it.

She jumped when the door opened. But it was only Elsie to say goodnight. A little later the phone rang. It was Bill. He wanted to know if he should come over.

"Oh Bill, I'd love you to, but… but…" her voice trailed off. Her niece, with impeccable timing, was standing in the doorway.

"Susie… is there anything wrong?"

"No, nothing… it's just that I've got such a frightful headache… I…"

Liz came over and put her hand over the mouthpiece of the telephone.

"Not tonight, Auntie. Don't you make any dates. Put him off; I don't want him round here tonight!"

"Susie…" she could hear his voice through the receiver, "are you sure it's just a headache? You sound frightened, somehow."

"No, I'm not frightened, dear, just a real splitter of a headache. I was going to bed when you rang…"

"I'm sorry. I'll not keep you in that case. I'll give you a tinkle tomorrow, eh?"

They agreed to talk early in the morning. Susan felt she would probably need the comfort of his voice by then. She replaced the receiver and looked up at her niece. "Now?" she asked.

"Getting impatient for it, are we?" she grinned. "No, not yet. I'm going to fix myself a snack first. I'll tell you when I need you."

"I shall be in my bedroom," said Susan in a low, dispirited voice as she left the room to go upstairs.

She paced up and down in the bedroom for a while; she stopped in front of the long cheval mirror and looked at herself. She was dressed. At least she could spare herself the indignity of having to strip in front of the lusting young lesbian. So she undressed, feeling like someone preparing for some weird judicial punishment. Naked, she looked around for something to wear. Was there any point in putting on pyjamas or a nightie? She decided against it since she would only be taking them off as soon as Liz entered the room. At any rate, she wanted to get this over with as soon as possible. So, no night-wear.

She started to put on a filmy negligee, then discarded it. Too sexy, too suggestive. She finally settled for a celadon candlewick dressing gown and slippers. The soft, tufted fabric felt comforting against her skin as she sat down on her bed to wait.

It was after midnight when Liz finally rattled the handle of her door. Susan had locked it. Slowly, she went over to open it and stood silently, waiting for her niece to order next move.

"Well, ask me inside!"

Her aunt stood back to let the girl pass. Liz was dressed in her habitual jeans and black shirt outfit, and she carried a bundle of sorts, something wrapped in what looked like a pillow case. Susan closed the door, hesitating briefly before locking it too.

She stood with her back to the door, watching as her niece sauntered around the room in a proprietorial, yet inquisitive sort of way. She picked up the lacy panties that Susan had discarded. Too late she realised that she had made her first mistake by leaving them on the bed. The girl opened out her underwear and looked inside, feeling the gusset in the crotch between finger and thumb. She wrinkled her nose disapprovingly.

"Oh Auntie Susie! Don't you wipe after you have a piss? It's all… moist!" she said, her face set in mock disapproval.

Susan's face flamed, partly because her niece had cheekily just used the familiar diminutive that only her husband or Bill ever called her by and secondly because of the unpleasantly crude implication she had made. To make matters worse, Liz brought the skimpy undergarment up to her nose and inhaled, smiling.

"Mmm! Cunt juice, I would say. Sorry… my mistake. I didn't think you'd be so eager! I see you've more or less stripped for action too. Come over here"

Her aunt looked at her aghast. Where had she learnt such disgusting language? With lead in her feet, she went over to her. Liz reached out and pulled the cord of her dressing gown, then took the lapels and wrenched the garment wide open. The girl was unable to suppress a sharp intake of breath at the naked beauty of Susan's generous breasts, curving belly and full, springy bush.

Her arms down at her sides, Susan stood with closed eyes as her young niece gazed greedily upon her torso. She felt a slight tug and then the dressing gown sliding down over her shoulders, down her arms as it gently slipped to the floor. At last she stood entirely exposed before the rapt stare of the young blackmailer.

She opened her eyes and looked with loathing at Liz's intent expression as she lifted first one substantial breast and then the other, to examine them briefly. Automatically she crossed her hands in front of her lower belly as the girl's glance dropped to that area. Roughly they were pulled away and she had to stand while Liz tried to push her hand between her closed thighs.

"Open your legs!" the teenager growled.

It was only prolonging the agony to make protests or disobey. She moved her feet about nine inches apart and gasped as ungentle fingers probed and prodded at her sex. Curious fingers, which started to separate her hairy outer labia, probe her dry, unreceptive inner lips and even scuttle back to lightly finger her anus. Susan screamed silently. This was going to be even worse to endure than she had thought.

Liz walked around her as if she were livestock at a market, looking, touching, stroking, probing. She was utterly absorbed and delighted, like a child with a new toy. Susan suddenly jerked forward as she felt two strong hands on her buttocks, first gripping them hard, then pulling them wide open, cruelly exposing the posterior view of her vulva and anus. It was like some warped medical examination only ten times worse.

"Do you have to do that?" she whispered.

"Yes, I do. I bet you wouldn't complain if it was Bill doing that to you!" Susan thought she could detect a small hint of jealousy in her niece's voice. She made a mental note of it, to be considered later. "I'm going to examine your cunt even more closely soon. It looks a pretty one, though, I must admit."

The touch of the girl's hands, feeling at her, made her nauseous. Now she wished she would carry out whatever dreadful, vile act she needed to in order to achieve satisfaction for herself and just get it over with. Meanwhile, Susan could only stand there and let her niece do whatever she wanted.

The girl was standing behind her now, her hands running up and down Susan's flanks. They slid around to her quivering belly. Susan could feel Liz's clothed body pushing against her back, the slight protrusions of her small breasts pressing against her, just below her shoulder blades, the rough cloth of her jeans against the soft cheeks of her bottom. Once more, her own breasts were being handled. She looked down at the hands clasping and lifting the heavy, creamy mounds, fingers inevitably finding her nipples and tweaking them lightly until they started to firm up. Susan clenched her fists, willing herself not to round on the girl and slap her hard. Then the intimate assault on her breasts ceased and they were allowed to bounce gently back into place again.

"Stay there – don't move!"

Liz undressed brazenly in front of her aunt. First the shirt came off, revealing a cheap white brassiere; she peeled off her socks and kicked off her loafers and then it was the turn of her jeans to be removed. Briefly, she stood in bra and panties. These too were unceremoniously discarded and Liz stood in front of Susan naked as the day she was born.

Curious, Susan could not but help look at her niece in this very different state. Her body, she had to admit, was sexy, although the very opposite of her own. The girl's skin was snowy white. High, round breasts the size of small apples were tipped with stiff, carmine, bud-like nipples which, like her big, sensual mouth, were a welcome relief to the almost monochrome quality of her naked body. Her lean frame held a sculptured ribcage and flat, muscular stomach, embellished by a slightly protruding navel. Below this jutted a prominent *mons veneris*, adorned with a thick, black pubic bush. Slim hips and long, coltish legs completed the picture. What a pity she has such an unpleasant, perverted personality, Susan thought sadly. She could be so attractive.

"Now, my beautiful Auntie, we're all ready, aren't we? Come on, I can't wait to fuck that juicy cunt of yours!" She grabbed Susan's wrist and hauled her over to the large double bed. Just what could she mean by 'fuck'? How could a girl possibly…? Susan suddenly felt as though she were in a lift plummeting down the deepest mineshaft. *Oh no!* Surely she couldn't… couldn't be considering *that* sort of sex…?

Susan knew only very little of lesbian encounters. Merely what she had gleaned from the very occasional risqué conversations with other army wives. Of course she had heard of hand-held dildos, as well as the strap-on variety, and those new, white plastic, bullet-shaped vibrators that you could now buy quite easily. Likewise, she vaguely understood what lesbians actually *did* with one another after a school experience that she had all but erased from her memory.

Aged seventeen, she had had the most terrible crush on a girl in her class at boarding school. Miranda had been very athletic and muscular. The passion she felt had been disturbingly real, especially when she had discovered that their feelings were mutual. They had consummated this fledgling relationship only once, behind the gymnasium, where a conveniently dense shrubbery meant detection was almost impossible.

The experience had been traumatic for Susan, who had just wanted to kiss and hug the object of her affections. But Miranda had had other ideas, and after some breathless French kissing, had raised hers and Susan's sports shirts so that her own small breasts could rub nakedly against Susan's far larger ones. The sensations had been so utterly thrilling for Susan that she had felt quite faint with arousal. She became very wet and perhaps she would have tolerated that degree of intimacy – had it gone no further. But of course, it did.

Miranda had abruptly stuck her hand into her friend's knickers encountering the warm slippery gash of Susan's by now sopping sex. Susan had at first frozen at this intimate – and mortifyingly revealing – contact; she was paralysed with uncontrollable lust by the other girl's attempts to masturbate her to orgasm with her fingers. But just before this could happen, by summoning all her willpower, she had somehow wrenched herself from the embrace and ran off, her face burning with shame. Later she had gratefully shrugged off the whole thing as mere teenage sexual frustration: what she had really wanted was a male, not some masculine female substitute.

With a sinking heart, Susan stood at the end of the bed while Liz reached down and selected something from the little bundle she had brought with her. It was about eighteen inches in length and made out of dark red rubber, which gave it a slightly surgical appearance. Susan looked at it for a long minute before she finally understood what it was. The rubber it was made of was stiff, but not too hard. At each end of the long flexible rubber shaft was a bulbous shape. A double dildo. Susan had once seen a picture of one in a filthy magazine that she had discovered while unpacking her husband's suitcase on his return from abroad.

Susan watched her niece reach for the dildo, which lay next to her on the bed. With the thumb and forefinger of her left hand, the girl held her labia open, while with her right hand she placed the head of the dildo against the wet opening. It was huge. At least twice the size of a real cock. For a moment, Susan doubted that Liz's cunt would be able to open wide enough to receive it. But then, as Liz moved the tip of the thing toward the wet inner flesh of the opening, she realised the elasticity of her niece's cunt would allow her to accommodate it quite easily.

The older woman stared in fascination as Liz's cuntlips stretched slowly to accept the gentle pressure of the rubber dildo. She watched open-mouthed, as little by little, her niece's feverish sex swallowed the fake phallus. A crossbar divided the shaft of the double-headed dildo at the midpoint. Liz screwed the rubber rod to the left and right as she worked it deeper and deeper into her pussy, which seemed to devour the firm rubber sausage's length until only half remained. At last the crossbar was pressing flat against the wiry jungle of Liz's pussy hair, protruding obscenely from the base of her bush and she let go of the rod.

"There… are you ready for a good fucking, Auntie? Because I am!"

Before the startled woman could answer, Liz was pressing herself against her, her sensual mouth open and wet against Susan's, her tongue attempting, unsuccessfully, to invade her aunt's mouth. Susan was revolted. The girl's hands dropped to her bottom, gripping the cheeks, pulling her closer. Her large, softer breasts were flattened by

Liz's smaller ones as they pressed hard against her.

"Put your arms around me, then," she whispered against her lips, her breath warm and surprisingly sweet.

Susan slid her arms around her niece's neck, but turned her face, unwilling to give the girl her lips once more. Her stomach was pressing against Liz's pelvis and she could feel the soft, disconcerting tickle of the teenager's pubic bush just above her own. But more disturbing was the feel of the rubber phallus that now nestled between Susan's thighs. It seemed to have a life of its own, from time to time brushing against her labia, twitching and moving like a real penis.

With a rising sense of panic, Susan realised that this girl, this teenager, was about to… to *fuck* her with the obscene rubber thing between her legs. Any minute now it would slide between the lips of her vulva.

"Open your legs – I want you to feel it against your cunt!"

Her legs opened and indeed she felt the stiff rod jerk upwards against her slit. Liz moved back and forth, rubbing it along her vulva, then made her close her thighs on it, trapping it there.

"Lie on the bed now… no, not that way," her niece snapped as she was about to lie back in the conventional way, with her head on the pillows. "Legs dangling over the bed, and get them well open. I want to have a good look at that randy slit of yours!"

Almost crying with shame, she obeyed, her bottom resting on the edge, her feet on the floor. Liz rummaged in the pillow case. She brought out a small torch.

"Oh you *beast!*" Susan moaned when she saw what the girl was bent on doing. "You horrid, horrid little girl!"

She tried to close her legs, but was prevented by Liz quickly

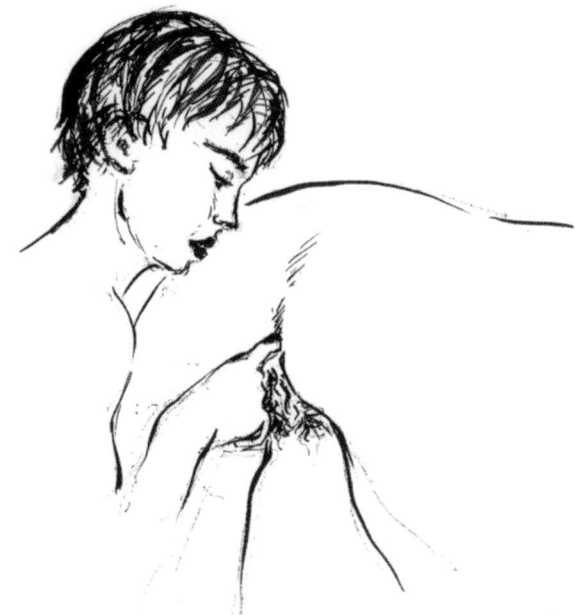

kneeling between them and getting an arm under one of her thighs, holding her.

"You stick to your side of the bargain, Auntie. I can always change my mind if you don't perform well enough. And be careful about calling me names, I haven't forgotten about that slap you gave me last night."

Susan writhed in embarrassment as Liz switched on the torch and looked directly up into her sex.

"Hold the lips open, like this," she was told, and felt the girl's hands on her sex for the first time. Whimpering with humiliation, she complied, parting her labia so that the teenager had a perfect view of the entrance to her vagina.

She lay back, her lovely naked body tense, her fingers spreading her vulva open for inspection, as her niece knelt between her legs with the torch. She jerked every now and then as Liz touched her clitoris or a finger poked into her vaginal tunnel. Even her anus was prodded and poked. She hadn't dreamed that the agony would be so prolonged. She had thought that at worst there would have been a short groping and furtive, mutual masturbation, the whole thing over and done with in a few minutes. But by the leisurely way that Liz was going about things, Susan could tell that Liz intended making it last nearly half the night.

"How long are you going to torture me like this?" she whispered. "For pity's sake, I've agreed to let you have what you want – why humiliate me as well?"

"This is what I want! I know you're getting impatient for a good fucking, but really Auntie, show a bit more self-control. I'll give you that in a minute!"

"Oh, God!" She tried another form of appeal: "Liz – I'm your Aunt Susan – your *mother's sister!* Surely that should mean something to you!"

"Umm... yes! It does! It makes it more sexy!"

"Would you do this to your own mother then?

"Oh, Susie, you bad woman! Now you're putting ideas into my head! She probably wouldn't let me, though!""You... you're a *monster!*"

"I've warned you about calling me names." She got to her feet. "Now, then. Get your heels up on the edge of the bed and keep those knees well apart. I'm going to fuck you now!"

This was it Susan did as she was told, lying on her back, heels on the edge of the bed, her knees splayed wide. She felt terribly exposed and vulnerable, now, as her niece stood looking down at her. The long, rubber phallus rose up from her loins in a sick parody of male genitalia. She saw that the bulbous head was even formed like a glans penis, roughly conforming to the shape of the real article.

Liz moved in, her hands resting on either side of Susan who, looking up, her body cringing as her niece lowered herself down on to her. She felt the contact of the rubber penis against her slit once more and Liz's hand reached down between them to guide its head in.

It was a fruitless action, however. Susan's cunt appeared to be dry and utterly impenetrable. She was nervous as a kitten and nervousness often made her unable to lubricate. Liz responded by removing the dildo from her own vagina with a slight sucking noise, pulling Susan back so that she was lying properly on the bed, her head on the pillows. Then she said, in a softer voice than usual, "It looks as if I'm going to have to do something to make you feel quite a bit sexier."

Liz's hand reached forward to touch and caress her breasts and Susan experienced another new sensation she had only known once before: the gentle, physical seduction of another female's hands. She gasped, momentarily closing her eyes, as she heard the girl's lewd chuckle.

"Oh, I thought so. You're a tittie girl, aren't you, Auntie?"

The long, gentle, slim fingers caught at her nipple, rolling it and squeezing it in a tender, understanding way that only another female could know. Susan began to tremble all over at the forbidden strangeness of the situation. Her upbringing had never accepted this sort of thing, but at the moment her whole being was tormented by her unfulfilled lust, the sexual frustration that her husband's long absences and her initial contacts with Bill had only succeeded in exacerbating; now there flew to mind the almost-forgotten schoolgirl encounter of a dozen years past. Now she found that she couldn't resist, even if had she wanted to, her handsome young niece's advances.

The alien fingers crept over her with a feathery softness as they gently forced her down. She closed her eyes even tighter as she felt the girl's soft lips engulf the nipple of her left breast, all the knob-like areola, all of the berry-like nipple with a swiftly flickering tongue that sent urgent, taunting messages radiating outward along nerves to her brain...

Slowly, Liz slithered up her body until their faces were level with each other, and her thigh crept up Susan's twining around it, her soft, curling fleece of pubic hair brushing warmly against her own. Susan felt a wetness there that was not her own. Not yet, at least. Liz's big, sensual mouth came down upon her own. Those full, pliant, soft lips found Susan's with an agile possession, and her sweet, knowing tongue fluttered into her mouth.

And this time, in spite of her shame at the thought of another woman kissing her so intimately (or perhaps because of it), Susan could not help responding. She sucked at the invading tongue as Liz's hand trailed over her tormented body with enthralling touches, running over her large breasts, her sides and back, their bodies finally locking together as the caressing hand reached her generous buttocks and pulled them apart to stroke the raw little anus delicately with her finger.

At last, Liz raised above her, taking Susan's left breast in her hand, her fingers teasing the still distended nipple. She let her eyes rove over the lovely auburn-haired woman's voluptuous nakedness. Finally, her voice trembling uncharacteristically, she said, "You're a beauty, Auntie, I've got to admit! And I'm going to make you spend like a fountain... no, like a bloody volcano!"

To her astonishment, Susan moaned, "Oh yes, yes, please ..."

"Just you wait, lover," Liz panted, and commenced to slide down her aunt's trembling, passion-filled body.

Susan raised her head to watch in half-revolted captivation as Liz nestled her face into the hollow of her opened thighs. She felt the soft kisses on her skin, on the tender creases, felt the hot puffs of breath, and then the magic tongue licking the cleft, simply licking in long strokes from the bottom to the top, not entering yet, but bringing an involuntary slight lifting of the loins with each slow up-lick of tongue on sensitive labia.

Susan's clitoris became hard in seconds, and it hardened even more as it peeked out further to enjoy a grazing tickle from the tongue. She hissed and rolled her head slowly back and forth on the pillow. Liz eased her tongue inside at the bottom of the cleft and drew it up, up... up towards the tingling little pink bean.

Susan's throat worked insanely. She held her breath, then exhaled sharply at the delicious contact.

Suddenly, the gentle taunting was over.

Liz pressed her mouth closer. She reached up with both hands and played hard with Susan's breasts, while her mouth became hungry, open, hot, with nothing but a soft, slippery spear of muscle invading the now yielding wet gash before it, nothing but tongue lashing at

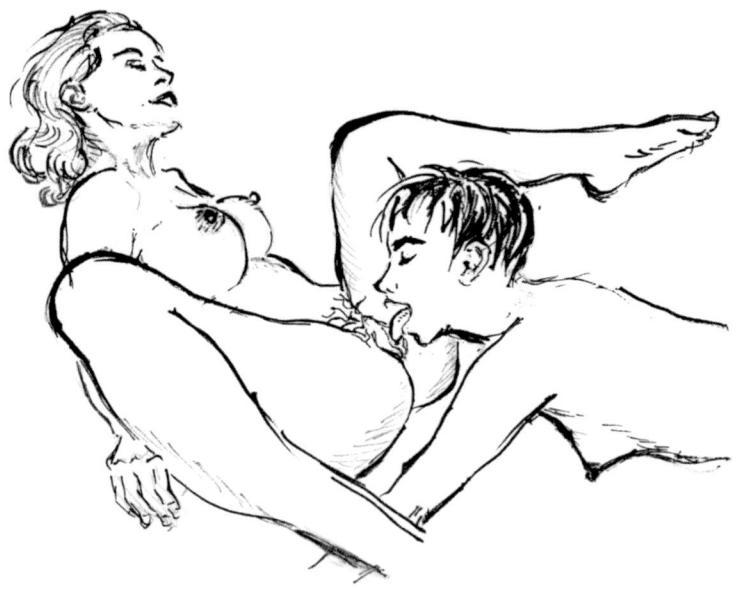

the erect clitoris, tongue everywhere in her throbbing cunt, slippery in the juices, eel-like in the vagina, and always returning to the sensitive, tingling clitoris.

Susan moaned and thrashed uncontrollably. Liz laughed wantonly and continued to suck and lick despite the increasing difficulty of remaining in contact with her aunt's bucking loins. Minutes passed and Susan's belly rippled. She commenced to pant explosively as her loins curled up, pressed up with vibrant tension to bring the magic tongue tighter to the quivering centre of her body.

Liz was gasping, sucking air in short surges, hardly ever breaking the fervent, lashing contact of her eager mouth... tongue... lips... even her nose was buried, immersed, sometimes, during the wild depravity of her lovemaking in Susan's wet, steaming cunt.

"Ohhh... ohhhh... I can't stand it!" Susan screamed. "It's too much... simply too much...!" Her voice died in a strangled mixture of sob and sigh and then broke out again in a high-pitched wail as her passion overflowed all bounds and swept through her loins. She twisted in the grip of her sweet agony, twisted and writhed and did not break with the open mouth glued to her cunt while the flickering magic tongue played like summer lightning over her clitoris and sent that lightning surging through her body to her brain.

She endured the pleasure, gasped, groaned, clutched Liz's short black hair with clawing fingers... at last, shuddering violently, then relaxing... or trying to relax... as Liz continued, refusing to stop.

"Oh God... that's enough! Oh, stop... please..." Susan begged her niece weakly, not really wanting it to stop, but cringing with the sharpened sensation. Liz eased away from Susan's clitoris. She plunged into the vagina, tasting the slightly salty secretions, licked again the now flushed swollen cunt-lips, kissed the trembling inner thighs.

"Dear God!" Susan gasped as she drew in great, shuddering breaths. She was enervated, drained, lethargic. She could not push the girl's head away. She could not close her thighs. Oh God, she still wanted to be fucked! She rolled her head to stare at the long, thick, hard cock that lay where Liz had discarded it and Liz caught her eye.

God, she wanted it filling her, those slim hips of Liz thrusting it into her. She sobbed aloud with her frustration and Liz returned to her voracious tonguing of the hard little bud of her clitoris. Susan convulsed. Her stomach muscles went rigid as her hands locked at the girl's head, wanting, yet not wanting, her to stop.

Again, she spasmed inside, climaxed once more, her heart slamming wildly in her chest, her mind awash in pleasure that flamed, her lungs a bellows, animal-like sounds emitting deep within her chest as her eyes glazed and her mouth hung limply open, a little trickle of drool running down the side of her mouth.

"Please" she begged, "do it now"

Liz chuckled darkly and withdrew her wet, glistening mouth from

Susan's palpitating cunt, raising her head slowly.

"Yes, finally I think you're ready, Aunt Susan," she smiled.

Susan could not help but return a grateful, if wanton, twitching smile of her own.

As the sweating Liz knelt up between her thighs, entirely of her own accord, Susan raised them up and spread them wide so that her knees pointed in opposite directions and her heels were almost touching her full bottom, while new sensual spasms of hazy delight at what was to come taunted her still throbbing pelvic area. Now, she would get fucked! She was so open, so ready… Surely, now, *now…*

But with Liz, nothing was ever that simple.

"Oh, we are eager, aren't we! But first, Auntie, you have to return the compliment I just paid you. And you know something? I think I'd like you to lick my arsehole a bit, too. I've always liked that." She laughed at what must have looked a comical expression of horror on Susan's face. "But first, my dear Aunt, let me get on my hands and knees so that you can lick my little brown hole with your tongue, mmm?"

Liz gave a little shudder of delight as she assumed that position, while Susan got to her knees in dull abhorrence at the thought. To perform such an act on a man was one thing, not that she ever had, but upon a woman… she didn't think she could do it.

But Liz had already waggled her buttocks back toward where she knelt… beautifully tight, rounded, white, moon-shaped buttocks, and Susan could see the hairless, puckered brown opening as Liz lowered her shoulders to the bed, thrusting the area back toward her. Susan's eyes dropped to the long dusky pink slit of the girl's sex, with its hair-lined lips only slightly opened, and she could see the enticing pink flesh beyond. Small, sparkling droplets clung to the fleecy lips, and suddenly she sensed herself moving forward as if drawn, until the musky scent stung her nostrils and she lashed out with her tongue, going down deep toward the handsome girl's clitoris just as she had done to her only moments before. She found it clasped within the inner petals, her own lips coming in contact with the soft pubic haired, fleshy folds of her cunt as she stretched her tongue to its entirety, its tip stabbing at the erect bud and raising a deep groan from the teenager.

Slowly Susan swept upward, licking her tongue-tip several times against the long clitoris, then backward toward the round viscous covered opening of her vagina, plunging in far enough to feel the rippled walls of hot flesh nibble and milk at her tongue then out to taunt her urethra before travelling on up the satin-smooth vale between her buttocks to the crinkled mouth of her pulsating anus. She continued to lick, her tongue failing to discriminate between cunt and arsehole, with mounting passion.

Oh, it's wonderful! The delicious taste of her cunt... I love it! Susan's head reeled: am I really a lesbian too? she wondered. Why am I enjoying this so? She returned to her task in hand, and lavished her most sensual tongue caresses upon the small, twitching orifice until Liz gave a little shudder and said, "Enough!" and rose up.

"Quickly now, on your back, get ready…"

Liz once more slid the dildo into herself and, holding its protrusion tightly, brought its head towards Susan's cunt. And pressed it home.

"Oh God, no, Liz, *stop!*" screamed her aunt. "It's too big… much too big! You'll kill me with that thing"

"Shushhh! Elsie might hear! Besides, if it fits me, I don't see why it shouldn't feel fine in your precious little cunt…"

Liz pulled the flanges of her aunt's cunt apart with the fingers of one hand while with the other she continued to try to work the rubber dildo inside. She turned it first one way and then the other in an attempt to screw it in. Finally the tapered tip began to penetrate.

When, at last, Susan's cunt had opened far enough to accept the entire bulbous head of the dildo, she gave a long, low moan of pain.

Liz knew that the entry was hurting her aunt. For reasons that she was still trying to understand, that moan of pain was exciting, too. Her clitoris was twitching and throbbing with excitement as she watched herself, with a series of short violent jerky motions, drive inch after inch of the rubber cock into the older woman's tight cunt.

By now Susan's moans of pain were gradually turning to sighs of pleasure. Liz could see her body moving up and down as she matched the driving rhythm of her niece's fucking. Liz was moving her hips up and down like a man, fucking the life out of her victim, her pert buttocks bouncing and rolling as she threw her body wholeheartedly into the task. Each time she came up, the dildo's shaft slipped out of both her cunt and that of Susan, until it bridged the space between their sweating bodies, held in place only by the two bulbous heads, which were swallowed by the two tight, clasping vaginas.

Then as Liz's spare frame crashed heavily down on top of Susan's, the dildo was buried in both cunts until nothing but the little rubber crossbar separated them. Liz began moving her bottom around in little circles as she made the traditional in-and-out motion that was a parody of the reproductive act. Now both of the women were panting excitedly as the artificial prick brought them to the brink of orgasm.

And then, in a perfectly timed duet, both women began to sob and groan in a rhythmic staccato that signalled the advent of their mutual orgasm. The voice of the novice was somewhat muted by her unwillingness to accept the situation, but her passion was nevertheless obvious. Liz's shouts were loud however, as if she were proudly proclaiming her arousal to the world.

Had Susan's housekeeper chosen that moment to enter the room, the sight of the conjoined pair would have riveted her. At last Liz, still panting with the strain of her efforts, rose to her knees, pulling the thickly lubricated dildo from the her victim's cunt with a slight slurping sound. Then, as she rose to her feet, the stiff rubber rod still jutting from her hairy cunt, she sighed a long sigh of completion.

"Oh, that was beautiful," she said. "Sometimes I wish I could have one of those flesh and blood cocks that men want to fuck us with. Then I would have been able to feel that scrumptious cunt of yours wrap itself around me.

Susan raised herself on one arm and looked up at the girl. She suddenly wanted her to go, to get out of the room as soon as possible. She desperately wanted to be alone.

"All right," she said quietly. "I'd like to go to sleep if that's agreeable to you."

"Well, no, as a matter of fact, it isn't. You see, Auntie, we have some rather important, unfinished business to take care of."

Chapter 6

"Unfinished business? But what could you possibly..."

"Bend over and touch your toes, sweet Susie!"

"I beg your pardon?"

Liz's voice hardened, her demeanour became harsh.

"Do what I say or you'll regret it a great deal!"

"What for? What are you going to do?"

Liz had turned to once more rummage in the pillowcase. When she faced her aunt again, she had one hand behind her back.

"What! You haven't obeyed me? Do as you're told and bend over at once!"

"I want to know what you intend doing to me."

"You didn't think you were going to get away with slapping my face, did you? And the snide, disrespectful remarks since I came here? I don't forgive things like that, you know."

"What... what are you going to do to me?" whispered Susan,

comprehension slowly dawning.

"I'm going to punish you with a good caning!" And Liz showed her what she held behind her back – a long, thin, willowy cane. Susan flinched and jumped back as Liz swished it through the air close to her.

"Come on! Bend over and take your medicine!"

Susan looked around wildly; she was naked and helpless; she knew that Liz was slightly taller and she guessed she was stronger, too. In any case, she could cut her to pieces with that vicious-looking cane before she could get to grips with her. She tried to get to the bed for her discarded dressing gown, but her niece jumped in front of her, swishing the cane from side to side, perilously close to her breasts. Her hands came up to protect them as she fell back. The teenager advanced on her and she continued to back away until she felt the cold glass of the wardrobe touching her bottom. She stood, holding her large breasts fearfully, her face flushed, her eyes on the cane.

"No, Liz – please, you mustn't. I let you have sex with me. Isn't that enough?"

"The sooner you bend over and let me get at that beautiful bum of yours with the cane, the sooner it'll be over. But I'm not going to wait too long."

She made a feint at Susan's soft belly with the point of the cane. She dropped her hands protectively with a gasp, letting her breasts fall. Immediately the cane flashed up, the tip prodding at the underside of her left breast. Liz laughed at her cry of pain.

"Ohhh!" She touched the spot tenderly. "You… you could injure me like that!"

"Well, let's see your backside, then! Why won't you take your stripes like a grown-up should and get it all over with? I'm not leaving until I've caned you!"

"I could scream for Elsie."

"Go ahead – let everybody know, not only that Bill has been up you, but your own niece, too. That'll give them all something to think about!" She laughed in Susan's face, then her eyes glinted, her mouth twisting in a terrible sneer. "I told you I'd make you pay for that slap you gave me."

"You're certainly not going to cane me!"

"Your choice. Caning now or tapes to husband in the morning."

Mention of the tapes drained a lot of the defiance from her, but to allow her to lay a cane across her naked buttocks was somehow unthinkable. The whole thing was unreal – she was her aunt, for God's sake! This sixteen-year-old was her niece – yet she was the mistress of the situation, too. Susan cowered, naked, before her, trying to think of some plea, an appeal to some remote spark of decency in her, that might dissuade her from administrating this shameful punishment, which, she suddenly realised, she was going to have to submit to eventually.

"Come on – you're wasting time." She swished the cane imperiously, grinning when she saw her aunt flinch. "You told me you wouldn't change your mind."

"I agreed to go to bed… to have sex with you. I didn't know that flagellation was going to come into it."

"You should have been nicer to me, shouldn't you?"

Liz was flexing the cane in her hands and there was a strange, predatory, excited look in her eyes as she gazed at her victim's nakedness. Susan could swear that she was sexually aroused once again.

Susan knew, then, that she would have found some other excuse to cane her, no matter how she had first reacted to her proposition. Liz was a budding flagellant, her main sexual thrills coming from whipping another human being. Perhaps she was her first victim – a guinea-pig! At her age, surely she hadn't had the opportunity to practice her sadistic lesbian inclinations. She tried one more angle.

"I'll not submit to a caning," said Susan quietly. "Give my husband the tapes if you must, but I will not allow you to beat me."

She saw the disappointment on Liz's face; the girl looked down at her cane and then back at her aunt. The way her eyes burned into her, Susan half expected her niece to start hitting her wherever she could reach with the cane, but she stood her ground and waited to see what the reaction would be.

"OK, I'll send the tapes off in the morning," came the sullen reply.

"I think you're rather silly. You've had me once and..."

"Yes. A free ride, wasn't it!"

"...you could have me again for the next few days, and all that money at the end of it. Think what you'll be passing up, all for the sake of inflicting pain on a helpless adult. Is it worth all that?"

"You know my parents aren't exactly hard up. The extra cash would have been a nice little extra pocket money, but I can do without it. My parents buy me whatever I ask for."

"And sex with another woman?"

"Oh, you're not the only girl I've had sex with. I started at school. Trouble is, most of them won't stand much punishment, and that's what I've always liked and wanted. And I've had men, too. In fact there's one in town who's taught me most of what I know. I think you'll like him when you meet."

"I doubt it," said Susan, fervently hoping that she never would meet this sadistic boyfriend.

Liz swished the cane irritably and looked over the enticing nakedness of her lovely aunt.

"I'm not so sure. I think some women love corporal punishment. And that you could be one of them. You just don't know it yet."

Susan's memory flashed back to the early days of her marriage, when she had allowed her husband to spank her a few times by way of experiment. He hadn't seemed to be very interested, yet she had, admittedly, found it rather thrilling. She had achieved a very satisfying climax, too, although later she told herself she would have attained it through the normal channels – and without the sore bottom afterwards!

"Have you ever caned someone before?"

"No, but I know all about it. I've got lots of books and pictures on the subject. I've had this cane for a long time and I experiment on pillows and cushions and things and imagine it's a woman's backside. Don't worry, Auntie. I could make a good job of caning someone's bottom, all right!"

"You really want to cane me, don't you? No matter if I had welcomed you into my bed with open arms, you'd still have wanted that. I think you'd get as much of a kick out of that as sexual intercourse."

"Maybe more!"

"You realise that's a perversion, don't you? To get more pleasure out of inflicting pain on a helpless member of your own sex than…"

"I'm not here for a lecture! Will you or won't you?"

Susan saw that she was lost. She now either accepted a caning at her niece's hands, or the tapes went to her husband. She glanced at the cane and Liz grinned, flexing it to show her how supple it was. She shivered at the thought of having it across her behind.

"I'll give you another minute to make up your mind, then the whole deal's off and I'll have fucked you for free."

Liz laughed as Susan turned away, the colour flooding her face again.

"Just think! you'll have gone through all that sex with me for nothing. Not that you didn't seem to enjoy it rather more than you made out you would."

"Shut up! Let me think!" She put her hands to her ears and went over to the bed. She sat down and draped her dressing gown around her shoulders.

"What's a few strokes of the cane, anyway? A little pain and a sore bottom for a day or two." she pursued.

"How… how hard would you give it to me?"

"Oh, as hard as I wanted to."

Susan knew that she would find no quarter with her sadistic teenage niece. She would beat her just as hard as she was capable of. Would she be able to take it? Could she bear to stand still while the shameful thrashing was inflicted on her by this perverted girl? The pain was going to be awful. That thin, willowy cane, coupled with the teenager's sadistic drive, would tax all her reserves of strength. And afterwards – she might not be able to get about for a while. She just knew that Liz would have no pity, show her no mercy as she beat her.

And the alternative? Those damned tapes to her husband and the exposure of Bill and herself. The disruption of three lives for a long time to come. Divorce courts, rows, publicity. Wouldn't it be better to suffer pain and humiliation for a short while rather than that.

"How many strokes would you want to give me?" she asked in a low voice.

"Well… for the face slapping and the insults, I think six good hard strokes on the bottom would fit the bill."

"Very well. I'll submit to it." Susan's voice was dry with fear and shame as she got up from the bed. She stood looking at the cane for a moment, screwing up her courage, then, taking a deep breath, she drew herself up and pulled the dressing-gown from her shoulders.

Naked, she stood before her niece, her beautiful body tall and straight, the firm breasts proudly out-thrust.

"Well? I'm ready," she said, simply.

Liz strolled over to her, literally licking her lips as she looked at the lovely woman she was about to thrash. The blood pounded in the teenager's ears; at last she was going to do what she had dreamed of for so long: flog a beautiful, grown-up woman! And there she stood, waiting for it, naked. Her lovely aunt, of all people!

"Bend over where you are and touch your toes." That harsh, authoritarian voice again.

Resigned now, her spirit just about broken, Susan bent over, her fingertips just touching her toes.

"Straighten your legs." The victim gave a little groan. Always the careful attention to detail, she thought. Liz viewed her bent posture. "No, I think it would be better if you gripped your legs just below the knees. It would push your bottom out a bit more. That's right… like that. Better!"

Her face red with shame and her bottom tingling already in anticipation of the coming caning, Susan obeyed quickly, wanting the ordeal to be over as soon as possible.

"Turn to the left a little more, so that the light is right on your behind. There! Now arch your back." Her niece was like some demanding director getting exactly the required position for shooting a film.

Susan's hands slid higher up her legs as her back arched.

"No, more than that."

The little sadist knew what she was about, thought Susan, arching her back still more and feeling the skin tighten as her bottom stretched tautly.

At last, Liz was satisfied and there her aunt bent, naked, her pale, full-fleshed bottom now tight and stuck well out, awaiting punishment, her normally deep cleft spread wide and shallow, her labia even slightly open in the position demanded.

Susan waited, grasping her legs tightly while Liz viewed her, touching her bottom and the backs of her thighs; she gave a little start as a finger poked into the cleft and prodded her anus.

"Oh for pity's sake, cane me and get it over with! That's want you want, isn't it?"

There was more touching and stroking, then her hand pushed its way in between her thighs, fingering the slit of her cunt.

"Do you have to do that?" Susan whispered. "What is the purpose of humiliating me further? Haven't you done enough in that respect? You're going to cane me now, inflict pain, shame me, so why don't you get on with it? You're getting your heart's desire!"

"That's all part of it: looking at you bending over all naked, your bottom stuck out waiting for me to cane it. The worse you feel, the better I like it. All right then, Aunt Susie – here it comes!"

Susan tensed her bottom and clenched her teeth. Her niece lifted the cane right up and made it whistle as she brought it down, right across the crown of her taut buttocks.

The hissing intake of breath and sharp crack of the cane on flesh were almost simultaneous. Fiery pain lanced through her bottom. She half straightened, then forced herself to bend down again.

Five more strokes.

Her niece's eyes gleamed at the long red stripe her cane hand raised on the beautiful globes of her aunt's bottom. The hissing of her indrawn breath as she received the stroke had been music to her ears. Now to see if she could make her victim cry out, beg for mercy. That would be the supreme pleasure.

Up went the cane for the second stroke.

It hummed as it came down and cut into the flesh, the report echoing around the room, Susan's mouth opened to yell her pain, but by great effort of will, she clamped it shut. The pain was awful and she desperately wanted to touch the weal to see if Liz had drawn blood. That would hold things up, though, and she wanted it over as quickly as possible. She remained in position, trying to control her breathing and keep her body from shaking. Four more to come and already the pain was intolerable. She took a fresh grip on her legs and awaited the remainder of her punishment.

A sobbing cry started to well up from deep in her chest as the third stroke bit into her; it landed low down on the fleshiest part of her buttocks. God! The little demon knew how to use that cane! Somehow, she managed to choke back the cry and remain where she was, though the temptation to run was almost overwhelming. If Bill – or her husband, for that matter – could see her now"

"Hmm. Your bum looks much prettier now, Aunt Susie. Three lovely red welts across both cheeks. Are you enjoying it?"

The naked woman remained silent except for the sound of her

heavy breathing, buttocks tensed and ready for more punishment that she knew would surely come.

Liz took a step back this time and brought the cane round from the side. It was low, terribly low and caught Susan right across the tops of her soft, unsuspecting thighs, in the tender crease just below the buttocks. A startled cry was hidden in her gasp of pain as she jerked upright, both hands going to her bottom without actually touching it. Her fingertips gently traced along the hot, raised weal of the last stroke, her breasts heaving as she fought to control herself.

Her niece stood back and watched her, trembling with the erotic lust the scene roused in her. Her aunt's voluptuous, naked body taut, head thrown back, full breasts thrust forward and heaving mightily, as she reached behind her to touch the red weals Liz had just inflicted on her backside.

"I'm waiting, Auntie; you still have two more strokes to come."

Not missing a chance to humiliate her aunt as much as she possibly could, Liz tapped the underside of one of her breasts, making it jiggle and quiver.

She looked at Liz briefly as she bent forward again, her eyes swimming with tears and her lips trembling. Her niece was jubilant when she realised that Susan was so close to giving in and becoming abject. A cruel smile played over her lips.

Not quite knowing how she managed it, Susan found herself gripping her legs again, her bottom thrust out and in position for the rest of the brutal caning.

The thighs, thought Liz, bringing the cane round and almost jumping in as she delivered the fifth stroke. She almost had an orgasm as she heard her aunt's sharp cry of pain. She waited, hoping for yet more sounds of suffering from the older woman. But Susan sensed that this was what the girl wanted and apart from a hissing sound as she sucked the air in through clenched teeth, gave no other sign of the agony that she was experiencing. Instead she stayed in the shameful position, waiting to receive the final stroke of her 'punishment'. Both thighs and bottom were on fire now. She couldn't control the trembling of her legs, but she refused to give in to the sadistic treatment of her perverted, lesbian niece. When alone once more, she would give way, but not in front of her.

Liz thought about giving the final stroke on the backs of her aunt's thighs again; the trembling of her legs was not lost on the cold-blooded teenager, and she felt that one more to the thighs, a little higher than the previous one, near to where that little pink split bun of her quim peeped back at her, might well bring this proud woman to her knees.

However, she could not resist the shapely bottom and decided on inflicting the sixth cut there: there was still room down on the fleshy part.

Susan dimly saw the cane lift out of the corner of a tear-wet eye. She drew in her breath and held it; the cane thrummed, cracked.

Her breath left her lungs in an explosive, sobbing gasp as the willow seared across both cheeks again, seeming to wrap itself around the globe of the right buttock, towards her hip. She half straightened, then sagged back into her punishment position. Every breath was a stifled groan of pain and large, heavy tears dripped down to the carpet. Her bottom and the backs of her thighs felt as though they had been scalded. Her 'punishment' was over.

Slowly, excruciatingly, she began to straighten. She knew she was going to have difficulty in walking for a while.

"Just a moment, Aunt Susan!" her niece's voice once more cold, authoritative. "You have to wait for my permission to rise after you've been punished. I have to examine your stripes before you get up."

She bent over again, not wishing to incur another thrashing – which she was sure would be given to her at the least excuse. She sensed Liz kneel behind her to inspect the damage she had caused. She jerked and gasped as the girl touched each burning weal. When Liz got to her feet again, she remained standing behind Susan, and although she couldn't see anything, she sensed some sort of activity going on behind her.

"You've been well caned. You really ought to congratulate me on making such a good job of it, seeing that it's my first time. So it's time to show your appreciation."

She moved round her and stood close to Susan's lowered head. The red, bulbous tip of the double dildo swam into view, and Susan could vaguely smell her own sexual secretions on its rubbery length.

"Take it in your mouth and make it wet. I'm going to do you from behind now."

Susan hesitated… surely not again… and from behind! That would hurt so much now because of her recent thrashing.

Liz grasped a handful of the heavy chestnut hair that had fallen over her face and tugged, forcing her head up.

"Now suck it!"

She tugged on her hair again, harder this time, pulling her head closer to the rubber phallus. Susan jerked her head away, sickened, as it was pushed against her lips.

"Go on – suck it, or I'll give you another six strokes!"

She knew that the little bitch would, too. Her stomach lurched as she started to open her mouth.

"I can't…" she protested feebly.

"You can and you will, or else I'll bring the cane down across those big tits of yours!"

Susan submitted and her niece started thrusting the dildo in and out of her mouth, deeper every time until the end was bruising the entrance to her throat and causing her to gag. Her nose pressed up against her niece's pubic bush and she could smell the arousal of Liz's gash. After what seemed like an eternity, the ordeal came to an end.

"Now, keep your legs wide apart and your hands on your knees and stay in that position until I've given you another good fucking."

She knew that she had no choice in the matter. Every liberty she had allowed so far made it easier for her niece to take still worse liberties with her body. Liz wasn't stupid, she realised that Susan would be unwilling to throw her hand in after letting her get so far with her aunt.

She braced herself and, opening her legs wide, rested her hands on her knees to support her upper body.

This time, Liz didn't bother with cunnilingus. She was too eager and merely spat copiously on her fingers and wiped them on Susan's once-more dry slit, pushing open the lips and running her middle finger along the hairy split and then deeper in until she had parted the inner labia and was encountering the residual juices that had occurred from their earlier lesbian coupling.

Liz held her aunt around the hips. The head of her dildo was pressed against the opening of her vagina. She pushed and once more the rubber shaft glided smoothly up Susan's cunt. She closed her eyes, hating what was happening to her, yet unable to deny that there was a certain thrill of submission, of being subjected to something that was entirely outside her control.

Then she opened them again with a sharp yelp of pain as the rough pubic hairs crushed against the painful weals that decorated her bottom. The next two or three minutes were agony and Liz knew it, making it intentionally as rough as possible for Susan.

Little moans were forced from her with each thrust, but she didn't attempt to get away, and Liz knew that she wouldn't. How ever much she lacked experience, the young lesbian more than made up for it by being strongly intuitive. She guessed that Susan had vast, untapped reserves of erotic potential, that her aunt was a molten furnace of sexual frustration and in order to exploit this to her own ends she only had to find the flash point of her libido. For some reason, perhaps because it would suit her own ends, she chose to think that Susan was, deep down, a strong masochist. And she was not far wrong.

As she endured this painful ordeal, Susan's treacherous memory drifted back to a time shortly before her engagement to Peter. She had become involved with a married man, briefly but significantly, and had fallen a little in love with him. He had never caned her but he was a passionate spanker and had more than once taken her over his knee for some pretended transgression and given her a dozen painful slaps on her bottom. Secretly, she adored these little 'punishments', although she always pretended merely to put up with them.

Later she had met Peter and her married lover had wisely decided that their affair should end. Susan and her lover had met one more time to say their last farewells and naturally, he had told her sternly that she had to be punished one last time, too. Susan's mixture of guilt and lust was perfect for the occasion and she had received no less than a dozen hard spanks on each of her luscious, naked buttocks, which went through several permutations, from white to pink, from pink to red and from red to an angry burgundy hue. Then he had made her kneel down and had taken her roughly from behind, his belly and thighs slapping hard against her burning bottom, each of his thrusts a delicious agony, until she could bear it no more and her world exploded in a burst of orgasmic bliss.

This was simply not the same! she kept telling herself as the girl's huge rubber penis thrust in and out of her vagina. Noooo… she mustn't… she mustn't get aroused because Liz would see… see the juice flow from her… her *cunt!* The vulgar word popped into her mind without bidding… *what is happening to me?* she thought desperately, *I'm becoming no better than my sexually perverted niece.*

She started to think of Peter, of anything that would bring back a sense of responsibility and reality, but it was no use. The combined sensations of pain and helplessness, the brisk, insistent thrusts of the dildo, all conspired to make her wet, shamefully wet, and worse still, she could feel those little tendrils of orgasmic bliss curling around her sexual centre, small flames of fulfilled desire licking at her erotic core.

Suddenly, the thrusting stopped. Susan almost moaned with disappointment. She had been so close!

"You may get up now, Susie."

Susan crawled over to the bed and flung herself down on it, trying to hide her arousal. She felt her juices slippery between her thighs, oozing from her labia. She was experiencing something between emotional hysteria and sexual ecstasy. She didn't know whether to bring herself off with her fingers, then and there in front of her gawping niece, or sob her heart out. But whatever she did would have to come later. She couldn't let her persecutor see either weakness – sexual or emotional. Why didn't Liz just go? She'd had everything she wanted. She had several more days to torment her, for heaven's sake! She raised her head to look at her young torturer.

"Why d-don't y-you leave m-me alone, now?" she whispered, drawing a quick, trembling breath between every word as she fought to keep back the deluge.

"Want a quiet little weep on your own, eh?" she grinned nastily.

"Please… go!"

"Just another quick look at that lovely striped bum, then I'll leave you in peace."

Susan winced as she felt Liz's fingers tracing along her weals; then the girl made her cry out with a sharp slap on the lower part of her bottom.

"Not bad, for a start. Just wait until I really get my hand in. I'll just have time to become a real expert before I leave. Thank you for letting me use your gorgeous backside for learning on, Auntie. Well, sweet dreams!"

Then she was gone.

The beaten Susan let herself go then. For a long time she lay on the bed, great, heaving sobs wracking her body. Utterly shamed, her thighs and buttocks still on fire, she felt as if she had come to the end of the road. Exhaustion swept over her like a warm, comforting blanket. She slept.

Chapter 7

Bill called her the following morning to find out how she was. She was able to tell him brightly that she felt fine again. However, that posed another problem – he wanted to take her out. If she said she didn't feel quite up to that yet, she would have to invite him round, thereby posing yet another problem – she could hardly do other than ask him to sleep with her.

Could she go out with him and not invite him back with her?

Hardly – he'd run her home, anyway, so she'd be back where she started. Either way, with their relationship on the footing it was, he would think it odd if she didn't ask him to stay.

She made a quick calculation and decided she couldn't plead that she was having the curse, either, because when the real one turned up he would more than likely be around and also because if he knew anything about safe periods, he would spot the lie.

To defy her niece's 'commands' would probably treble whatever punishments he intended giving her next – maybe even a flogging with the whip she had so foolishly mentioned – then the skin would really be flayed from her back!

"Susie," said a patient voice over the phone. "Have you fallen asleep again, my love?"

"Mm? Oh, sorry, darling! No – I was just working something out." Her chin came up then. To hell with Liz the lezzie! She'd let Bill take her out and bring him back with her afterwards. She would take whatever punishment when he had gone and count it worth every stroke she was given. "What time do you want to pick me up?"

"Around seven-thirty?"

"I'll be waiting."

For the rest of the day she shut all thoughts of Liz and her cane out of her mind, concentrating on her date with Bill.

She was quite ready by seven o'clock and it was only then that she thought she might stave off at least some pain, by telling her niece of her date and pointing out that she couldn't do very much else without making Bill wonder if there was something wrong. If it did no good, well – to hell with the little bitch – twice!

She went up and knocked on the door of her room, but there was no answer. She knocked once more, then tried the handle. Locked. She looked in every room but there was no sign of her.

"Have you seen Liz, Elsie?

"Yes, she went out about half an hour ago; she didn't say where she was going. She never does at this time."

"Why, does she often go out around six-thirty, then?"

"Oh yes, very often. I'm never sure what time she gets back: I thought you knew about it."

"News to me." Neither was she worried.

When Bill saw her he whistled.

"Susie, you look absolutely stunning!"

"Shh! Elsie's about," Susan whispered, but she couldn't help smiling at the sincerity of his compliment. "Glad you like me, though."

She wore a gold lame dress that hugged her body and showed off her exciting cleavage and straight, creamy shoulders. Her shapely legs were shown off, too, the skirt not quite reaching her knees. Bottom, hips and breasts were accentuated, but not in a vulgar way.

He held open the door of the car and patted her bottom as she got in.

"What would he say if he could see me right now, only bare?" she wondered. "Or worse still, two nights ago?"

Now her caning showed as just six faint pink lines.

Bill took her to a night club with a floor show. Though she enjoyed it, her mind kept straying back to the house and her niece. Was she there now, petulantly swishing the cane and devising new methods of chastisement while she waited for her?

Still, she refused to be cowed. Somehow, while Bill was with her, her subjection to her niece seemed to be something remote and hardly even real.

When he drove her back from town, she asked him in for a drink. Once in the library, she stood very close to him, her body touching his, then boldly slipped her arms around his neck and offered her lips for kisses.

Once in his arms, with his lips on hers, she was gone. Liz and ten more like her couldn't have scared her. She pressed herself in, moulding her body to Bill's.

"Darling!" Her voice had become smoky, sexy. "Stay with me tonight? Hm?" She wriggled against him, her thighs parting slightly against his, to be sure he cast the right vote.

"Thinking of trying to talk me out of it?"

"Do you really need that drink?"

"Like a hole in the head!"

"Let's go up, then. One more kiss first. Mmmm… we'd better go up now before I strip right here for you!"

She paused at Liz's room. Not a sound and no light showing under the door. If her niece was in, she hoped she wouldn't wake up until late morning. If she wasn't, what the heck was the little bitch up to? Whatever it was, would she please keep doing it!

In her own bedroom, she locked the door, made sure the window was secured and drew the curtains, aware of Bill's adoring eyes on her the whole time. She allowed herself a quick glance in the mirror. Hmm… she *was* rather gorgeous, at that!

Now she had to be careful. It was true that the marks of the caning were only faint, but they were still visible, and if Bill noticed them there was only one explanation. She must make sure that she faced him while she undressed. To improve her chances of avoiding detection, she turned off all the lights except one of the bedside table lamps. It cast a warm, soft, shadowy glow over the room.

Bill was only too happy to have Susan's smiling face and wonderful breasts in view as they both swiftly removed their clothes. He was impatient to get to grips, as was only too apparent from the accelerating tumescence of his sizeable cock. Susan couldn't help thinking, Is that all for me?

Stripped, she drew on her black silk pyjama trousers that she had worn on their first night together, but without the bolero top. The effect was stunning – as she intended: the gleaming black silk of the pyjama bottoms that came up to her bellybutton was contrasted by the creamy whiteness of her upper body, her full, ripe breasts, out-thrust and gently swaying as she moved.

By the way Bill looked at her, by the size of his jerking, hardening cock, she knew that he was soon going to pull the pyjamas down again and taken her where she stood. Thrillingly novel as that would have been, the risk of him discovering her cane marks was too great, so she slid swiftly into bed and under the covers, though still seeing to it that her breasts were in sight and available.

Once he was in bed beside her, of course, the pyjama bottoms were soon off and she even turned to let him stroke her now smooth bottom. With her bare front pressed tight against him and his arms about her, her passion flared quickly.

She took his hand and pulled it down the front of her body, lifting one thigh to open herself up to him, guiding his hand to the wetness between her legs.

"Ohh, Bill, darling, I feel terribly sexy tonight!" she breathed in his ear.

"Mmm, you do indeed!" He bathed his fingertips in the warm, slippery squashiness of her cunt. "Oh, Susie, your fanny's so lovely – all wet and ready!"

"I know, you could easily slip in there without even a push."

"Give the blighter a chance and he'd find his own way up."

Bill heard her gasp as his fingers found her slippery little clitoris.

She disengaged his arms and rolled on to her back, pulling him with her to get him to mount her.

"Darling… this is terribly urgent! I'd hate to have the climax that I feel coming on all by myself – it's not good on an empty fanny!"

She spread her eager thighs as he covered her, her hand going down to grasp the thick, manly cock and guide the head to her longing entrance. What a difference between his prick and… but no, she mustn't spoil the heaven of this moment by thinking about… about…

"Darling," she husked as he sank the full length into her, stretching her wonderfully. She felt his penis throb as it went up her all the way until their pubic hairs met. Unwanted, another comparison flitted through her mind... her husband's cock was just not in the same category as his brother's. "Dar... OH!... I... uh... ohhhh, yes!"

She bucked suddenly and jerked herself up at him so that the hilt of his shaft thrust against the screamingly sensitive bud of her clitoris. Then she was moaning and clutching convulsively at him, spending wildly. He held her close through her orgasm, keeping his cock well up her, kissing her open, panting, mouth.

"My! That was a quickie!" he grinned when she relaxed.

"Mm – I felt it coming on, that's why I needed you in me so quickly. I've needed that for the last three days, and it was absolutely marvellous! No – don't take him out – you've got to do it yet and I'll have another one coming on in a few minutes. Would you mind if I get really lewd?"

"No, not at all – why?"

"I-I want to ask you to do something."

"What?"

"Fuck me!" she whispered, her mouth against his. "Fuck my... cunt, darling." She gave a deep, shuddering sigh, holding him tightly. "Fuck me as hard as you know how!" And, wrapping arms and legs about him, she started the four-letter movement without waiting for him.

The rhythmic slap of naked body on naked body, soft sighs turning into deep moans.

A small, high-pitched cry; an urgent, panted, last-minute instruction. Frenetic, accelerated movement, an upheaval, a sob, a groan, a faint squelching sound as the male sperm was passed to the female. Then the waves gradually receded as the flood-tide ebbed.

"Wow! What a fantastic orgasm that was!" Susan lay back, weak and happy. "I can't remember ever having had such a knock-out. And twice in quick succession!"

"I think you drained me dry. What a suction you put on – have you got a small pump working down there?"

"No darling," she purred. "I just have a very, very sexy fanny! Are you complaining?"

"No fear!"

Chapter 8

The next day dawned with a sleepy, but very happy, Susan reflecting how perfect life was – or could be – as she lay her head across Bill's manly chest. But this pleasant reverie only lasted until her lover roused himself in order to leave before anyone else was stirring in the house. Susan was aware of him dressing with as little noise as possible, then leaving the room as silently as a fading shadow, pausing to plant a kiss on first her left, then her right, nipple. She smiled and then drifted back into a deep slumber.

Liz was an unwelcome presence at the breakfast table.

"Disappointed last night?" she asked.

"Disappointed?"

"Yes – when I didn't show up."

"Hardly! I did wonder where you were, though. After all, I am still responsible for you to your parents; you are still my sister's daughter, no matter what has passed between us recently." And she made it clear by the tone of her voice that she hated all three roles.

"It was for your benefit. I wanted to give you a little surprise, a treat, even. I think I told you that I had something in mind for you, something you'd really enjoy? Well, I've arranged it all: you'll be having it tonight!"

"Oh? What vicious little humiliation have you dreamed up for me this time?" She tried to keep her voice light and disinterested, but already she could feel those butterflies in her stomach.

"I'll keep it as a surprise, I think. You'll enjoy it all the more."

Her mouth tightened as she rose from the table, her breakfast almost untouched. She was glad Bill had slept with her last night and fervently wished that she could be transported back into the comfort of his arms now. God only knew what tortures the young pervert had thought up for her. But as she left the room she became aware of another, very unwelcome, reaction to Liz's news. She was wet. She could feel her arousal and she hated herself for her lack of control. Good God! How could it be true? Was she turning into some sort of flagellatory masochist?

They agreed to have sandwiches for lunch and Susan took hers, with a newspaper and a book, into the garden where she ate them alone. Liz spent most of the afternoon in her room, probably asleep, Susan guessed, preparing herself for her aunt's ordeal later that evening.

But at about six-thirty, Liz went out; when eleven o'clock came and passed and she still hadn't returned, Susan began to hope. She sat up until midnight, then went to bed, breathing a sigh of relief as she switched off the light. She was rather curious as to what her niece was getting up to, but was certainly not complaining!

The next thing she knew was that the room was flooded with light and Liz was standing beside her bed, grinning wickedly down at her.

"Bet you thought you were going to be disappointed again, eh, Auntie?"

Her heart sinking, Susan sat up, blinking in the light.

"What time is it?"

"Only one-thirty."

"Surely you don't intend doing anything at this hour? I did wait up until twelve; I thought it was going to be the same as the other night."

But her niece couldn't care less.

"Come on – up you get! Out of that bed!" Liz threw back the bed clothes and whistled… "*Sexy!*" she breathed. "*Very sexy!*"

She was wearing the black silk pyjamas again – this time, complete with bolero. She got out of bed and stood waiting, holding the bolero across her chest to cover her breasts.

Liz gripped her upper arm roughly. "You're coming into my room tonight – that's where I have your surprise waiting for you." Susan felt herself being led towards the door. Unwilling, dreading every step, she allowed herself to be led along the passage to her room. The door itself was closed, but light shone from beneath it. Liz turned the handle, pushing the door a little way and looking round it into the room, still keeping a tight, almost painful, grip on Susie's arm. Then she turned back to her, grinning even more broadly.

"Now for the big surprise, Auntie Susie."

She pushed the door open and walked in, leading her forward.

"I'd like you to meet a friend of mine – and yours, too, very soon, I hope!"

Liz pulled her right into the room and Susan recoiled with a gasp of horror.

"This is my beautiful Aunt Susan!" the pale teenager announced dramatically.

"Aunt Susan – this is my very good friend – meet Vernon!"

"No need to stand on ceremony, love – I feel as though I know you already."

The youth that was sitting in the armchair by the window got up and came forward to greet her, jerking a thumb back at the tape recorder.

"Might as well shake hands, though. We're going to know each other a lot better before the night's out."

He walked over to the stunned Susan and grasped her nerveless fingers, held on, and stroked up her arm with the other hand, his eyes all glittery.

The boy was about Liz's age – a little older, perhaps even just eighteen. He wore only a string vest and a pair of underpants. He was tall and lanky, with dark, greasy hair that was slicked back. Like

Liz, there was an unhealthy pallor about his skin, though while at least Liz looked attractive, Vernon's general appearance was that of something that had crawled out from under a stone.

"You see, your Liz would like me to give you a proper seeing-to!"

Susan came to life at last and pulled her hand away. She looked at her niece in shocked horror.

"You – you *animal!*" she grated, her voice hoarse with anger. Then she turned on her heel and went straight back out of the door.

Two pairs of hands grabbed her and dragged her back in again, Liz immediately locking the door. Susan turned to demand to be let out, and, as she did so, the gangly youth gripped her bolero at the top and wrenched it down off her shoulders; he had it down and off her arms before Susan could do anything about it. The bolero was flung into a corner and she had to stand naked to the hips, hands inadequately trying to hide her breasts from Vernon's scrutiny.

"Blimey! You *are* a lovely piece of overtime, aren't you, love? You're good enough to eat!"

A hand reached out and touched the exposed side of Susan's left breast. "Firm, too! Liz, you're a treasure! I'm going to enjoy every second!"

"Why have you brought this… person into my house?"

"Watch the language, love. Not so much of the 'this person' business. I could make it hard on you tonight." He grinned at Liz. Come to that, I could make it hard on you in other ways, too, couldn't I?" He laughed at his own joke.

"We both could, Vern!"

"Come on, darling, let's have a look at those smashing tits of yours, they fair make my mouth water! I wish I'd come back with you before, Liz. Look what I've been missing!"

"I refuse to go any further with the deal until you tell this… youth to get out of my house!"

"Coo – posh Roedean accent with it! You were a clever girl – right on the mark with those tapes. I taught you well, didn't I? You ought to be proud of your niece, Auntie Susie – uses her head, she does, and no mistake! Of course, it was me who set her up in business, as you might say. Taught her all I know."

"What… what was that you said?" asked Susan faintly. "What was that about teaching her and setting her up in business?"

"Oh, we're partners, Auntie," grinned Liz. "I've known Vern since I came for the summer holidays two years ago."

"How did you get to know a person like this?" She looked the near-naked lad up and down, noting with distaste that the bulge in his tight Y-fronts seemed to have grown much larger while they had been talking.

"All right," he said defiantly, "so I took your niece's cherry. So what? She wanted to loose it and I obliged."

"But she was only fourteen then!"

"She knew just what she wanted, though, even then. Though it seems she's getting a taste for her own kind nowadays…" and he gave Susan a lewd, meaningful look. "But she still enjoys a good fuck and I still give her one now and then. In fact, we had one just before we woke you up. But don't worry, I've not spunked yet. Plenty left for you, darling!"

He pointed at the door. "Liz and I have got things nicely set up for *you*, love. Make sure you give us a nice fuck afterwards!"

Susan looked at the door and her stomach felt sick with dread. There, at each corner of the frame, they had nailed a stout leather strap with a buckle.

"You see, Aunt, I kept on thinking what you said the other night. Remember when you suggested I might try flogging you with a whip? Well, I thought it might be a good idea, and, as you appeared to be keen on it, I bought those straps and nailed them up. See how it works? You put your wrists in the two top ones and your ankles are fastened to the lower one and there you are… all nicely stretched."

"I refuse to have anything to do with you as long as this… youth… stays. Now, please let me go."

"I do wish you'd call me Vern – sounds much more friendly," Vernon complained.

"Aw, come on, now Auntie! You're not going to give in now, are you? After going through what we did the other night and letting me fuck you with the dildo – surely you're not going to let all that go down the drain?"

It was just what Susan herself had been thinking – to have gone through all that for nothing!

"I haven't refused whatever you want to do to me; I just don't want him here while you do it."

"Oh, but he's going to help," Liz almost whined.

Vern smiled nastily. "It's like I said, lady. Liz and me are partners."

"In blackmail!" snapped Susan.

"Now look here – we've had enough messing about; if you have any intention of carrying on, you'd better stop playing hard to get, the longer you make me wait, the more I'll take it out on your skin when I do start." Liz had dropped her mock wheedling and her own sweet naturally vicious nature was taking over.

Vern, however, kept it up. "See – I've brought you a present, love," he grinned. He turned and fiddled with the catches of a small case. Susan was forced to revise her opinion of his age. He looked more twenty-plus than eighteen, she thought. He opened the case and turned back to the beleaguered woman. "There – how about that?"

Susan jumped back in panic as a long, slim whip cracked close to her ear. She jumped back again as the tip flicked out once more, cracking within a couple of inches of her breasts. She protected them with her hands and, as she did so, her niece took the opportunity of darting in and wrenching her pyjama trousers down to her knees. The whip cracked again and she gasped as she felt the wind of it ruffle the hairs of her mound. Again it flicked out, whispering just below her chin, making her jerk her head back. She stood there, petrified, her hands covering her breasts, the pyjama trousers about her knees. She dared not let go of her breasts, in case the youth gave her a full-blooded lash across them; she trembled for her sex, so kept her legs tightly together.

As the whip continued to flicker all around her, keeping her backed up against the door, she watched the bulge in his underwear expand even more, and now, to her horror, she could easily discern the outline of what seemed like an enormous, semi-hard penis. This horrid game was making him… hard!

Her niece stood watching the scene, her eyes going from one to the other like an umpire at a tennis match. Finally, Vernon lowered the whip, laughing. He sat down on the bed and Susan relaxed for a while, raising no comment when she drew her pyjama pants up again.

"I can see by your eyes that you're going to love having it proper!"

"You had her scared there, Vern," grinned Liz. "You needn't have worried, though, Susie – he's an expert with the whip."

"I trained as a circus performer a few years back. Before I joined the fairground. There are some skills you just don't lose. Why – I used to be able to pull a cigarette from someone's mouth with a whip at twenty paces."

Susan felt horribly naked as the fairground lad kept eyeing her. Risking her niece's wrath, she retrieved her bolero and felt a little better with her breasts hidden from those penetrating eyes. But Liz was too interested in her hero's reminiscences to take any notice.

"I can't wait to get Auntie Susie strapped up on the door. Do you want to grope her first?

"Grope me?" Susan looked at her in alarm. "What do you mean?"

"Give you a good feel. And I can tell you, my fingers are fair itching to do it!" supplied Vernon. "Yes, I think I'll do that, then I'll give you a lesson in how to whip a woman. We can strap her up now, if you like. She'll struggle for a bit when I start groping her."

"I want a few strokes at her, too!"

"And you shall have them, my girl, after you've watched me. There's more to inflicting a whipping than just swinging your arm, you know. You could damage her if you didn't wield the whip properly."

"No, I will not be whipped by him or in front of him! This is all too humiliating – I can't go through with it this time." Susan felt she had to make some sort of stand. It was as if they were talking about some object, not a human being with feelings and emotions.

"Oh, come off it, Susie, Vern's going to whip you and then he's going to fuck you – you know you're going to give in – eventually. So why prolong the agony? You're only wasting time."

While the awful truth of Liz's last statement was dawning on Susan, she dimly heard Vernon say, "To whip a woman is to master her. Never argue with her, young Liz. You're either going to whip her, or you're not. You want to give her a good whipping, don't you?"

"You bet I do!"

"And watch me give her a fucking afterwards?"

"Can't wait to see you getting that lovely cock of yours up her!"

"Right!" Vernon suddenly dived at Susan and got a grip on one of her arms. "Get the other, quick!"

She grabbed Susan's other arm and now she stood, a victim between her two tormentors; she had been about to put up a fight, but she didn't see any point in it. The coming hour or so was going to be hellish, she knew. Far worse than when she had submitted herself to her niece's cane and revolting lesbian practices in her own bedroom. Now she was going to be flogged by an expert in the use of a whip. But before that she was going to be humiliatingly groped and handled obscenely. The lash was going to sing and crack about her naked body. And any minute now they were going to remove the scanty covering and lead her over to the door to be strapped and held in position for punishment.

Feeling rather like a woman from an earlier age must have felt when about to undergo a penal whipping, she allowed them to lead her to the door. They looked at her in surprise at her sudden capitulation.

"Going to be a sensible girl about this, eh?" laughed Vernon.

"I have no choice," Susan said, fighting the tremor in her voice.

"That's the spirit. Let her go, Lizzie. She won't get try to get away now. Take your pyjamas off, love. Let's see some bare bod again."

As Susan slipped off the bolero, Vernon went over to the bed to fetch the whip. He brought it back, coiled in one hand, held down at his side, almost as though he didn't want to frighten the his victim by letting her see the instrument of punishment. Susan, however, had a perverse curiosity now – she wanted to take a closer look at the object of fear and humiliation, like a rabbit fascinated by a snake.

"May I see the... whip?" she asked quietly.

"With pleasure, love," smiled Vernon, handing it over. "And while you're getting acquainted with my little tickler, I'll get stripped for action"

Vernon removed his string vest and briefs, leaving him quite naked. Susan could see that his uncircumcised penis was enormous – far the biggest she'd ever seen, and she quickly turned her attention back to the object in her hands. It was of smooth leather, slim and tapering to almost nothing from the thick, fairly heavy stock, the whole being some three and a half to four feet in length.

She handed it back, then drew her pyjama trousers down from her hips and stepped out of them. Now her body was fully bared and the youth and the woman eyed each other for a moment, as if sizing each other up. Vernon held the whip in his right hand, uncoiled now, letting it trail on the ground.

Liz, too, stripped naked.

"Ready now, love?" asked Vernon, not unkindly.

Susan nodded and turned her back to him, placing herself against the door and raising her wrists to the leather straps at each upper corner, having to lift on her toes to reach them. She knew this position thrust her bottom out, but then it was supposed to, wasn't it?

Vernon let Liz do the securing. She pulled each strap tightly around her aunt's wrists, so that there was no possibility of her pulling free, then buckled them.

It was rather worse with her legs. They were roughly and widely pulled apart and the ankles shackled. Now she was braced tautly against the door, her body stretched, arms and legs forming an 'X', bared and trussed, ready for her flogging. Once again, she felt terribly helpless and vulnerable, but the thing that worried her most just then was the fact that her legs were held so wide apart, leaving the long, slim gash of her sex exposed – supposing she became aroused… it would be so apparent. So obvious to them. And that would be the ultimate humiliation. Already, the mere hopelessness of her situation was causing a sort of masochistic flutter in her psyche – she did her best to banish it from her mind, but her thoughts were racing, out of control.

She waited, wondering when Vernon was going to begin the whipping. Then she remembered that she had something else to come first as she looked over her shoulder and saw the naked Vernon moving in on her, his cock making little upward jerks as it became increasingly erect.

Arms slid around her waist and the warmth of his body was pressed against her back. She felt, too, the hard shaft of his cock as it nestled between her thighs. Her stomach was caressed, the hands dropped lower, fingers combed her luxuriant pubic hair, moved outwards to smooth down over her hips and thighs. Up and inward again, fingers dipping below her pouting labia. There was nothing she could do about it, her legs were stretched so widely. The fingers probed, pressing open her vulva, finding her clitoris, teasing it knowingly.

The fingers were gentle and Susan found the sensation not unpleasant. And the knowledge that it was a strange male's hands that were roaming over her body was exciting, part of her mind had to admit. Kisses were pressed to the nape of her neck, her shoulders, her ears. A hand slid up the front of her body, then, gently pulled back on her to bring her breasts away from the door. Her firm mammary glands were held, squeezed gently, the nipples stroked against rough, leathery palms; Susan bit her lip when she felt them stiffening. Crisp pubic hair rubbed against the cheeks of her bottom while at the same time, Vernon's big penis moved slightly against her hairy outer lips.

Susan could feel herself lubricating. She knew that if he felt her down there with his hands… he would feel the slipperiness, then it would be all over. They would know that she had lost the last bastion of dignity that she possessed, and she could not bare to think how these two perverted criminals would gloat.

"Please, may I be whipped now, and get it over with?"

"If you want it that way."

The arms tightened about her for a moment, the shaft between her legs gave a little lurch, then – nothing.

"How many strokes am I to receive?"

"How many strokes of the cane did you give her the other night, Liz?"

"Six. Four on the bum and a couple across the backs of her thighs."

"That's all right to start her off. How many do you want her to have now?"

"Um – let's see – she hasn't been very nice to me, has she? How about giving her a dozen lashes?"

Susan listened to the discussion on how much punishment she was to receive, still only half-believing that it was happening to her, Susan Barrow.

"Make it ten of these. I'll give her the first seven and you can give her the last three. Ten strokes," said Vernon to Liz.

Fear and shame filled her in equal measures as she braced her naked body against the door. Yet there was a third emotion that rose up behind the others – like some obscene descant – lust. It was a ghastly arousal that Susan could have well done without, but it was undeniably there, and growing stronger by the second. And this even though her arms were already beginning to ache and her wrists were uncomfortable. Her legs and thighs felt as if they might easily cramp. She really was painfully stretched, her buttocks thrust out and taut as a drum. Susan started as the stock of the whip tapped her shoulder.

Chapter 9

"Brace yourself."

The words struck terror into Susan's heart and she couldn't help a fearful glance back to see how imminent the pain was.

Vernon was several paces to her rear and on her left. Her niece about the same distance behind her, but on her right. Both pairs of eyes were focussed on her vulnerable, white body. She saw Vernon's arm lift, the long whip flicked back. Susan turned quickly away, shutting her eyes.

Swwwwissshhhh… CRACK!

"Ungggh!" The grunt of pain was jerked from her as the scalding line was traced straight across her shoulders. One. She braced herself again.

Swwwwissshhhh… CRACK!

"Aieee!" Another fiery stripe was laid a scant inch below the first. Two.

Swwwwissshhhh… CRACK!

Susan choked down the vocal acknowledgement of her pain that time, but she didn't think she'd be able to for long. This man knew exactly where and how to lay on each stroke, and had that much more strength than her niece and, of course, was vastly more experienced. Three.

Swwwwissshhhh… CRACK!

"Arrghh!" That one drove the grunt from her as it landed just above the tender flesh of her waist. Four – and already her back was on fire.

She writhed in her bonds as the fifth stroke cut into her, wrapping itself across the top of her buttocks and over her right hip. Fiery agony. Shame and pain were almost overwhelming – and the stripes burned into her from shoulders to hips.

The whip whistled again and the lovely naked woman jabbed her pelvis against the door as the leather smacked into the soft flesh of her bottom, bringing back sharply the memory of the recent caning. Six.

There was a short pause in her thrashing and she hung, shaking, in her bonds while they whispered behind her.

"Well, I'm sorry Mrs Barrow – I promised to show her how to make you cry out without hitting a vital spot. This is the last stripe from me, so I'm making it a good one – hold on tight!"

The whip sang, cracked.

"Arghh! Unggghh! No… no… ohhh, please – have pity! Oh… my breast…. haven't I been whipped enough?" The tip of the whip had gone under her arm and flicked across the right side of her breast. It had hurt like hell.

"No you haven't! It's my turn now!" said her hateful niece.

"Give her a minute or two to recover from that last one."

"So, can I whip her now?"

Susan hadn't even the energy to *think* what she'd like to do to her niece. That last cut of the whip had been agony, the whole breast ached, but stung viciously along the side where the end of the whip had flicked.

"Go ahead then," said Liz's mentor, "but don't try cutting in at her tits – keep to that lovely back and bum."

Susan was surprised to see that he no longer had an erection. Unlike his protégé, Vernon was not sexually excited by whipping his victims. His thrill was more one of professional pride.

"Whisssshhh… CRACK!"

Without warning, the whip snaked out and caught Susan's buttocks. She arched her back like someone stretching and yawning, but her mouth was open in a silent scream of agony.

Twice more the whip flew and twice more Susan jerked, arched her back and stifled a cry. It was over. Liz and Vernon untied the straps and let her down from the door and she fell on to Liz's single bed. She lay a little awkwardly across it, and from this position, she could see the tape recorder, half-hidden under the bed, and thought – there is the source of all my troubles. She could also see that, just where the carpet met the floorboards, some signs that one of the boards had been prised up.

So that's where she hides the evidence she thought dully.

"Just look at her gorgeous striped arse, Vern!"

"Yes, it's a beauty… just waiting for a good fucking!"

"No, please not that," said Susan faintly. "I don't think I could bear it."

"Oh, you'll not only bear it, I guarantee that you'll love it!"

Vernon knelt behind her prone body and, grasping her by the hips, pulled her up into a kneeling position. Her bottom was cocked up, her knees spread wide, the skin stretched taut as a drum. There was a pause as her audience of two viewed her critically. Conscious that her buttocks were drawn apart, she realised that in this position she would be showing everything she had to the two perverted adolescents – even the lips of her sex were stretched.

Fingers stroked her outer labia, then they were exploring further.

Vernon swore softly.

"Would you believe that! She's all wet!"

Susan wanted to cry with humiliation. It was true! It seemed that she could no longer control herself in that respect.

"Go on Vern – fuck her. Take it from me, she's a good fuck, is my Auntie Susan!" And Susan's niece burst into peals of unpleasant laughter as the older woman felt Vernon's cock enter her and thrust violently in and out with no concern for the comfort of her lacerated bottom. But she liked it like that, she thought, bitterly. She had brought this all upon herself by screwing Bill. And now she was paying the price – by being whipped and fucked by two sadistic teenagers.

Susan tensed. I must get a grip of myself, she thought, as the first tendrils of orgasmic pleasure licked at her groin like little tongues of flame. Oh no! Please don't let me... and almost to her relief, Vernon withdrew. It was a short respite, for almost immediately she felt the firm head of his cock nudge her anus.

"No, no! I beg of you," she panted wildly, slamming her body flat on the bed once again. "Not – not my – my bottom – you'll kill me! Please – don't do it there!"

"Shut up and keep your arse still, or I'll give you some more of the whip!"

"I'll do anything – use my mouth – my vagina!"

"I'd better give you some more of the whip, I think, and keep on giving it to you until you learn to stop jerking about! I've tried your cunt, and now I want to have your backside. And I will fuck you there, if I have to keep you here all night!"

"I've never had it there before: I'll be too tight – you'll never get in there!"

"I'll get in there all right. You're going to get bum-fucked. If you want to be whipped again first..."

"Noooo! I'll do it!" Susan almost sobbed.

"No more fuss?"

"No," she whispered, broken.

"Then get your legs wider and stick your bum up more!"

"I can't," moaned Susan, and it was true. She was utterly spent.

"Liz," said Vernon "try and get a pillow under her to lift up her arse for me."

Liz hurried to oblige. Her aunt had stoically taken everything that they had dished out, and she was anxious to see how she would accept a buggering. From her own experience, she knew that Vernon had an enormous cock, and it couldn't fail to hurt her when he shoved it up her ass. This would be interesting.

She took a pillow from the head of the bed and placed it on the mattress next to Susan's shapely arse. She reached around under her and squeezed one of her softly rounded globes in her hand as she lifted her aunt up off the bed. She knew that as she pulled up on Susan's bottom, livid weals would hurt, but the older woman didn't utter a whimper of complaint. She couldn't wait to get her own cock – her double-ended dildo – into her. And she knew her chance was coming soon.

She stuffed the heavy pillow under the prone woman, and as she did so, she saw the angle of her pelvis changing. Her tight brown anus was visible now, pointing towards the ceiling. It looked so small and helpless, nestled in the downy valley between the big round hills of her buttocks. Vern's thick cock bulged with excitement, and Liz could see that this was going to be a tight fit. The thought made her cunt wet with desire.

She drew her breath in sharply as Vernon mounted her, his stiff cock probing for the tight opening into her virginal anus. He drove forward, his cock floundering against the luxuriously soft flesh of her bottom-cheeks. "Looks like I'll need a little help, Liz" he muttered. "You don't mind do you?"

"Of course not," Liz chuckled. "It's her arse, not mine." With a snicker, she moved forward and, taking Vern's cock in her hand, guided it to the tight brown pucker of Susan's anus. She placed

the thick purple head against the tight opening and said, "Any time you're ready." Vernon answered by humping his hips forward, driving at least two inches of his cock into the tight hole.

"OOOOW!" cried Susan. This was unlike any other pain she had experienced at the hands of these two so far. But it was soon superseded by a lesser pain, more a sensation of discomfort.

In her usual perverse way, Liz found the sound of her aunt's agony exciting. But, as Vernon's prick inched its way into the tight nether passage, the opening stretched to receive it, and eventually Susan's moans of pain changed to ones of pleasure.

"All this has really given me the horn," Vernon murmured. "I don't think I'm going to last very long in here. She's close, too, but you'll have to finish her off for me." With that, he speeded the rhythm of his thrusts. Liz could see the wet shank of his thick cock as it slid easily in and out of the rapidly expanding opening to her aunt's bowels.

"Well, here I come!" cried Vernon. "Oh Mrs Barrow, get ready to have your pretty little belly filled with a hot load of fresh spunk! I hope you can take it! This is going to be one hell of an enema! And here I come!" Vernon's words faded out in an uncontrollable sigh of orgasmic release as his heavily swinging balls let loose jet after jet of obscenely flowing white spunk, filling her anus to overflowing, and running down the round cheeks of her arse to wet the bed below. Her body was thrashing about as though she was trying desperately to arrive at a climax of her own before he withdrew from her. But it was to no avail, for as soon as Vernon's cock had finished spewing its measure of thick, warm sperm, he dismounted, leaving her moaning in frustrated desire and her drenched anus obscenely open for a moment.

Susan lay on the bed, face down, moaning still with shame and pleasure. When she sensed Liz climbing on to the bed to replace Vernon, she was utterly passive to being turned over so that she lay on her back, then equally unresisting to the girl's lesbian ministrations as she roamed her hands all over her body, finally ducking down between her legs to take her clitoris and nuzzle it gently between her lips.

"Yes!" she screamed… "Yessss… lick me, make me spend, Liz… ohhhh!" The intensity of her orgasm shocked her. She bucked and thrashed like a madwoman.

Chapter 10

"Strip! We want to see the marks of your last thrashing." Two days later they were gathered in Liz's bedroom. Susan stood in front of Vernon and Liz, her head held high, her eyes flashing defiance. Giving them both a look of hate, she raised her skirt and unclasped the suspenders; she had a bit of a struggle to get the skirt high enough over her hips to lower her panties, but finally made it. Then she had another struggle to pull the roll-on up and expose her bottom.

She had to stand like that, bending forward slightly, while they inspected the marks of her most shameful punishment. She felt fingers tracing the painful weals, pinching and prodding the flesh. Other fingers felt between her legs.

When the groping was finally over, she straightened up, still keeping her back to them.

"May I cover myself now?"

"No. We want to see the rest of the marks, especially the one that Vern gave you along the side of one tit."

Susan made no useless protests. They assumed that she wanted to get the ordeal over quickly. She unzipped the dress at the side and back and removed it, took off her slip and unclipped the strap of her bra. Leaving her knickers still hanging around her knees, she stood holding the cups of her bra on her breasts while they examined the marks of her whipping. She cringed as she felt Vernon's hands moving over her body, stroking her flanks, her back, her buttocks. Then, without warning, they all saw the bedroom door open.

When he saw Bill come through the door, Vern looked troubled. He knew that this was all wrong. Liz, on the other hand, just looked furious. But Susan was already relishing this reversal of fortunes. Bill was a big man, over six feet tall and solid, built like a rugby player. "This changes absolutely nothing, Aunt Susan!" spat Liz. "If he so much as threatens us, the tapes will go off in the post today."

"Oh," said Bill casually, "I suppose you mean these tapes?" and he produced the package that Liz had already threatened to post once before.

"Who gave you… where did you…?" the colour drained from Liz's face. "Doesn't matter anyway," she muttered sullenly, "I've got copies."

"I don't think so, Liz. And if you have, then you won't mind if I do this…" and he threw the package into the fireplace, then briefly bent down to put a match to the fire, which was soon blazing merrily. "You see, it doesn't take a technical genius to work out that if you only had one tape recorder, you wouldn't be able to make copies. And although you possibly could have made arrangements to have that tape copied, somehow I doubt that you or this sadistic young oik here had the means to do it. Now shortly after your last encounter with Mrs Barrow, she rang me and asked me to come round to see her. You two had gone on some nocturnal jaunt, so Liz's bedroom was conveniently free to explore. We soon found the tape. There were no copies, because there was no second tape recorder to make them, was there?"

Vernon suddenly looked scared and much younger.

"We were just having a bit of a lark, see… the money, well, we weren't really serious," he volunteered.

"Oh, I think you were. I think you were carrying out a classic blackmail on Mrs. Barrow, no less. You threatened to expose her if she didn't agree to being treated to a vicious, sadistic beating by both of you. And to being sodomised. You expect us to believe that the seven hundred and fifty pounds you asked Mrs Barrow for was a joke, as well?"

Liz looked more defiant than confident.

"Oh that. Well, what if we did blackmail your precious girlfriend and give her a good thrashing or two? So what? You'll never be able prove it, will you?"

Susan bent down behind the sofa and stopped the tape recorder with a 'click'. As she straightened up, she gave Vernon and Liz a triumphant smile.

"I think we can safely say that we can now, Liz."

Vernon started to blubber. Liz looked even paler than usual, her eyes darting around the room as if to find a hole to hide in. There was a long, pregnant silence.

"Take the rest of your clothes off, all of them. Both of you. Naked. *Now!*"

It was Susan who had spoken. Bill looked at her, surprised. But there was steel in her voice and his look of wonder turned to admiration. Sheepishly, the two young blackmailers undressed.

"Bill, hand me that whip. Now, young lady, I want you to start sucking Vernon's cock. Suck it until it's hard as wood."

"Well, what if I refuse?" sulked Liz.

"Then you'll get this!" and so saying, with a flick of an experienced wrist, Susan landed nine inches of whip across Liz's rump. Even though Susan had not put much effort into it, the lash hit hard enough to make the girl squawk in pain and scuttle over to where Vernon stood. She knelt down, taking his big penis in her hand, then craned her head forward and started to suck it. It quickly grew stiff.

Bill gave a low whistle. He had leaned against the wall to watch the two teenagers undress, but now he chose to sit down on the bed to watch Liz fellating Vernon. How could Susan – his sweet, modest, sensitive Susie – have been changed into this vengeful harpy who seemed so impervious to the indecency of the situation? Good God! What had they done to her to make her like this?

"That's enough. Now – Bill – put her wrists into the lower straps on the door and tie them tight," said Susan, flicking the whip impatiently. As if in a daze, Bill complied; Liz was well and truly restrained, her bottom sticking up in the air."

"Right, you, Vernon – take her. Take her up the arse! Bugger the stupid little dyke silly! If you do it well, things may go better for you."

Vernon didn't need telling twice. He knelt behind the girl's rump and spread her bottom cheeks wide. For lubricant, he used saliva. There was a stifled groan as the outsized cock burst into Liz's rectum in a single determined thrust. After a few thrusts, the excitement became too much for him, and he started to moan and quiver. This was the moment that Susan had been waiting for. Without mercy, she started to flog the helpless youth, the long lash of the whip snaking out again and again until Vernon's back and buttocks were criss-crossed by angry red weals.

He roared in agony and yet he knew better than to withdraw from Liz until Susan had finished with him. When eventually she did, he succeeded in pulling himself off the helpless, prostrated girl, and collapsed sideways in a heap. Susan, with a particularly nasty glint in her eye, took up the cane that she had kept nearby and started to lay into her captive niece with a similar energy. Liz screamed with pain and begged her aunt to show her mercy.

"What mercy did you show me, you little bully? Show you mercy? I think not!" Susan spat at the girl, her teeth grinding with anger.

She continued to apply her punishment with such rage and energy that finally Bill had to intervene, though not before the girl's bottom and upper thighs bore stripes similar to, or worse than, those of Vernon.

Liz was past screaming. She wept silently, her whole body heaving with sorrowful, self-pitying sobs. Meanwhile Bill had thrown Vernon his clothes and instructed him to get dressed and leave.

"And if you ever think of contacting my niece or anyone connected with her again, we will have you put in prison, make no mistake!" added Susan as the boy slunk out of their lives forever.

Liz was left in her kneeling position for another hour or so. The boy's viscous spunk had dribbled down her inner thighs from her seemingly forever-stretched anal sphincter. Her pale skin still bore the marks of Susan's thrashing and would, by the look of it, bear them for some days to come. She was a sorry sight and even Susan felt a pang of compassion for the teenaged girl. She quickly undid her bonds and raised Liz to her feet.

"Oh Aunt Susan, will you ever forgive me? You won't tell my parents what happened, will you? Please?" Once more, Liz's body was wracked by remorseful sobbing.

"Get dressed. I've telephoned your parents who are coming to pick you up soon. I've told them that you've been involved with some nasty sort of local boy and that you've had a kind of emotional breakdown. Which is not so far from the truth really. So yes, when you're showing signs of having grown up a little, perhaps one day you can come and stay again. But it won't be for a year or two."

Liz was speechless. She simply put her arms around her aunt's neck and hugged her in pathetic, silent gratitude.

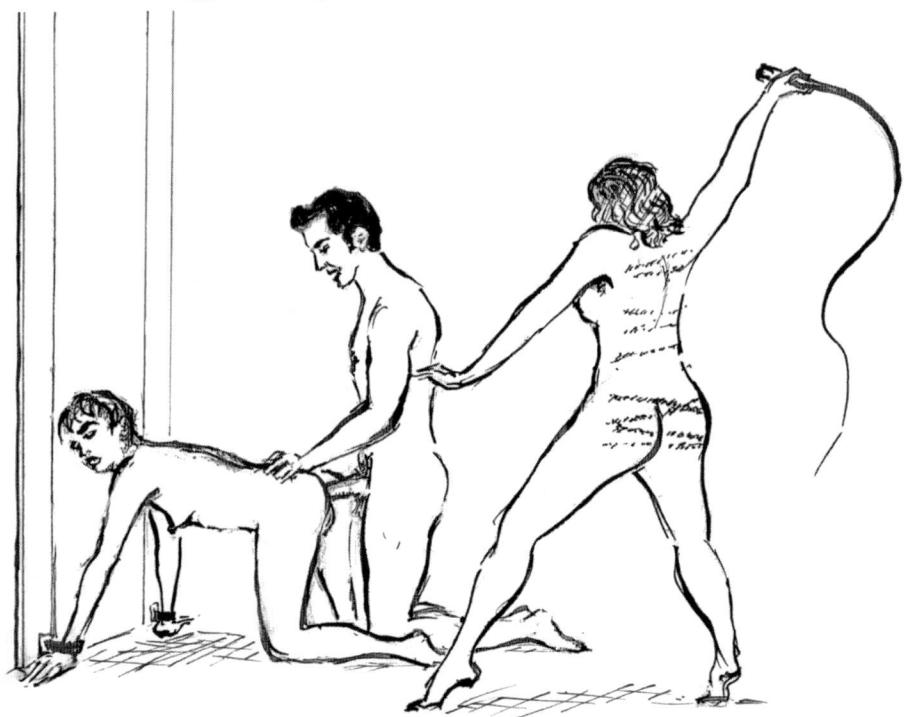

EPILOGUE

Some months later, Elsie brought a letter to Susan at the breakfast table. As she opened it, her heart missed a beat. It was from her solicitors. She read it out aloud.

"Dear Mrs Barrow, etcetera, etcetera… we are pleased to inform you that your husband has agreed to an amicable divorce on the terms we have outlined to his solicitors."

She was aware of a presence on her right, and slowly looking up, she beamed at Bill.

"Oh Bill, it's too good to be true. I'm free!"

"Hmm, at least you won't have to change your name when we get married!" was the dry riposte. "But I'm glad Peter understood. He's no fool, that brother of mine." I think that this definitely calls for a celebration. And as you're still in your nightie, shall we say your bedroom in five minutes?"

"It's a deal!"

Lucy Golden

Robin's Tale. Picture This

Robin's Tale. Picture This

Lucy Golden

I hadn't suspected my husband of having an affair until I found the pictures on a spare memory card which fell out of his jacket when I was tidying up. I would have thought nothing, not even bothered to look at them except I had been looking for the photos I had taken at Steph's graduation because I had promised to send some to her grandmother, Paul's mother. Only these photos weren't the graduation.

These were of a girl in her mid twenties, so a couple of years older than our daughter Steph. She was sitting, at the start anyway, in an oversized rattan chair and was trying to look like a cowboy, wearing a chequered shirt, jeans and a stupid pink stetson. By the last one, she was naked. Other than the stupid hat, she was completely naked, standing with one leg bent, her hands on her hips trying to look mean. I skimmed through them, and then studied them more carefully, and my initial assumption that Paul was having an affair faded a little. She was obviously posing, and she was against a very unconvincing background, a studio of some sort. I still couldn't work out where Paul might have got them from, but the more I looked at them, the more artificial they seemed: try as she might, the girl did not convey any real spark of sexual intimacy. She was a fraud, and with that thought in my mind, I worked through them all again.

She was certainly attractive, long slender legs and irritatingly thin arms, thick long hair that fell appealingly round her face, framing her wide eyes. And it could have been a pretty face, elfin, I suppose it would be called, with sharp strong features set in a wide and honest innocence, except she would have looked so much better if she had not been trying quite so hard. The make-up was too heavy; the clothes too impractical; the poses too deliberate and artlessly provocative. Above all, in almost every case, the smile was just too practised and constant. The one exception was the photograph I kept coming back to. She was half turned away, her bra was unhooked, but she was still clutching onto it, about to lower it off her breasts but had not done so yet. And she was looking at the camera and laughing. In this one photograph, just this one out of the thirty seven there (oh yes: I counted them) she was actually laughing, sharing a joke with the person behind the camera. The person? Who was I fooling? Sharing a joke with Paul. There could have been no-one else. I tucked them back in his jacket, but I didn't say anything when he came home that evening. When I looked the next day, the card was gone.

The images settled in the back of my mind for several days until the next part of the puzzle appeared: a photography magazine which fell open too easily at a certain page of studios for hire and among them, prominent at the top of the page, Capital Studios, only ten miles from where we lived.

But those were quiet days. This was the first summer that we had let the children go on to the holiday cottage ahead of us; I wasn't worried with the two of them together. Philip was inviting his new girlfriend for part of the time but Steph was always sensible. However it made for rather an empty house while Paul was out at work, and left alone, aimlessly drifting through those long days, the implications of what I had found sank into my mind, sluggish like a sodden log, lurking and occasionally rising back up to the surface before sinking down to fester a few days longer.

And then in a quiet moment, when I was on the computer looking up flights for our own holiday, I found myself going to the studio, finding all the details, the pictures of their resident models, and yes, there she was, the slightly gangly girl who I had come to know and whose pouty smile had flitted so often through my mind over the last month. 'Alice is friendly and very easy to work with, happy to work with amateur or professional photographers to whatever level you require.' All her statistics: age (22), breast size (34B), waist and hips (22 and 35).

What made me take the next step? I don't know. I was disappointed at the deception, but not irrationally so; we had never lived in each other's pockets. But it was supposed to be 'our' camera, in fact it had been my mother, not his, who had given it to us. And the website made it all so easy: 'Click here' for enquiries, 'Here' for bookings and finally 'Here' to confirm. I didn't want anything too soon, so planned a good safety margin so I would have time to back out, but that option was closed: 'Alice will be heading off to sun that gorgeous body on a Mediterranean beach from July 25th, so get your bookings in soon!' And I did.

The place was easy to find: an industrial unit in a small estate and in the tatty little reception area a man was laughing into a telephone while a girl, The Girl, I realised: Alice, offered me half a curious smile and went back to fiddling with her mobile phone until the man finally wound down his telephone conversation.

"Sorry about that, love. Now. What can I do for you?"

"I'm Robin," I said. "I made a booking."

They both stared. "Oh," he offered finally. "Sorry, only we don't get many ladies. I had assumed you were a man."

"I'm not," I answered, as I had done so many times before when my name was mistaken for masculine. 'Is that a problem?'

"Oh no. Not at all. Right. Yes. This is Alice..." and so he proceeded with the introduction, showed me the studio, went round turning on the lights and seemed surprised that I knew how to use the equipment. "It's twenty five pounds for the studio and you pay Alice direct. I'll be just outside if you need anything." He shut the door firmly when he scuttled out.

Left alone with Alice, I was glad to drop the defensive confidence and stared round at the range of sets: a bedroom, featuring a massive bed; a lounge, with a vast cream sofa and a scarlet chaise longue; a dungeon, with manacles and ropes; desolate in the corner, stood the rattan chair where she had sat for Paul's photographs. I felt her watching me as I examined it all, dropped the camera bag and turned to smile at her, looking for something to say.

"People always assume I'm a man. It annoys me. Hope you don't mind that I'm not."

She shrugged. "Fine with me; I need all the work I can get and things have been bloody quiet recently. Plus I'm off on holiday next week so I'm saving up for that."

"Where are you going?"

"Greece, well an island off Greece. I don't know much about it but my boyfriend knows it well and says it's nice."

"I'm sure it will be. We go to the islands a lot, pretty well every year and they really are lovely."

"Good." Maybe it seemed as strained to her as it did to me, or maybe her private life was not to be shared with someone like me, a mere client. "Anyway, I'm glad of any work I can get and you didn't come here to chat about holidays' and her smile, her real smile that had come across only in that one photograph, lit up her face for an instant. 'Where do you want me? On the bed? In the living room?"

"I don't know, really. Which is better?"

She shrugged again. 'Entirely up to you. What do you want me to do?'

"I don't know, actually. To be honest. I've never done this before."

"Well you're the boss," she said, sitting down on the edge of the bed. "It's your call."

"What do people normally want you to do?"

"Mostly they want me to take all my clothes off and open my legs."

"Oh."

Perhaps she could see that her sharpness had rather taken me back, because she smiled again and stood up. 'Shall I start with some standard poses and we'll see how it goes from there?'

It went well enough. She stood up and began posing and I began taking photos. Most of the poses I recognised from Paul's pictures, and others were standard billboard type: obvious visual cliche. After half a dozen she began to unbutton her blouse, slowly, one button per frame and when that had been dropped away she stood for a minute in her bra, a sleek lacy thing in virginal white, seductive and meant to be shown off, to be shown off by a girl with a figure like hers. She reached round to unfasten it and it was only then the inevitability of the process fully sunk in, that I fully understood the implications. I was shut in this private room with this girl, a stranger, and she was going to stand there and take all her clothes off simply because I was there watching her and photographing her.

She half turned away, unfastened the hooks and then peered over her shoulder at me. She had laughed to Paul; she didn't laugh to me. I wondered what he might have said, but already she was turning half back and lowering it bit by bit until the top sliver of her nipples appeared.

More, and the whole nipple was visible.

More, and the whole breast was exposed, both breasts: rather attractive, not as big as mine, but a much better shape. Younger and firmer, although the nipples were quite small: she had never fed a baby. I glanced up and she was watching me watching her.

"Very nice," I said quickly. "You're very lucky."

This time the smile wasn't the real one. "Thanks."

"I mean it" but I wasn't getting through the barrier she had built on a lifetime of insincere compliments. She peered down at them, her bra swinging at waist level.

"I'm planning on having a boob job actually. As soon as I can afford it."

"Why? They are lovely! Nice shape, perfectly good size! Don't mess them up."

Another sad laugh. "It isn't likely I'll ever be able to afford it anyway." She turned on the standard sexy smile and cupped them in her hands, half turned away and waited for me to take the next shot. Then she rubbed her palms over them. 'And my nipples won't stay up.'

"Lucky you! Mine won't go down and that has frequently been highly embarrassing."

She was starting on the skirt, a short denim thing which she steadily un-popped, unzipped and slowly edged down over her bottom. A pair of very pretty and very skimpy knickers appeared which, naturally, matched her bra; glamorous, and similarly designed to be flaunted, to frame and display, not to support or conceal. They didn't cover much of her cheeks and anyway, as soon as the skirt was off and she had faced forwards, sideways, other side, back, after that she started on the knickers. For an instant I was going to tell her to stop; that it wasn't necessary, that I didn't know what I was doing there or why I had come or anything, but my experience of photography has always been to watch through the viewfinder, to record the events; never to interfere. So I said nothing, crouched there watching her as she took her knickers off.

She was completely shaved, which I had expected from seeing Paul's pictures, but it was still mesmerising watching her edging her knickers down and seeing all that delicate intimate skin appear, the little crease and a sliver of her inner lips. All the while she was edging them down, she was turning coyly, spinning it all out but finally she stood up, waved the knickers once in the air and dropped them on the floor. I glanced at my watch; fifteen minutes had gone by, and I had booked the studio - and booked her - for an hour.

She peered at me from under her fringe, saw me checking the time. "Do you have to go?" she asked.

"No! Not at all. I just..." She didn't help me, stood unashamedly naked, one leg half bent, casually palming over her nipples with a slightly superior frown: at least fifteen years younger than me, but I was still the pupil. I couldn't think how to carry on. "Just... Just, you know..."

"What?"

"Well. I'm not sure what to do now! I mean I could spend the next three quarters of an hour taking more pictures of you in the nude but I kind of feel they'll all be pretty similar."

"Would you like me to play with myself?" She hadn't even blinked; just the same calm tone as if she had asked whether she should stand up or sit down.

I was stunned and hid behind more questions. "Is that what most people want?"

She giggled. "No. Mostly they want to fuck me or they want me to give them a hand job, but as they know I won't do that, they ask me to play with myself. I'll do girl/girl; I don't do boy/girl."

She was settling down onto the long sofa, propping pillows under her head as she talked and then, with one knee bent up against the back and the other hanging off the side, she lay back and ran her hands over her breasts, pinching her nipples up between her fingertips a few times. One hand slithered down her stomach and stretched down between her legs, she sighed, closed her eyes and the fingers started twisting, trembling, stroking.

I was mesmerised. She was a bit older than my daughter, but not much.

So could Steph ever do something like this? I couldn't imagine her posing for photographs she had always been a quiet, private and modest girl but perhaps with someone special. Letting someone else in on the intimacy of so private an action, could there be any greater expression of love than that?

Of course, I had never seen a girl do this to herself in any circumstances before, and to do it so openly was unbelievable and utterly hypnotic. I couldn't take my eyes off the sight and it was not until she giggled that I looked up and saw her eyes open again, watching me, laughing at me.

"Sorry, I wasn't wa..." I felt myself blushing and fiddled with the camera again. "You're so... I've never... Sorry."

"You're meant to watch," Alice laughed again but didn't stop stroking herself as she spoke, even lifted up her hips to settle more comfortably into the cushions. "That's what I'm here for, for you to watch." She licked two finger tips and then ran them in a slow tight circle round her nipple.

"Well, to take photographs," I corrected her.

"'A photographer is only a voyeur taking notes.'"

I laughed. 'I like that. Who said that?"

"A photographer; one of my regulars."

"It's very good. But you don't mind people watching?"

"It depends who it is," and her head turned towards me, her eyes holding me as she licked her fingertips again and ran them round the other nipple, slowly, carefully. "It's rather nice with you. Different, from normal." And she turned back.

"Different?"

"Yes, you know. More relaxed."

"You don't look as if you have trouble relaxing."

"I suppose. Maybe I'm better with women than men."

"I thought you didn't get women?"

"No, I mean if I'm doing a girl/girl shoot."

"I see." I didn't but a little sigh from Alice and her eyes were shut again. I carefully took a photograph, but the noise of the shutter and the brilliance of the flash felt intrusive. I wanted to record what was happening, but at the same time I didn't want to interrupt her, distract her. Nor stop watching her. Her tongue appeared, ran along her lips and slid back in. The fingers kept working. A soft gooey slurp escaped from between her legs.

"How does that work, then?"

"What?"

"A girl/girl shoot."

"It depends." She was silent a moment although her fingers hadn't stopped moving and the other hand was now enfolding her breast, rubbing round the bright nipple, squeezing and massaging.

"Depends?" I prompted.

"Oh, you know. Who the photographer is. How I'm feeling. Who the other girl is. Whether I fancy her."

"Whether you.. I see."

I didn't see, of course, so she laughed at me again, her little face curling up and the eyes sparkling. "Shocked?"

'Surprised. No: you're right. I'm shocked. I didn't know you were... gay, whatever the word is.'

'Bi, actually. Aren't we all?'

'I don't think so. I mean certainly I'm not. I've never...'

'Then what are you doing here now? Why are you paying money to watch me take my clothes off? To watch me masturbate?'

'It's not to watch. Photography is what I have always done, even professionally at one time.'

'"A photographer is just a voyeur taking notes,"' Alice repeated and this time we both laughed.

"Not in my case," I said although I was aware that I was still watching and she was still giving me something to watch because she hadn't stopped stroking round her breasts although the hand between her legs was still. Briefly. It started again, a long slow slide down until the extended finger touched her bottom and then back up.

"Rubbish! Why else would you be here?"

"Other reasons."

"Being?"

I hid behind the camera a moment, making unnecessary adjustments. I felt stupid, realising I should have expected and prepared an answer to this question. Not that it would have helped, as it turned out, because that would have been an answer for some tart who was trying to seduce my husband. Not for the person I had found: Alice, who was real, trying to be friendly, trying to make me feel less awkward and yet was stretched out in front of me casually masturbating. A prepared concealment would not have been fair to Alice. She deserved the truth. "I found some pictures of you. I think my husband probably took them."

This stopped her and she sat up, pulling her knees up and crossing her ankles.

"Who is he?"

I had stopped too, was no longer pretending any interest in the camera. "His name is Paul."

She shook her head, "That doesn't mean anything to me. Does he come regularly?"

"No! Well, I don't know. Not as far as I know. I suppose he could. I only found one set of photographs."

"Recent?'

"As far as I can tell. Your hair was a bit longer."

"I had it cut last month. What kind of pictures? What was I doing?"

So I told her everything, how I had found them, described the chair, the stupid cowboy outfit.

"Oh, God! That!" She laughed, running her hands through her hair, shaking her head, all that nervous stillness dissipated in embarrassed recognition. "I remember. That was a group shot, club thing. Those are always just so tacky. I hate them but Danny thinks they are good for business. I can't see it myself because people almost never come back."

"So he's not..." Not what? I no longer knew exactly what I feared and her question didn't help.

"Not what?" She waited for an answer, watched me, read me with all that experience which I still didn't have. "He's not shagging me, if that's what you thought."

"I just didn't know what to think."

She shrugged. "He came and took some photos. It's what men do. Forget it. He didn't even come on his own; he needed the security of a crowd of mates. It's barely a full step up from buying Playboy or something. Not as far a step as going off to a strip club."

"I didn't know." No, I didn't, but she did. This child knew more about this than I did; knew more about men in general and that included my own husband.

She saw my doubt and misunderstood it. "Stop worrying. Its nothing. Not a threat. Nothing."

"Ok."

She sat staring at me, shoulders hunched, knees clamped together, hands clasped, an earnest seriousness on her face. 'Really.'

"Ok," I managed a smile. "Thanks," I said although I don't suppose it was very convincing. I picked up the camera again. Twenty-eight shots taken and none of them probably worth keeping. "I suppose I'd better go."

"Why? We've still got more than half an hour." I didn't find an answer. "What do you want me to do now? Or shall I just carry on?"

"I don't know. What do you want to do?"

"You're the boss."

"I don't feel like the boss."

"Shall I carry on then? It was just starting to get nice actually."

And when I didn't stop her, she lay back down again, her legs as wide apart as before, her pussy open and welcoming, her fingers digging in there, sliding between her lips and then two curling round deep inside. When they came back, they were shining and she spread the shine round the outside of the lips and across the top. Everywhere. I took another picture, because that was what I was nominally there for and it saved me having to look into her face and acknowledge that I knew she was looking into mine.

The silence was comfortable between us, I suppose because there was no pretence. I knew she was masturbating; she knew I was watching her. I did wonder how long she would go on for; presumably she would stop before she felt she might actually have an orgasm.

"Even so," her voice was low and calm, "even if you didn't know what the position was with your husband, what made you decide to come here? I mean to book all this? Book me? You could just have turned up if you wanted to find out what was happening."

"I don't know. I wanted to know what he saw in you I suppose. What you offered that I don't." The explanation sounded silly. "Apart from being younger, prettier, and less familiar of course."

'Don't put yourself down.' More advice from a girl who should have been taking advice from me. She lapsed back into silence, and the next time she spoke, she didn't even open her eyes. 'You can come a bit closer you know.'

I took a step forward, just one, and squatted down to peer through the viewfinder and she looked over to me, the beginnings of a lost, far way, concentrated determination seeping into her eyes, and the slight trembling in her mouth. It was a smile, knowing and experienced, and even slightly mocking. She even reached out her hand to me. 'I don't bite.'

I shuffled a little closer still but her hand kept reaching for me until she could take mine, squeeze it and at last was satisfied. "That's better" she said and she turned to face me more fully, both feet now on the floor, her thighs so wide apart that she was entirely open to me, her eyes smiling and welcoming me.

I took a few more photographs, but I was hypnotised by the easy openness of her manner. I could never do that myself, and until today had never imagined anybody else could. Once more two fingers of one hand had burrowed far up inside her while her other forefinger churned little circles round her clitoris. She trembled, quivering all over, tensing her thighs and lifting up her hips as a low grunt of pleasure growled out from her throat.

She had closed her eyes again, concentration twisting her face as if agonised, her tongue emerging to run smoothly across her lips and her eye lids fluttering, quivering. Her fingers pulled out from inside, slurping as they slid down, her scent coming with them, an enticing scent that was familiar and yet not exactly like me, but she lifted her hand immediately to her mouth, with no hesitation licked it clean and giggled when she looked up at me and saw my stare.

Now the hand slid up to squeeze at her breast, pressing it flat, pulling it out, fingertips turning little rings round her nipple and then the palm smearing it against her ribs. Briefly her hand moved across to the other breast but then abandoned that and slid back down between her legs, dipping underneath her other hand.

"I like feeling something inside when I come." The two fingers pushed back up inside, stirring, squelching and twisting while one little fingertip from her other hand continued grinding round her clitoris. She was panting now, every breath a soft cry that could have been pain or pleasure or both while the tensing, twisting of her thighs forced her legs even wider then clamped them shut, trapping her hands before the cycle started again.

For a second her eyes fluttered open, locked with mine and she smiled again before another twitching grimace wiped it away and she settled back down. There was a deeper grunt, and her legs spread wide, set to embrace anything and everyone as the speed of those wild fingers increased again and that seemed to be enough. She let out a series of grunts, growing steadily louder and more aggressive as her whole body went rigid and she clamped her hands tight over her pussy, racked and quivering, sweating, panting, crying.

Eventually she sighed: a deep long moan that transformed into a giggle as she opened her eyes, saw me still dumb struck and her face softened back into innocent smiles, into the elfin girl she had been before. Her legs slid back together and straightened out in front of her and she ran her hands up the whole length of body, up over her face and through her hair. For a minute she paused there, her hair all held up in an untidy clump on the top of her head and the gentle sweetness turned serious once more.

"Shall I tell you something? Loads of the guys who come here want to see me masturbate, probably one a week. That is the first time ever I haven't faked it." She let the hair fall again, giggled and her whole body relaxed. "I like having you watch." Her legs stretched further, until her feet were touching me, and her toes tickled along my thigh. "So! Now you."

"What?"

"Now you. Your turn. Put down the camera and take your clothes off."

"No! Alice, that's not what I came here for, it's not..."

"Stop arguing. Do it." She stood up, reached to unwind the strap from my wrist and lifted the camera out of my hand and nodded at the indentation her own bottom had left on the sofa. "There, sit down." And maybe she knew I couldn't do it because she took my hand and turned me, eased me back until I was sitting, perched awkwardly on the edge. She squatted down in front of me and her hands slid down to my waist, took hold of the bottom of my shirt and started pulling it up.

"Look, Alice ..." But without meaning to, I had let her raise my arms and the shirt was already up covering my face, over my head, away and Alice was standing over me again, straightening it out and laying it down like a careful mother. I folded my arms, covering the stupid vest that I had not thought was ever going to be seen, ashamed of how weak I was in the face of this girl's confident insistence. I tried to exert an authority I didn't feel, to address her the way I did Steph when she tried to take control. I reached for the shirt again. "No, Alice, I don't want to."

A tug of war would have been silly, but she wouldn't relinquish it. "Why not?"

"I just don't. I can't."

"You're not going to try to pretend you never have!"

"No, I don't mean that but..."

"Then what is the problem?"

"Everything, I don't know."

She squatted down in front of me again. "There isn't one." And she slipped off one of my sandals, "You see?" Then the other one, settling them neatly side by side.

"Please Alice ..." But it was a pathetic protest, transparently insincere, that she ignored, simply reaching for my vest, pulling it out of the skirt waistband, tugging it free and lifting it off me. The bra was ancient: practical and comfortable, but as far removed as it was possible to be from the glamorous wisp that Alice had been wearing. But first she went for my skirt.

I didn't help her, but I didn't do anything to stop her. I had given up protesting so I just watched these slim delicate fingers neatly unbuckling the false belt, slipping the button through its loop, sliding the zip smoothly down. It all worked so easily for her dainty hands, as if all these fastenings were made for someone like her, not for me, whose stubby clumsiness always struggled, who could never make undressing look smooth, effortless or sensual. And those thoughts distracted me, so that I barely noticed the skirt was being pulled out from under me, nor that I had, without thinking, lifted my bottom to allow that to happen.

My knickers were even worse than my bra: big and sensible in a faded burgundy red which clashed horribly with the pink of the bra. I looked ridiculous, felt ridiculous and could not look Alice in the face. She pretended not to notice the full horror but dropped down onto the sofa next to me, and perhaps it was a relief that there was immediately something else which needed my attention: she was reaching round to unfasten my bra.

"No, please, Alice..." But I was too late. Her nimble efficiency already had the hooks free and she was sweeping the straps down off my shoulders, pulling it away from me as I tried clutching it. She took hold of my wrist and lifted my hand away and then the bra was gone and my breasts were tumbling out into the air, the wide dark circles round my nipples emphasising how pale and podgy was the rest of my breast. The nipples were erect; of course they were, full and red and greedy as they always are. I looked up to catch Alice staring and quickly covered them with an arm and a hand.

"Don't!" she said pulling my wrist away again. "They are lovely. You are lovely." Her hands were cool on me and they lifted my breast, cradling it in both her palms with the thumbs brushing over the centre. "How beautiful," she whispered. "What beautiful nipples." And her head bobbed down and kissed me, kissed the nipple, kissed a second time and then her lips closed round it and I felt a soft gentle sucking while the tip of a tiny tongue ran trembling rings round me.

"Please, Alice?" But I hadn't made clear what I was asking so she simply murmured an agreement that reverberated through my body and suckled all the more. I felt the beginnings of an excitement that I did not want to acknowledge.

When, finally, she stopped, she twisted to look up at me, still cradling my breast as if it were a sacred cup. "You are lucky." Gently, reverently she released me and knelt down on the floor again. For a second neither of us moved, just stared at each other. There was only one step left for us to take, but I couldn't move and would have stayed there for ever if Alice had not reached forward to take the thin elastic of my knickers and begin to ease them down. Her earlier admiration and flattery helped me through this and again I lifted my hips to let her pull them out from under me, sliding them down my thighs, my legs, my feet.

She tossed them away and laid her hands on my knees applying only the slightest pressure but I gave in and let them be spread wide, allowing her to run the backs of her hands up my thighs, so lightly up the insides - where do girls her age learn so much? I wouldn't have done that then and I don't think I could have done it now - but it was so gentle, like a slow moving wave that sent a low swell running ahead of it so that, although she stopped her hands well before the top, that swell continued and rocked over all those most sensitive parts which were now exposed and waiting right in front of her eyes. I felt more naked than I had ever been in my life.

Squatting back, evidently contented with where she had led me, she grinned up into my face. "There!" she said and ran her hand back up my leg again, up further this time, right to the top and before setting off down the other side, she crossed though my pubic hair, dawdled and ruffled at the growth. "You're gorgeously wooly!"

I thought back to her own sleek smoothness and to a succession of half-read, half-remembered articles in months of colour supplements, all discussing treatments I had never wanted. "Is it too much?"

"No, not at all. Either have it all or none of it; there are no half measures. It is those disgusting little narrow strips of coarse stubble, intended to look so cute, those are what is really gross."

I didn't argue. How could I, when she was so much wiser than me? Her quiet certainty revealed a world which I knew nothing about, but that ignorance was my choice. Married for twenty years, and faithful - except for one slight stumble - all that time, of course things had all moved on and I had been left behind. I hadn't really minded, but now this girl's calm assurance unsettled me, raised thoughts of my children again: roughly her age, presumably with similar experiences to her, would they too pity my ignorance?

But I was still sitting there with my legs wide apart, my entire body exposed to her while she, similarly naked and yet so much more comfortably so, crouched in front of me, her palms now sliding up and back along the inside of my thighs. Just once the hands came up to meet in the middle, the thumbs running one purposeful sweep up the length of my lips before she pulled away, jumped up and arranged the cushions on the end of the sofa again.

"Here, move up into the corner." She patted the cushions, directed me up until I was sitting diagonally along the sofa, arranged one leg, knee bent against the back, the other leg also bent, flat on the seat while Alice took a place on the opposite end. "There! That's better. Now you will be comfy and I can watch you."

That was clear. The way she had arranged me left me totally open and accessible and I quickly brought up my arms and hands to cover myself. My breasts seemed so saggy compared to hers: hanging where hers bounced. Her stomach had a single neat crease where she was sitting up; mine seemed softer, podgier. Her pussy still glistened, and its neat shaved honesty seemed somehow more intimate, more clearly understanding its purpose. Mine was natural and untrained. And she was staring at me, doubtless making exactly the same comparisons. She smiled. "You're gorgeous, you know. So much more feminine."

"I don't feel gorgeous."

"You look it," and she moved up to sit on the arm beside me. Her fingertips trailed across my shoulders and chest and then her voice came in a low whisper. "May I touch your breast?"

"Yes, I suppose so." I watched her fingers trail down to my nipple, to circle it, enclose it and pull it up. I don't know why that made a difference but it did, and that simple contact freed me to edge my own hand over my stomach, down through my bush and to run my fingers down my lips.

I hadn't realised how wet I was, and didn't like to think too closely what might have caused it. Watching Alice? Having her see me naked? The anticipation of what I was about to do? Whichever it was, my resistance was evaporating and having her dainty fingers trailing round my nipple was surprisingly effective. My nipples are sensitive, but stroking them myself doesn't have much effect and Paul is often too rough.

She didn't stop the stroking, but she moved round to kneel on the floor beside me. "There! Now I can see you better." Her other hand ran slow sweeps up and down my thigh, comforting and affectionate without being too intrusively stimulating. She watched intently, focussing on my fingers circling round over my clitoris and I lay back and closed my eyes.

I had never done this with anyone else in the room and would have been mortified if I had thought anyone might be able to see me. Now it seemed natural, comfortable and almost innocent. I never have wild fantasies, so just lying there enjoying the reliable stimulation of my own fingers, Alice's delicate stroking across first one breast and then the other, the slow caress along my thighs and the feel of her breath on my skin, all of these together were growing increasingly seductive and I felt a shiver running down me, tingling in my legs, sending little darts through my skin.

"You smell wonderful," Alice whispered. She lay her head down on my thigh and her hand moved off the top of my thigh and started running the same long sweeps up and down the inside. They were undoubtedly getting steadily closer to the very top until our fingers brushed against each other. It was just once, but for a while her sweeps shortened, stopping before they might touch anywhere too intimate, but I could imagine what she was looking at, guess what she was thinking, and maybe what she was wanting to do. I didn't dare lift my head to look in case I broke the spell, but I was getting wetter, closer, heard my own breathing rasp out and a little cry that I hadn't expected. Alice's sweeps lengthened again and this time there was no embarrassment when our hands touched, no question that she was repeatedly running her fingers up into my bush and over my lips.

"Don't you like to stroke your lips?" she asked softly.

But I didn't want to talk, just feel. "I like this. I've always liked this." And I carried on with the steady regular circles around and over my clitoris.

"Don't you like to feel anything inside you when you come?" I didn't answer, didn't know for certain what she meant. "It's much nicer with something inside to squeeze on."

I was getting close, very close, and I shivered again, clenched my bottom and lifted my hips and it was going to be very soon. One of the girl's hands was still running round and over my breasts, the other was sliding slowly up and down my thigh, but this one stopped. I was almost there when I felt her little fingertips dig between my lips, long slender fingers wormed their way up inside me and that was enough to tip the balance. I think I screamed as my fingers rubbed harder and of course she was right about this as she had been about so much else. It was lovely having something to squeeze on when I came, clamping my hand over myself, feeling her hands on my breast and her beautiful fingers stretching up inside me where I could squeeze them and hug them as the tremors overcame me.

When I was calm again, I looked down and saw her gazing up at me. Slowly she pulled her fingers out of me, held them up to display the sheen, and then, as easily as she had when it had been her own liquid, she put them in her mouth. "Mm. Yummy."

We laughed and we hugged and we even kissed, nothing too passionate but I meant it and I do think she did too. We were sitting together like that, comfortably naked, hugging, quietly at ease, when there was a discrete knock on the door.

"Nearly time."

She dropped one light kiss onto each of my breasts, "Wonderful breasts," she said and stood up and started gathering her clothes from the other side of the studio. I needed to do the same, but didn't want it all to end so soon and wanted to work out how I could ask about meeting again and while I thought, I watched her.

"Thank you." She was disentangling the straps of her bra but she turned and smiled at me. "That was a lovely shoot to end on."

"To end on? Are you stopping? I thought you were just going on holiday."

"Yes, I am, but I'm not sure how long for or when I'll be coming back. You see Philip's got this villa place on the island, well his family have, and he and his sister are out there already. I am going out to join him, but we can stay there for as long as we like. And then, even when I do come back, I don't know whether I will do any more modelling. In September he starts his second year at Bristol and we were thinking I might go down there and share his house, find a job down there."I slumped down on the sofa. "Philip?"

"Yes, he's my boyfriend." She had turned away and had her back to me and I couldn't move. I just sat hypnotised as I watched my son's girlfriend pulling on her jeans.

Michael Faraday *has been a professional illustrator for many years. His very first professional commission was for the legendary Gordon Grimley of the Odyssey Press. He took a degree in art history at Oxford and now lives in a quiet East Anglian village.*

Michael Faraday

The Ten Commandments

thou shalt not have any other God

... make any graven image

... take the name of the Lord in vain

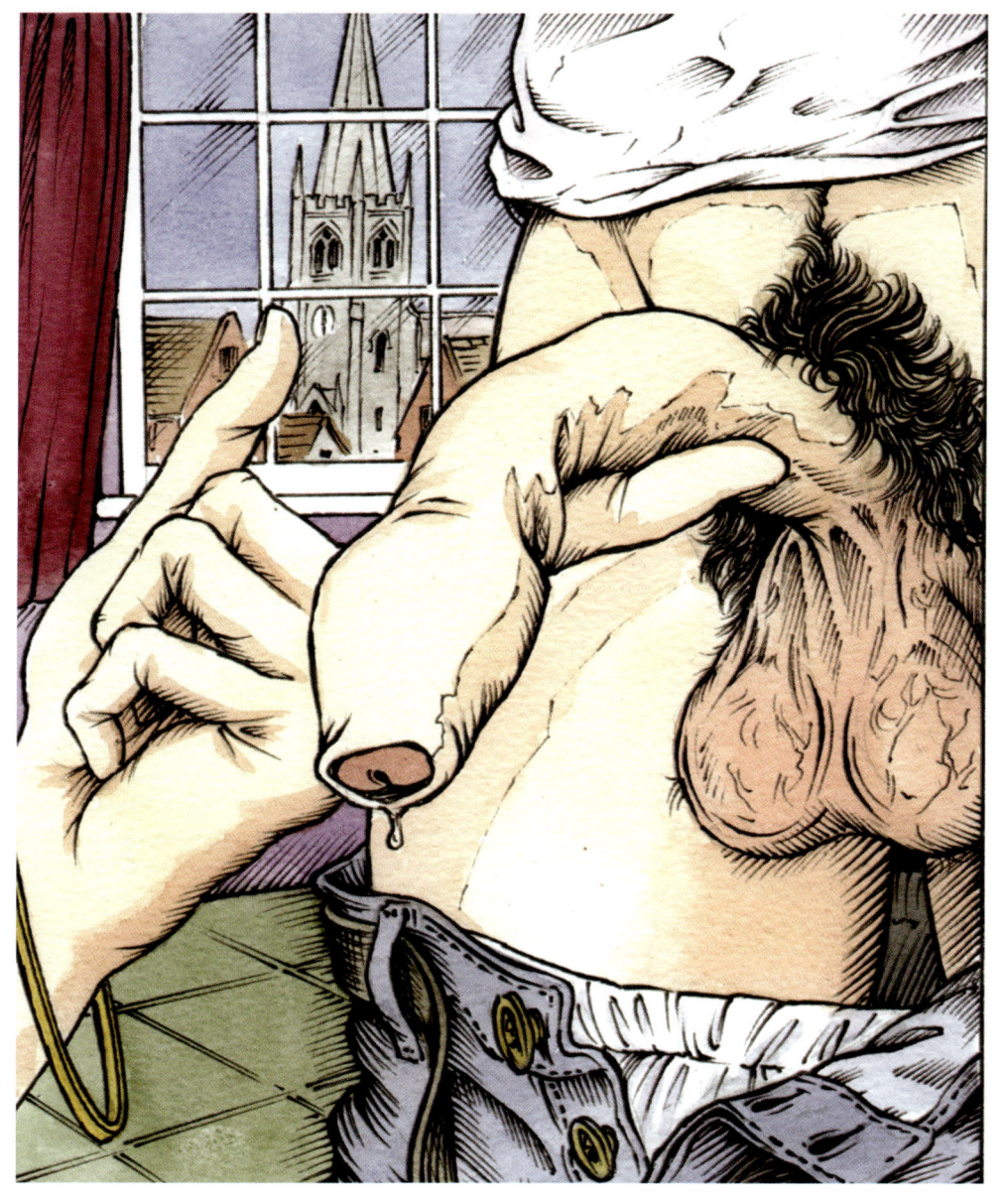

... work on the Sabbath

thou shalt honour thy father and mother

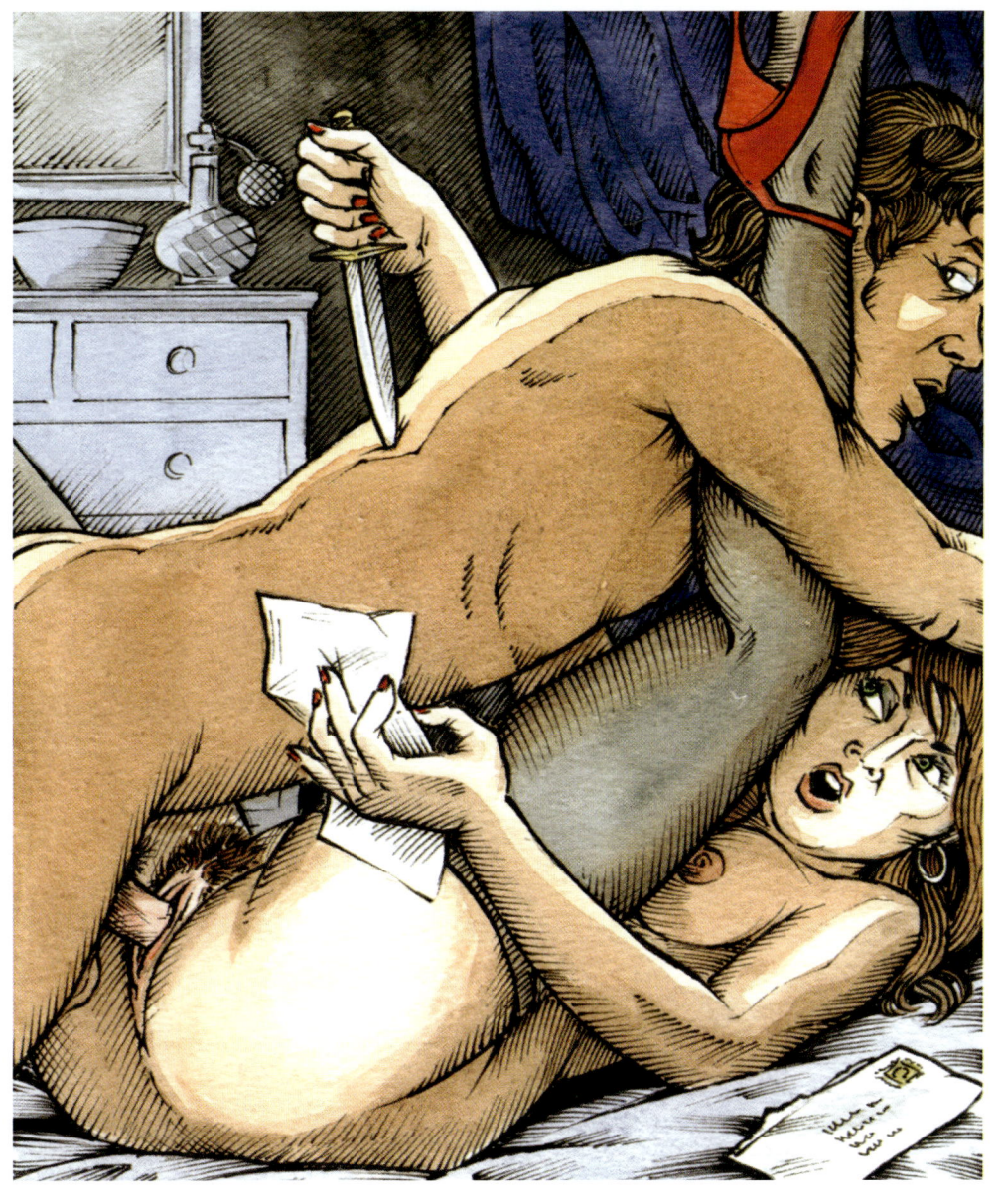

thou shalt not kill

... commit adultery

... steal

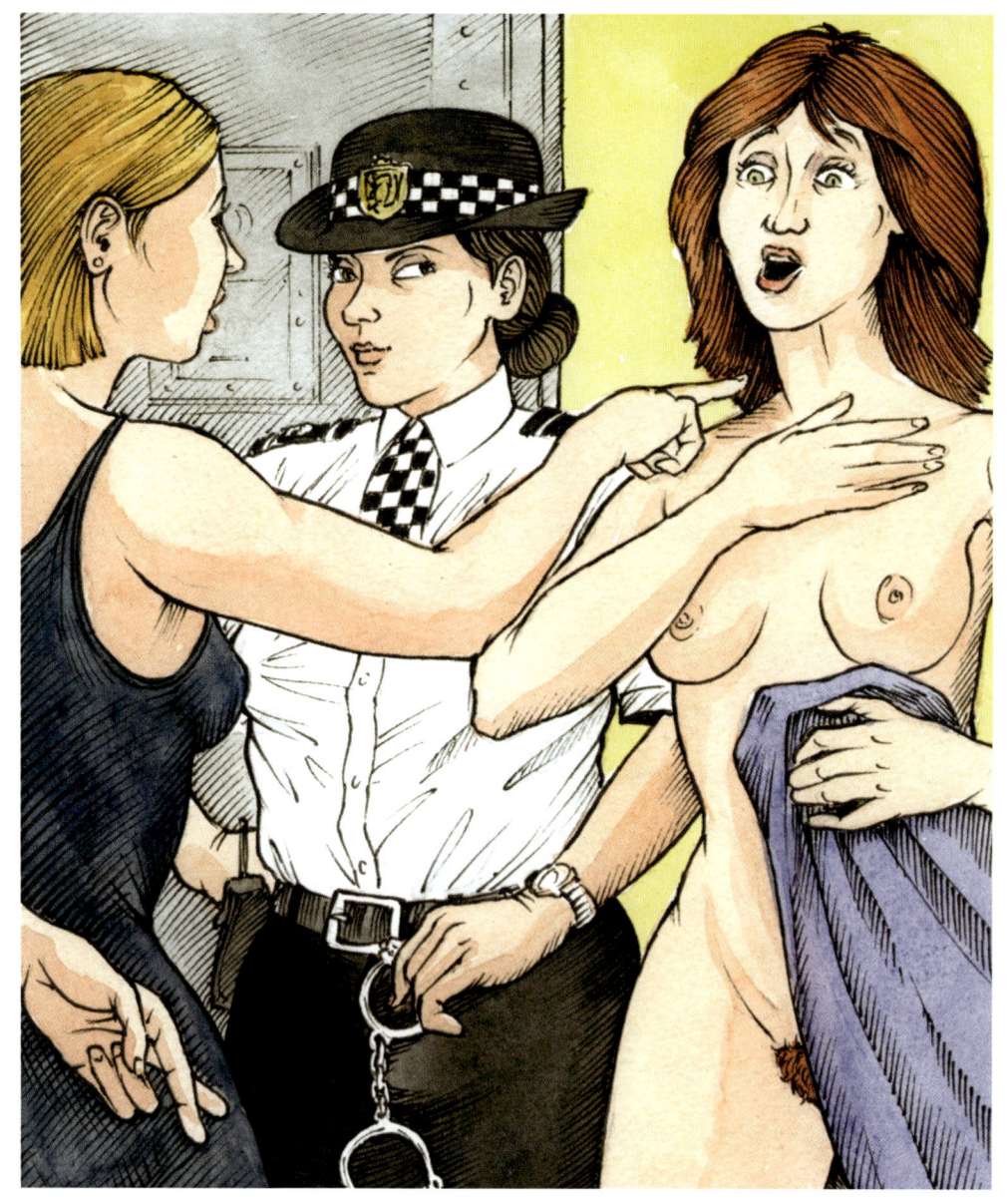

... bear false witness

... covet thy neighbour's wife

Tilly

e following pictures come from three photo sessio
had with a friend, both in and out of the EPS offi

Think of SEx as The Erotic Review's wicked, but literate, uncle (we guarantee this magazine will never be for sale in WH Smiths). The Independent described us as the magazine that 'leaves the smut behind'. Well, up to a point, Lord Copper. With writers like Stephen Bayley, Jonathon Green, John Gibb, Kate Copstick, Alison Spritzler-Rose, Tilly Johnson, Katie Kelly, The Bakewell Tart and other sex-fiends too numerous to mention here, the smut, if ever left behind, soon catches up, thank God. And then there's the illustrators, the grown-up comics, the photographers, the high-minded art and the shameless porn. And Christopher Peachment, our editor, who makes sure your SEx is always entertaining, if not always smutty.

In 2007 you can get SEx delivered to your door monthly. for a laughably small subscription fee of £20 to keep the writers in thigh-length rubber boots and butt-plugs. Don't delay. Rush to buy your subscription now at www.eroticprints.org or www.thatSExmagazine. com. It could be the sexiest decision you'll make all week.

Some of the many other titles available from the EPS:

BEYOND THE TOP SHELF: Eric Wilkins £17.95

Wilkin's view of his model's untrammelled charms evoke a time of relative innocence, before the silicone implants, the shaven vulva, the mandatory tongue stud and any number of dehumanising, Barbiesque, sex-doll attributes which can often make this type of imagery so lacklustre today. A tribute to those earlier models and, of course, to Eric's photographic art. This book contains images of explicit sex.

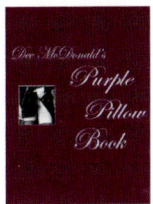

Dee McDonald's Purple Pillow Book: £14.95

The Erotic Print Society's former secretary makes her own definitive erotic choice: a sex therapist's view of the juiciest, earthiest and most intelligent stories and images. Sparkling with sexy wit, the second EPS Pillow Book is positively stuffed with fun and fornication: non-stop arousal. **Emily Ford's Pillow Book** (£9.95) and **Charlotte Webb's Pillow Book** (14.95) are also still available.

THE ART OF SARDAX: Sardax £12.50

In the world of Sartopia, men are worthless, but not entirely useless. They can, for instance, become sexual playthings for women. For the male of the species, pain is transmuted into pure, masochistic pleasure, while the female is diverted and entertained.With over 75 classic Sardax images beautifully reproduced with accompanying erotic texts, this is a must-have book for any who love male servitude.

THE YOUNG GOVERNESS: Phoebe Gardener £7.50

From our Past Venus Historical imprint: Kate Spencer's job as governess to a young girl in a large country has seemed idyllic. However, she is soon drawn into the Followers - a mysterious group who take pleasure in forcing young women to perform perverse sexual rituals.

Orderline: 0800 026 25 24
Web: www.eroticprints.org
Email: eps@leadline.co.uk
Order our fully illustrated, 176-page Catalogue for £5.00 only (post-free in UK)

why not visit us at
www.eroticprints.org?

you could be surprised by what you find...